The Last Crystal

The Last Crystal

FRANCES SCHOONMAKER
The Last Crystal Trilogy
Book 3
Illustrated by the author

Auctus Publishers
Havertown, Pennsylvania, United States

AucTus Publishers

606 Merion Ave., First Floor
Havertown, PA 19083, USA

Softcover ISBN 978-1-7327882-4-4
Hardcover ISBN 978-1-7327882-5-1
Electronic ISBN 978-1-7327882-6-8

Library of Congress Control Number: 2019950738

for Shannon Spas and Leslie Dunlap
All grown up by the time a doting auntie could afford to
take her nieces and nephews on graduation trips,
this trip on the Santa Fe Chief is for you.

Contents

PREFACE

If this is the first book you've read in *The Last Crystal Trilogy*, you may want to know about what happens before. In *The Black Alabaster Box*, the Willis family sets out for California on the Santa Fe Trail. Grace, who doesn't believe in magic, longs for her safe, comfortable home in St. Louis. She is just learning to enjoy life in a wagon train, when fellow travelers kidnap her. An unlikely heroine, Grace steps up to act in heroic ways, when it would have been much easier to cave into despair. In the process, she finds help in unexpected places. She also learns that there is such a thing as magic and there are some things only a child can do.

Book Two, *The Red Abalone Shell*, follows Grace's son, James. James finds himself on the steps of a church, with no idea who he is, where he is, or how he got there. His only clues are an old map, a red abalone shell, and a dog, Old Shep. Karl and Hannalore Matthias, a German-American pacifist family, adopt James. The United States is about to enter World War I. Anyone who doesn't believe in war is looked on with suspicion. As James struggles to piece together the mystery of his past, he learns what real courage is, and what it means to be a true patriot. In doing so, he discovers that his identity is linked to mysterious, magical events that define both his past and his future.

Book Three, *The Last Crystal*, is divided into two parts. Part One one begins on the famous Santa Fe Chief train in 1944, two years after the United States entered World War II. The Harrison children are about to find out that their journey on the Santa Fe Chief runs parallel to Grace Willis' journey on the Santa Fe Trail in unexpected and terrifying ways that spill over into Part Two.

Part 1

The Santa Fe Chief

Chapter 1

Loose Lips Sink Ships

It all started with a telegram on a rainy Saturday morning in April. At least that's what they thought. Actually, they were part of something that started long before then, before they were born. But they didn't know yet. It was just as well that they didn't.

J.D., the oldest, was the first to know about the telegram because he happened to be looking out his bedroom window. With his arm around Old Shep, he watched a drizzling rain destroy all hope of baseball practice. A bicyclist made his way up the street. "A telegraph messenger boy, bad news for somebody," J.D. said to the dog. The only people he knew who got telegrams got them from the Army. His father was in the Army. Now that the United States had entered World War II, a telegram almost certainly meant somebody had been wounded, was missing in action or, worse yet, had been killed.

Chapter 1

The bicyclist stopped in the street below his window. J.D. watched, frozen. The messenger boy opened the gate and walked up the path to their front porch.

A knock on the door sent Old Shep flying down the stairs. Spurred into action, J.D. raced downstairs after him, calling to the others.

Mamma was already at the door. "Telegram for Mrs. John David Harrison," the messenger said.

Mamma took the telegram, calmly thanked the messenger, and gave him a coin. She asked everybody to sit down in the living room. "J.D., would you kindly bring me the letter opener? It's on my desk." She sat down on the piano bench, facing them. Old Shep sat on the floor next to her as if he fully understood the gravity of the situation.

How can she be so calm? J.D. wondered, his heart pounding. He fetched the long, silver letter opener. Mamma was proud of that letter opener. It was a gift from her brother, their Uncle James. Nobody said anything. They were all too afraid of what the telegram was going to say.

Slowly, deliberately, Mamma opened the yellow envelope. They waited tensely as she read it to herself, hands trembling ever so slightly. Looking up, she said, "Daddy's alive. That's the most important thing."

At last she read it to them, "The Secretary of War regrets to inform you that U.S. Army Air Force pilot John David Harrison was seriously wounded on April 7, 1944. Further details will be forwarded to you as they become available."

That is how J.D., Mary Carol, Robert, and Grace Harrison happened to be at Union Station in Kansas City one night restlessly waiting for the Santa Fe Chief to Los Angeles. "We're lucky that Uncle James works for the railroad and could get tickets for the Chief," Mamma had told them, trying to sound cheerful. "Once you're on board, you won't even have to change trains. Uncle James will meet you in L.A. It couldn't be more convenient. The Chief's a famous train. You never know whom you'll meet on the Santa Fe Chief—movie stars, singers, politicians, famous baseball players—they all love the Chief, at least that's what your Uncle James says. And you never know what adventures are waiting for you."

"What will Old Shep do if you go away to take care of Daddy and we go to Uncle James?" Grace cried in alarm.

"We'll find somebody to look after him while we're gone," Mamma reassured her. But it wasn't necessary. Old Shep left as suddenly as he came. A little over two years before, right after their daddy left for the war, the black and white sheep dog appeared on their porch. Nobody was sure how he got through the front gate, but there he was sitting at the door looking at them as if he expected to be invited in. He looked exactly like the Old Shep Uncle James had when he and Mamma were children. So they called him Old Shep. Sometimes Mamma said it felt like Old Shep really was the same dog.

That was impossible, of course. It would make him at least 350 dog-years-old. Dogs don't live that long. Mamma said the other Old Shep left Uncle James unexpectedly, too, sometime just before he went off to college.

Mamma checked around to see if anyone was missing a dog. But no one came for him. By then they all loved him too much to do anything but keep him. Grace was especially attached to the dog. As far as she was concerned, Old Shep was a magical dog who came to comfort her in her father's absence. Robert might have pooh-poohed the idea, but J.D. reminded him, "Little kids believe in magic, Rob. A couple of years ago you'd have thought the same thing."

"It would be good fun if he were magic," Mary Carol said. She wasn't entirely convinced that he wasn't. There was something about him. "Wise— Old Shep is wise," she said.

"That doesn't make him magic," Robert said.

"Why not?" asked Mamma, smiling at him. "Your Uncle James says the world is full of magic. We don't notice it because we don't expect it."

"Yeah, but what good is it?" asked Robert, still unconvinced.

"If it makes Gracie feel better to think Old Shep is magic, maybe that's enough good," Mamma said.

The day before they were to leave for the train, Old Shep disappeared. Grace took it especially hard. Mamma tried to reassure her, "I guess he must know we're all going away. Maybe he'll come back when everybody's home again."

It was almost too much for any of them to bear— Daddy hospitalized in far away England, Mamma having to go away, and now Old Shep gone. Despite Mamma's attempts to reassure her, Grace spent most of the day with tears running down her cheeks. The least sound sent her flying to the door expecting to see him. But Old Shep didn't come back the next day either. They left for the train without seeing him again.

The Great Hall of the train station was alive with activity when they made their way through to the vast North Waiting Hall with its arched windows and rows of high-backed wooden benches. People were coming and going to far-away places, some of them to California through Texas, some to St.

Louis or Chicago and beyond. *It's like you can step into the train station and go anyplace in the world,* Mary Carol thought, places she'd only read or heard about.

It was eerily quiet in the Waiting Hall. Most of the passengers were dozing. Grace stretched out on the high-backed bench where they sat, her head in Mamma's lap, fast asleep. She'd cried herself to sleep before they left for the station. They had to help Mamma get her in and out of the car. When she fell asleep, Grace was amazingly heavy for somebody so tiny.

Mary Carol sat upright next to Mamma, wide-awake, feeling her responsibility as the oldest next to J.D. There was excitement in the air, more than the surface excitement of people coming and going. *Something is about to happen, something even bigger than the trip to California on the Santa Fe Chief,* she thought. It was something she couldn't name. She had feelings like that sometimes.

I don't ever want to forget this moment, Mary Carol thought, smoothing down the folds of her skirt. She was wearing her second best dress. It was red plaid with black, gold, and white crisscrossed stripes and a sash that tied into a large bow in the back. The skirt was full. With the war going on, even fabric was rationed. But Grandma Matthias made it for her from one of Mamma's old school dresses.

The only new fabric was the white collar. The dress was new to Mary Carol, though, and she loved it.

She looked around at other passengers who waited. The man and woman, who sat diagonally across to the left, were dozing. He was roundish with a carefully trimmed moustache that hung over his lip, like a brush. His hair looked as if he'd tried to paste it down with hair cream. It stood up where it was supposed to be covering his bald spot. He clutched a briefcase on his lap as if he were afraid it would get away from him. *Maybe it holds a map to buried treasure,* Mary Carol speculated, smiling to herself, *or gold and jewels.*

The woman was very pretty in an overly made-up sort of way. She looked much younger than the man. *I wonder if she's a movie star?* Mary Carol studied her. The woman's deep navy blue travel suit with wide white pinstripes looked very expensive. Golden, perfectly formed curls fell from under a fedora hat. Its creased crown and soft brim matched the navy in her suit perfectly. The way she delicately leaned on the man's shoulder seemed odd to Mary Carol. It was as if she didn't really want to put her head on his shoulder. *Maybe she's afraid she'll muss up her hair. Or, maybe she doesn't like him.*

Next to Mary Carol, Robert sat back to back with J.D. Their legs stretched out in opposite directions so Robert's feet were almost touching her. The Santa

Fe Chief was late, really late.

About an hour before they were to leave home for the station, another telegram came. Seeing a messenger boy at the door again scared the daylights out of everybody, but it was only from Uncle James. "Delay. Storm in Rockies left trees on track. Chief due in KC at 1:30 AM. Get some rest. Love, James."

They got to the station at 1:00 AM to find it would be another two hours before the Chief arrived. People couldn't have been nicer, though. A man from The Atchison, Topeka, and Santa Fe Railroad office came over to Mamma and apologized. "Margaret Matthias Harrison?" he asked. "Mrs. Harrison, I'm Joe Elliott. James Matthias told me to expect you and the children. Would you like to wait in my office? I have a couch. It might be more comfortable for the children."

"That's so very kind," said Mamma, "but I think we'll just stay here. We're already settled; we'll be fine."

"Well then, let me know if there is anything at all that I can do for you. I'm so very sorry for the delay."

Mamma thanked him again.

J.D. was wide-awake, too. Tired as he was, he couldn't sleep. He looked around at the others who waited, some of them sprawled on benches as if some magic had put them to sleep. He wondered who was going on the Chief and who was waiting for other trains departing from Kansas City. He pitied those who had been there since before 9:00 PM when the Santa Fe Chief was scheduled to leave. Not everybody had an Uncle James who could get tickets at the last minute when there weren't any to be had and could inform them about delays ahead of time.

On the bench directly opposite, a young woman dozed. J.D. decided she was going on the Chief. *Otherwise she wouldn't be asleep.* He made a mental note of possible Chief passengers to check against later: *Young woman in gray suit.*

His eyes went all around the station, taking in every passenger he could see. It was far too vast for him to see everyone. He noticed the man with the briefcase and the fancy woman beside him. *They'll be on the Chief,* he decided. *They look like the sort who'd be taking the Super Chief—the "Train of the Stars." I'll add them to the list. The Super Chief only runs twice a week. Maybe they're in a hurry.*

Robert wasn't speculating about passengers. He sat wondering if he was as prepared as he should be. His bulging knapsack was safely trapped under his stretched-out legs. He did a mental inventory of its contents, checking them against the essentials for

9

survival Grandpa Matthias had taught them during summers on the farm where Mamma and Uncle James grew up. "Everybody should know how to survive in the wilderness," Grandpa would say, a twinkle in his eyes as they set up a makeshift shelter or identified edible wild plants. It was a game for the others, but Robert took it very seriously.

Another delay. It sounded suspicious to Robert. *How long should it really take to get trees off the tracks in the mountains?* He'd read about how the Axis powers were doing everything they could to disrupt deployment of troops and materials essential to the war. *This could be an enemy plot.*

He watched as a group of soldiers entered the station. They stood waiting as if they expected to be called any minute. By some silent command, the soldiers begin disappearing through the exit to the trains. *Are they being deployed or reporting for training? Deployed.* Robert decided, because of the strained look on their faces. They'd be boarding one of the special troop trains that were added to the schedule at unpredictable times, going where nobody knew for sure, except the engineers and people who ran the railroads. *Uncle James might know, but he wouldn't tell. He'd say, "Loose lips sink ships."*

He noticed the young woman in the gray suit across from them. *She is only pretending to sleep,*

Robert concluded. Below the brim of her straw hat he could see that her eyes were slits. *She is watching everything.* Hardly anybody would be able to tell except Robert. He recognized it because it was a trick he had mastered, something essential to being good at secret surveillance. Robert figured he was pretty good at surveillance. Grandpa Matthias said that surveillance is essential to survival if you are ever in an emergency situation. *Is she watching somebody or is she waiting for something to happen?*

J.D.'s gaze swept back to the six-foot tall clock that hung at the juncture of the Grand Hall and North Waiting Hall. *Fifty minutes to go.* He was excited about the train trip, but troubled, too. He worried about Mamma going to England all alone and about Daddy. He felt the weight of responsibility in being the eldest. *Robert isn't going to accept my authority no matter what Mamma said to him. I'll have to strategize. Mary Carol's the one who strategizes— organized to the point of being bossy. Gracie I can manage. She can be a right brat, but she isn't likely to pitch a fit in front of strangers.*

A soldier in dress uniform took J.D.'s thoughts elsewhere. He sat at the far right end of the bench facing them.

J.D. was used to seeing soldiers, but this one was different. He was Japanese-American. Mamma said that after Pearl Harbor the government started rounding up Japanese, German, and Italian-American immigrants, putting them into internment camps. But nearly twice as many Japanese-Americans were imprisoned. "There's an old Japanese saying, 'The nail that stands out gets hammered down.' I'm afraid it's all too true," she explained. "It's not just about the Japanese bombing Pearl Harbor. Folks see Japanese people as being different. For some folk, that's enough to make them afraid."

Mamma knew about how hard it could be during war times. When she was a little girl, during World War I, Grandpa and Grandma Matthias were accused of spying because they were German-American and pacifists. It didn't matter that they believed that war is wrong. She never forgot how it felt to see her brother James trying to protect their daddy from an angry mob. Mamma could put up with a lot of things, but saying bad things about people who are different or think differently was not one of them.

J.D. wondered if it was hard being a Japanese-American soldier. He supposed it must be. *You probably have to be twice as good as everybody else to survive,* he thought. This soldier must be. He wore the three rocker stripes of a master sergeant. The soldier nodded at J.D. ever so slightly. Blushing, J.D. realized he'd been staring.

Mary Carol asked Mamma if she could go to the toilet. She really wanted to see how she looked before it was time to board the train, though she would never have admitted it. As she stood looking at herself in the mirror in the Ladies Room, she felt pretty. "I don't think it's being vain to feel pretty."

"I don't either." The young woman in the gray suit entered the Ladies Room. "We all like to feel that we look our best, don't you think?"

Mary Carol was embarrassed. She hadn't realized she'd been talking out loud.

"And you do look very pretty," added the young woman, disappearing into one of the toilet stalls.

Mary Carol waited until she was out of sight, then twirled around to try and see the back of her dress. Her skirt whirled out in a circle. Spinning around again she went faster and faster, until she was dizzy. She had just started spinning in the other direction to unwind when the fancy lady in the navy pinstripe suit stepped out of one of the stalls. Purse tucked under an arm, she hurried to wash her hands. Trying to get out of the way and stop herself at the same time, Mary Carol mis-stepped and spun right into the woman, knocking her purse to the floor. The purse flew open.

"I'm so sorry," Mary Carol apologized, face burning in embarrassment. Still dizzy, she rushed to help the lady gather her things. She picked up gloves and a handkerchief, but before she had a chance to give them to the lady, they were snatched from her.

"Don't touch my things. You've done enough damage," the lady snapped.

Humiliated, Mary Carol rushed into a stall and shut the door. She didn't venture a look out until the woman left.

The woman in the gray suit stood waiting at the entrance to the toilet, "You can come out now," she called softly. "It's safe. I'm just waiting to see if you are okay. Did you turn your ankle or anything?"

"No," said Mary Carol, fighting to hold back tears.

"It wasn't entirely your fault. The lady wasn't looking," the young woman said. "It was an accident and you were trying to do the right thing. I know she spoke sharply, but let's give her the benefit of the doubt. It's been a long wait for the train. Her nerves are probably a little frayed, too."

Mary Carol took her time washing her hands, then walked the long way back to her seat. She didn't want to walk past the fancy lady. When she got back the woman in the gray suit smiled at her. She was sipping a cup of hot cocoa.

The fancy lady was back in her seat. She and her husband were drinking something hot, too. The lady demurely held the handles of her paper cup in one hand, resting it on her other hand.

It wasn't long until Mr. Elliott returned. "We'll be making a boarding announcement in just a few minutes, Mrs. Harrison. Shall I call a Red Cap to help you board the children?"

"No need, but thank you, Mr. Elliott," said Mamma. "I'll want to see them to the train myself."

"Of course," said Mr. Elliott, apologizing for the delay again.

Mamma began trying to rouse Grace. Grace wouldn't rouse. J.D. helped lift her from the bench. Mamma carried her as far as the stairs down to the tracks. Grace was too big to carry all the way down. Mamma tried to get her to stand. Predictably, Grace went limp. "Oh dear, I should have let Mr. Elliott get us a Red Cap," sighed Mamma.

"All aboard the Santa Fe Chief for Los Angeles, California, stopping in Lawrence, Kansas; Emporia, Salina; La Junta, Colorado. . ." the boarding call rang out. Passengers hurried past them and down the stairs to the track level.

"J.D., why don't you go find us a Red Cap," Mamma said.

"May I help, Ma'am?" It was the sergeant.

"That would be so kind," said Mamma gratefully.

"Robert, you take Gracie's bag from J.D. and, J.D., you carry this gentleman's bag."

"No need," the sergeant smiled. He picked Grace up and placed her over one shoulder like a sack of potatoes, picked up his own bag, and started down the stairs. They followed, J.D. bringing up the rear.

The sergeant gently transferred Grace to Mamma once they reached a stopping place on the platform. She was stirring now.

"Thank you so much, Sergeant," said Mamma. "I see you are in the 442nd. My husband is in the Army, too."

The sergeant nodded and bowed ever so slightly.

J.D. looked at Robert quizzically. Robert shrugged his shoulders. He had a list of different regiments, but he didn't know anything about the 442nd either.

Now wasn't the time to ask. Besides, Mamma hadn't told the sergeant what their daddy did. Nor did she ask why the sergeant was going to be on the Chief, instead of one of the special transport trains that usually took soldiers from place to place. *Loose lips sink ships,* J.D. reminded himself.

Chapter 2

The Santa Fe Chief

The Santa Fe Chief pulled into the station, the lights glistening on its red engine. The children were so excited they forgot about being tired and sad—even Grace. A sharp intake of breath let it be known that she was wide-awake at last.

The bright red of the engine streamed back like a war bonnet on the silver of the train. Yellow-gold and black painted trim carried the line of the bonnet the entire length of the engine and stretched along several cars. When the train stopped, porters stepped out of the sleeper and bedroom cars where passengers were getting off or where they were boarding.

Grace sat on her suitcase and looked up at the people who were getting off the Chief while they waited to board. It was interesting looking under the train and at people's shoes from her low vantage point.

Grace admired a pair of high heel shoes with black toes and heels. *Those are called spectator pumps. Mamma has spectator pumps in brown and white. But she isn't wearing them.* A man hurried off the train just as the lady in the spectator pumps stepped forward. He checked himself in time to keep from knocking her down, but her purse and the magazine she was carrying fell to the platform. Apologizing, the man picked them up, handing them to her before rushing on. *He gave her the wrong magazine,* Grace noticed. Nobody else seemed to notice, not even the lady. It all happened so quickly.

A porter looked at their tickets. "Mrs. Harrison, next car down."

Mamma took Grace's hand. Still watching the lady, Grace stood and let Mamma get her suitcase.

"Are you all right, Miss More?" The porter hurried to her. "I was afraid that man was going to knock you flat."

"It was my fault," Miss More said. "I wasn't looking. No harm done."

Grace didn't hear the rest. Mamma pulled her forward.

"Welcome, Mrs. Harrison," said another porter.

"I'm Raymond Moses. The children will be in my car. I'll be looking after them until we get to L.A. I'm so sorry for the delay, but they held us up in Chicago. Mother Nature wasn't very kind to the tracks outside Raton, New Mexico. We couldn't have the Chief sitting on the tracks somewhere between here and Dodge City holding up train traffic. Don't you worry about a thing. I'll take good care of these four."

"I'm so grateful, Mr. Moses," said Mamma. "James Matthias had very nice things to say about you."

He gave her a broad smile. "Folk call me Raymond."

"*Mr.* Raymond then," said Mamma, "I don't want the children to be impertinent."

"Then Mr. Raymond it is." He turned to the children, "Your Uncle James is a big man with the railroad. He's counting on me to see that you four get to L.A. safely. I expect big boys and girls like you will make that real easy for me. Let me help these other folk, then I'll get you settled on board. The train will be moving shortly." He patted Grace on the head.

"Why do people always do that?" Grace whispered to Mary Carol.

"It's because they think you're a charming little girl."

"But I'm not," Grace protested, "unless I want to be," she added, grinning. It was the first time she'd smiled since Old Shep left.

"Don't we all know!" said Mary Carol, rolling her eyes. She gave her hand a squeeze, though. Being away from home was probably going to be harder for her little sister than for any of them.

Grace noticed an Army officer waiting nearby. He had very shiny shoes. *Maybe he is going to be in our car, too.* She wondered if he knew her daddy since they were both in the Army.

"George, we're supposed to be in this car," called a man breathlessly. The fancy lady and the man with the brief case hurried forward, putting themselves in front of everyone else.

Mary Carol looked the other way for fear she'd be recognized. "It's okay," Mamma whispered, misreading her reaction. "Mr. Raymond will see that everybody gets on board."

"You youngsters tell your Mamma goodbye and wait for me in the lounge just inside the car to the left," Mr. Raymond said. "That way you can wave to her when the train pulls out. Leave your luggage. I'll get it. Your beds are all made up. Let me get other passengers settled first since you're at this end of the car. We'll have to be quiet. Everybody's asleep."

He turned to the couple, looking at their tickets. "Mr. and Mrs. Hackworth, I'm Raymond Moses. I will be your porter. I'll be happy to carry that for you, sir. Your berths are second from the right at the top."

Mr. Hackworth swore under his breath. "A Red Cap has our luggage. I'm carryin' my own briefcase," he snapped. "I thought we were gettin' lower berths. How the h. . ."

Mrs. Hackworth cut him off, "Laverne! There are women and children present."

"How the *heck* do you expect me to crawl into a hole at the top?" Mr. Hackworth growled.

"I'm sorry. We have a crowded train," said Mr. Raymond. "Your tickets are clearly marked. If you will kindly step aside and let the next passenger board, it will make things easier. His accommodation is past yours."

It was the sergeant. Mr. Raymond directed him toward the front of the train. "I'll be right there to see you get settled, Sergeant Nakamura. Let me take your bag."

"Thank you, but I'm sure I will be fine," said the

sergeant stepping on board. He carried his own bag.

Mr. Hackworth scowled. "And one of *them* in our car to boot!" he grumbled, making no effort to keep his voice down. "I don't care if he is in uniform. He's still Japanese. Probably a spy, just waitin' to betray us."

"Good grief, Laverne," said the woman, stepping up into the car. "It is three thirty in the morning. Let's just get to bed. That cup of hot cocoa we had should put us right to sleep. You go first, I'll hand you your bag."

"And how the *heck* do you expect me to get my pajamas on up there?" Mr. Hackworth complained. "You think I'm Harry Houdini or somethin'?"

"Then go to the men's toilet," said Mrs. Hackworth impatiently. "I'll stay in our berth with your precious briefcase until you get back. You'll never get up there more than once. . . ."

They argued all the way into the car, with Mr. Raymond politely reminding them that people were asleep.

There were tears in Mamma's eyes as she hugged them and said goodbye. Mary Carol took Grace by the hand and climbed up the steps into the train. Grace was silent, her eyes big as saucers. Robert followed. J.D. was last to board. "I'm counting on you to look after everyone, Son. You know how Mary Carol and Robert can pick at each other. And Gracie is still young in so many ways. Try to be patient with them. A little kindness goes a long way." She hugged him close. "I wish it didn't have to be like this."

J.D. tried to sound strong and confident. "We won't let you down, Mamma." What he really wanted to do was cry. But he didn't. Mamma had enough to worry about. Mr. Raymond appeared at the door to the car. He stepped out, picked up their luggage, and nodded to Mamma. J.D. boarded with Mr. Raymond behind him. The door to the train closed.

"Now the adventure begins," said Mary Carol, letting out a big sigh. They pressed their faces to the lounge window. Mamma stood on the platform, the lights shining around her like a halo. She waved to them and blew kisses as the Santa Fe Chief pulled out of the station. They waved back. Just before she was out of sight, Mary Carol pulled herself away from the window, "Bad luck to watch somebody out of sight."

"Why?" asked Grace.

"I don't know. It's just an old saying," Mary Carol replied. "Anyway, we don't need any more bad luck."

"It's Old Shep! It's Old Shep!" cried Grace, face still pressed to the window. "He's right there with Mamma. He came home."

They all rushed back to the window. Mamma was out of sight now. The others looked at each other over Grace's head, thinking the same thing. If it gave Grace comfort to think Old Shep was there on the platform, then they shouldn't say anything to the contrary.

Mr. Raymond returned, giving instructions in a low voice. "Every car has toilet facilities. Ladies Room is right here off this lounge, girls. Boys, the Gentlemen's Room is off the lounge up at the other end of the car. Your beds are just up there." He nodded toward the long aisle that stretched the length of the car. It was a sea of maroon velveteen curtains enclosing what had been seats in the daytime. Ladders led up to the top berths. Their beds were in the second compartment to the left of the aisle.

"Tonight boys sleep up top; tomorrow night, girls. Turn about is fair play. Mr. Raymond's orders. Got that everybody?" Mr. Raymond had such a kind and friendly way about him that he made everybody want to cooperate. "I'll come get you in time to get ready for breakfast. Now get some rest." He pulled the curtains to their compartments closed.

Once they had their pajamas on, the boys made their way to the front of the car to the Gentlemen's Room. Robert looked into the next car while he waited for J.D. to finish his turn in the toilet. The car was just like theirs, a long corridor lined with maroon velveteen curtains. The young woman in the gray suit and the porter were standing in the lounge by the women's washroom. She handed him a hot water bottle. "I'd be so very grateful if you could fill this with hot water," she said. "Tap water won't do. The water needs to be boiling so it will stay hot. I hope it isn't too much trouble."

"No trouble at all. I'll just take this down to the dining car and have it back for you in a jiffy. I'm sure you'll feel better after a good rest. That long wait at the station was enough to put anybody out of sorts."

"Thank you so much," she whispered.

Robert hadn't intended to eavesdrop. He ducked back into his own car.

"Mary Carol," Grace whispered as they snuggled into their cozy bed, "Will Mamma go to England now?"

"She'll be on her way soon," Mary Carol said, still wide-awake from the excitement of it all.

"Do you think Old Shep will go with her?"

"I don't know, Gracie," said Mary Carol. She didn't want to hurt Grace's feelings. So she didn't say that even if Old Shep had returned, they wouldn't have let him into the station and Mamma wouldn't take him to England.

"Shouldn't we say our prayers, Mary Carol, for Daddy to be well?"

"Yes, Gracie. And for Mamma to have a safe trip."

"Is Daddy going to die?" Grace blurted out the question that everybody had been afraid to ask.

"Mamma says he's doing his best," whispered Mary Carol. "But he's going to need more help than they can give him at the army hospital in England. That's why she has to go help take care of him. By the time we get back, I expect Daddy will be home walking around everywhere."

Mary Carol wasn't convinced. She'd seen the last telegram that came while they were at school. She knew that if Mamma wanted them to hear it, she would have read it to them. But there it was on the dressing table. Mamma didn't tell them things she thought would worry them. The telegram said that Mamma should come right away if she could. Daddy wasn't even conscious. They weren't sure that *if* he lived, he'd ever be able to walk again. Mary Carol was really worried. She felt guilty for looking, but she wasn't sorry she saw it. *Better to know*, she thought. Even so, she couldn't bring herself to tell the others.

Up above, Robert whispered, "What if Daddy doesn't get well, J.D.?" Robert didn't want to say so for fear of worrying J.D., but he'd also seen the second telegram after it came. He felt guilty for sneaking into Mamma's room and was nearly beside himself with worry about their daddy.

"I don't know, Rob. We'll have to cross that bridge when we get to it. *If* we get to it," he added.

Despite the exciting prospect of the train ride, they all worried. But they couldn't have stayed awake if they'd wanted to. The train gently rocked them until, one by one, they drifted off to sleep.

Grace was last to fall asleep. She was afraid that the others were keeping something from her. She feared the worst. She already missed Mamma terribly. She wondered who would protect them if there were any bad people on the train. *What if there are enemy spies? I'm not very brave.* She reached over and touched Mary Carol, just to be sure. *Besides, Uncle James wouldn't let bad people ride on his trains,* she told herself. It wasn't much comfort. *I hope there aren't any bad people on the train. I'm not sure what I'd do if I ever met a really bad person.*

Chapter 3

Strange Goings On

It was still pitch dark outside when Mary Carol awoke. The train wasn't moving. Curious, she put on her robe and started to slip out of the compartment. A woman in a pink cotton robe was climbing down the ladder to the compartment just across from them. She looked like the woman in the gray suit who had been so kind to her at the station. It was hard to tell for sure in the dim light and from the back. The woman looked both ways as if she were afraid she'd be seen. Not wanting to embarrass her, Mary Carol waited, watching from the slit in their curtains as the woman hurried toward the front of the train and disappeared into the next car.

Slipping quietly to the lounge, Mary Carol looked out on the other side of the train. A sign read, "Emporia, Kansas." To the east, the first hint of dawn reached toward the sky, throwing pink light on the red brick station.

When she returned to their berth, Grace was breathing softly, still fast asleep. The countryside had changed. The tree-lined Missouri and Arkansas Rivers and the rolling hills of prairie grass were far behind. Land was so flat you could see for miles and miles in the early light.

Vast fields of winter wheat, still green, stretched to the horizon. Occasionally a clump of trees sheltered a farmhouse with its barn and silos. She wondered about the people who lived there and what it would have been like long ago before Westerners reached the United States. *Mamma said we'd be following the Old Santa Fe Trail. I wonder what it was like to go west in a covered wagon?* Uncle James was Mamma's adoptive brother. Mamma said Uncle James' birth mother went on the Santa Fe Trail in a covered wagon. Unfortunately, she died before Uncle James was old enough to learn what it was like. *Her name was Grace, too, like our Gracie. And she had a dog, Old Shep. There's been an Old Shep in our family for generations.* It didn't occur to Mary Carol that it might actually be the same Old Shep even though she allowed for the possibility that Old Shep might be magic. *There was something mysterious about that first Grace and about Uncle James, too.* Mary Carol puzzled over snippets of conversations she'd heard when the adults talked. Nobody seemed to know enough about it to satisfy her curiosity. *I'll just have to pluck up my courage and ask Uncle James,* she thought. She wasn't so sure he was the sort of person you could ask, though.

Cattle grazed on open land covered with dry grass, sagebrush, and tumbleweeds. The country began to look wilder with more open spaces where nothing had been planted. Now and then a lone tree stood like a sentinel.

Grace sat up. The boys stirred above. Outside their berth, curtains were still closed along the aisle. "Lets hurry to use the washroom before there is a long line," Mary Carol suggested.

Grace was not known for being cooperative in the morning. To Mary Carol's relief, she hopped right out of bed just before Mr. Raymond made an announcement about breakfast. It wasn't long before he came to get them. "I notice that you four are up bright and early. I thought I'd be prying you out of bed for the last breakfast seating."

"Did you get to sleep any, Mr. Raymond?" Mary Carol politely asked.

"It isn't my job to sleep," he laughed. "But yes, I did get some sleep."

Even though their uncle worked for the railroad,

none of the Harrison children had ever made such a long trip by train. They looked around with wonder as Mr. Raymond led them through the car. Closed curtains lined the aisle. As they stepped into the lounge of the car ahead of them, Mary Carol recognized a pink robe. It was the young woman after all. She stood waiting in a line to use the washroom, stifling an enormous yawn. Mary Carol couldn't help wondering what she had been up to in their car. *Maybe she got lost.*

"That's Miss More," Grace said as they made their way through the car.

"How do you know?" asked Robert.

"That's what the porter called her in Kansas City."

Robert grinned at her. "And I thought you were asleep the whole time."

"Not when we were getting on the train," said Grace. "I'm good at surveillance, too, Robbie."

At the entrance to the dining car, they waited to be seated. Mr. Raymond showed them a map of the train. "I expect you already know that the Chief is a legendary train. We go between Chicago and Los Angeles every day. The Chief is like a hotel on the rails. See this? Besides the lounges at either end of your car, there is a lounge with game tables and comfortable chairs right here." He pointed to the map. "There's the lounge-observation car, too. It has a glass-domed ceiling—I think you'll like that one, especially when we go through the mountains. The Chief usually has a lounge-observation car at the end of the train, but we are picking up a private car in La Junta, Colorado, this trip.

"Toward the back of the train are the bedroom cars. If you want to explore after breakfast, that's okay by me on one condition. You have to follow the rules. No running. No loud talk. No yelling. No sticking your noses into the private compartments in the bedroom cars and no gawking at other passengers. A lot of famous people still ride the Chief, and they like their privacy." Giving them a broad smile, he added, "A lot of not-so-famous people like their privacy, too. Everybody understand?"

They all nodded yes.

"Looks like we've kept the waiter waiting," said Mr. Raymond. "This is Mr. Elijah Bradford. He'll take good care of you."

Walking into the dining car was like walking into a fancy restaurant. The car was already busy with people having breakfast. Tables for four were on the right side, tables for two on the left. Tables were laid with linen tablecloths and napkins. They were set with more china, crystal, and silver than the children had ever seen on one table, even on Sunday when Mamma used the best china. There were fresh flowers, too. "What do we do with all these forks and knives?" asked Grace, eyes wide with wonder.

Mary Carol cringed, wishing she'd cautioned Grace to keep her voice down.

"Don't you worry about all this fancy cutlery," said Mr. Elijah, smiling down at her. "I'll tell you which ones to use as I bring your breakfast. But as a general rule, you start from the outside and work in."

He helped them to get seated at a table for four. Mary Carol looked at the bowls and plates so carefully set out before her. "You won't see those anywhere but on the Santa Fe Railroad," Mr. Elijah explained "We have our own china pattern."

"It's very elegant," said Mary Carol, searching for the right words. She didn't want to sound like a little hick from nowhere, but it was how she felt.

Mr. Elijah gave her a reassuring smile. "May I recommend the famous Santa Fe Chief French toast?" he asked. "It's a favorite of your Uncle James."

It sounded good to everybody.

As soon as Mr. Elijah left the table, Mary Carol gave Robert a disapproving look. "You should have left your knapsack with our suitcases, Robbie." She felt as if everybody in the car was watching.

"My knapsack stays with me," he said firmly.

"What do you have in there, anyway, Rob?" J.D. asked. "Nothing dangerous, I hope."

"He's brought enough to last out an enemy invasion," whispered Mary Carol sarcastically.

"The thing about emergencies is you never know when you'll have one." Robert grinned. He was serious, though. "Daddy said that with the war going on, we should always be prepared."

They never knew for sure where Daddy was or what he was doing, except that he was in England and flew dangerous missions. They were pretty sure he'd lost his plane over enemy territory once before and escaped. They'd heard Mamma talk with Grandpa and Grandma Harrison in low tones. When they asked, Mamma said she wasn't certain, and besides, it was a war secret. She wouldn't say any more about it, and said they mustn't talk about it either.

J.D. lowered his voice. "Daddy wasn't so lucky this time." He didn't want to worry the others, so he said no more. He was plenty worried, though. He'd read the telegram on Mamma's dressing table, too. He wouldn't have gone into her room uninvited, but he saw it open on her dresser as he walked past. If it was bad news, she might not tell them. Now he carried the information like a heavy burden.

Mr. Elijah returned with freshly squeezed orange juice. "I'll be right back with your French toast and your milk."

"M-m-m," said Mary Carol, eyeing the French toast when it came. She tried to sound grown up, "This is one time I agree with Uncle James."

"Golly, look at this!" exclaimed Robert, not at all worried about what people around them might think. "Everybody has their own pitcher of syrup."

"Robert!" Mary Carol whispered, "Keep your voice down."

"Let's try to look on the bright side," said J.D., quickly changing the subject. "Uncle James is boring, yes. But he will let us do just about anything we want."

Robert's face broke into a broad smile. "We're missing the last month of school, too. That's a plus."

"At least the train trip is fun," said Mary Carol, "even if we are stuck with Uncle James all summer."

Grace poured the entire contents of her little pitcher of syrup onto her toast. "I like Uncle James," she said, floating a patty of butter on top of the pool of syrup. Mary Carol held her breath, hoping it wouldn't spill over onto the beautiful tablecloth.

"You like everybody, Gracie." Robert said.

"No, I don't. But I like Uncle James. He believes in magic."

Robert rolled his eyes.

Mary Carol swirled a bite of toast around the plate to load it with just the right amount of syrup. She was careful not to spill any on her pretty dress. They all had a change of underwear for the trip, but they were supposed to make their clothes last both days.

"Anyway, the main point is, we have to do this," said J.D. resolutely, "so let's figure out how to make the best of a bad thing."

"The *main point* is Mamma needs us to," said Mary Carol. "So does Daddy. So we've got to, fun or no fun."

"How come Uncle James isn't in the war?" asked Grace.

"He's chicken," said Robert, smirking.

"That's not fair, Robbie!" exclaimed Mary Carol. "He's a conscientious objector."

"Same difference," said Robert, rolling his eyes.

"No it isn't, Rob," said J.D. "He doesn't believe

in war."

"Neither does Mamma. That doesn't make her chicken." said Mary Carol. It was the tone of voice she used when she wanted to remind Robert that he was almost two years younger and didn't know as much as he thought he did.

"Then I'm a conscientious objector too," said Grace firmly. "I wish Daddy hadn't gone off to war."

The train came to a stop as the children were finishing breakfast. A sign across the front of a station house read, "Newton, Kansas."

"That looks like Old Shep!" exclaimed Grace. She could see a big black and white sheep dog looking up at them from the platform.

"Where?" asked Robert.

"Right there, next to that lamppost," said Grace with certainty.

"Oh," said J.D., motioning for the others to keep quiet. He couldn't see a dog, but he didn't want to upset Grace.

Mary Carol didn't say anything. She just put her arms around Grace. "We miss Old Shep."

"Maybe he is guarding us on the trip," said Grace. "I'm going to watch for him at every station."

J.D. sighed. *It doesn't seem to occur to her that*

Chapter 3

Old Shep would have to run faster than the train to keep up with us.

Chapter 4

Sensitive Information

They started back to their car eager to see how it looked when the beds were put away. Most of the berths had been restored to seats. They met Miss More coming toward the dining car. She looked refreshed and pretty. The children politely stepped aside to let her pass.

She paused, smiling. "That was some wait in Kansas City, wasn't it? Except y'all didn't get there till nearly one o'clock. How'd you know the train was going to be so late?"

"Our Uncle works for the railroad, Miss More," Grace said proudly.

"You know my name?" Miss More sounded curious.

"I heard the porter call you Miss More when we

were getting on the train," said Grace, suddenly feeling a bit shy.

"You're a good listener," laughed Miss More. "Why don't you call me Dolly? It makes me feel so old to be Miss More. You're going all the way to L.A., too?"

Gracie enthusiastically nodded "yes" before anybody thought to stop her. Mamma had cautioned them about telling everybody their business.

"Maybe I'll see you around then. I'm a good listener, too." She gave them a mischievous smile. "I know that your family name is Harrison and you are Grace, Mary Carol, J.D. and Robert. But I'm not sure who is who. Except I'm pretty sure you aren't J.D. or Robert," she said, looking at Grace. Her eyes sparkled. "If you get bored later today, I'm always good for a game of charades or something. Okay?"

"I like her," said Mary Carol as they made their way on through the cars. *There has to be some perfectly good reason for her to have been in our car early this morning. After all, she was very nice to me,* she told herself.

"I like her too," said Grace. "She knows more than people think she does."

"Where do you come up with these ideas about people, Gracie?" asked Mary Carol.

Sensitive Information

Mr. Raymond had already restored most of the seats in their car when they returned. The seats were like high-back benches upholstered in a soft, comfy fabric. Each seat held two or three people. They were grouped so that a set of seats faced each other, one looking to the front of the train and one backward, making a compartment. To the children their compartment seemed like a cozy, velvety hideaway. Heavy curtains that had given their "bedrooms" privacy were now tied back between each set of seats. There was plenty of room. Uncle James had not only managed to get tickets, he arranged for them to have a whole compartment to themselves.

Most of the seats in their car were occupied. They didn't see any other children—not surprising since school wasn't out yet.

When Mary Carol saw who sat across from them, she thought her heart would skip a beat. In the forward facing seats were Mr. and Mrs. Hackworth. She could feel the red creeping up her neck. The occupants of the rear-facing seats were probably at breakfast.

"Thunderation, Irma!" Mr. Hackworth frowned. "We're stuck next to *them*. Reckon it comes from bookin' our tickets at the last danged minute. We shoulda had a bedroom but, no, you insist we have to leave on *this* train. We couldn't possibly wait another day."

"You're right Darling, this isn't the Super Chief," Irma Hackworth said soothingily as she adjusted her hat. "One would have hoped those seats would be occupied by somebody worth getting to know."

Mr. Hackworth's stiff, white collar and patriotic red, white, and blue patterned necktie held back a collapsing double chin. *How in the world did he get up the ladder to the top berth and back down again?* Mary Carol wondered.

In contrast to her husband, Irma Hackworth looked like somebody on the front of one of the movie magazines in the beauty parlor where Mamma got her hair done. She was wearing a fresh white blouse with her navy blue and white pinstripe suit. She was even wearing silk stockings—hardly anybody had silk stockings with the war going on. Her white gloves were neatly clipped to her purse with a golden glove holder.

Mr. Hackworth put his hand on his head, "I have a busted head. If I didn't know better, I'd say I'd had one too many whiskies last night. Between that and a bunch of snivelin' brats swarmin' all over the place, how am I supposed to get any work done on this here proposal to Lockheed-Vega?"

He shouldn't be saying something like that, thought Robert. *That kind of thing could hurt the war effort.* Lockheed Aircraft supplied airplanes to the Army.

Daddy told them to be tight lipped about any information related to the war. "Things have a way of getting to the wrong ears," he'd cautioned. "Sometimes what seems to be the least important little bit can be significant."

Well, at least nobody else heard. The information is safe with me, Robert reassured himself. *But there could be people on the train who'd give their right arm to see a proposal to Lockheed.* Robert looked around. He felt particularly sensitive about anything related to airplanes, since their daddy was in the Army Air Force.

"Come on, Laverne, darling. Let's get to breakfast before they quit serving," said Mrs. Hackworth. Looking in the mirror in her compact, she ran a powder puff over her nose. "Maybe we'll meet somebody interesting at breakfast. We'll ask to be seated at a table for four. I'm perishing for a coffee. I have a splitting headache, too. I slept like a stone, though. Not at all like me, especially on the train."

Grace and J.D. wanted to explore before they did anything else. Robert experimented with a detachable desk. Mary Carol hunkered down in the far corner of their compartment, looking under the seat, hoping to stay inconspicuous until the

Hackworths left. "You should stash your scouting gear here, Robbie."

"Nope," Robert was resolute.

"What was that you shoved in your pocket before we left home, Rob?" J.D. asked, keeping his voice down.

Looking a bit sheepish, Robert pulled out an old tobacco tin filled with matches. "Just in case we get stranded and have to camp out."

"We're on the train! When did you plan to camp out?" Mary Carol scolded, her head still under the seat.

"You're a Boy Scout, Robbie," said Grace. "You can make a fire with sticks."

"Yeah, but it doesn't always work so well. Besides, it takes a long time," said Robert. "Ask J.D. He's a scout, too."

"Probably a good idea to put those away." J.D. lowered his voice, "I have a feeling Mr. Raymond might not approve, not to mention those two across the aisle."

Mr. Hackworth groaned as he stood, hand on his head. "Criminy! Feel like I been slipped a Mickey Finn. Reckon somebody was tryin' to get at my plans last night?"

"Quit being so melodramatic, Lavern," Mrs. Hackworth said as they set out for the dining car. "The only thing we had to drink was that cocoa at the train station."

Mary Carol popped back up as soon as the Hackworths were gone. "What's in your pockets, J.D.?"

"That's for me to know and you to find out!" retorted J.D., a little sharper than he meant. He was impatient to explore the train, but he took Mamma's charge to look after everyone very seriously. *I can't ask them to be kind if I'm not,* he reminded himself.

"Please, can't we just go?" begged Grace.

As they were leaving they could hear Mr. Hackworth calling in a loud, demanding voice, "George, you there, George! We need to be seated somewhere away from that hornet's hive."

"Why does that man keep calling Mr. Raymond, George?" asked Grace.

"Maybe they got him mixed up with somebody else," said Robert.

"They must not have seen his name posted up there." J.D. shrugged, nodding toward the front of their car where a placque read, "Raymond Lincoln Moses, Porter."

They walked the full length of the train, both ways, looking over every car without running, pushing, or spying on people in the bedroom cars. "Let's go back to the lounge observation car," suggested Mary Carol when they got back to their seats. "Maybe we'll be able to see the mountains from there."

They were still in flat lands. There wasn't any sign of mountains from the observation car, but they were hopeful.

"My notebook!" Robert jumped up before they were settled. "I had it out right after we got back from breakfast. I'll make it snappy." He was gone before J.D. could remind him that they were supposed to stick together.

"Hutchinson, Kansas. Next stop Hutchinson, Kansas," a conductor called. The others watched as the train approached a massive red brick depot. Grace pressed her nose to the window. Sitting back on the platform was Old Shep. He looked up at her. "It's Old Shep again," she said.

"Where?" asked Mary Carol.

"Right there, can't you see him?"

"You have better eyesight than I do, Gracie," said J.D.

"Can't we go see him?" pleaded Grace.

"Oh, Gracie. Rob isn't here," said J.D. "we don't dare take the risk of somebody getting left behind."

Grace looked at him with disappointment in her eyes. But she didn't protest.

Meanwhile, Robert found his notebook in their compartment just as the train came to a halt. He was headed back to the observation car when he heard Mrs. Hackworth's voice coming from the opposite direction.

"I just need a breath of fresh air." She was talking to Mr. Raymond.

"Yes, Ma'am," said Mr. Raymond. "We'll be here no more than ten minutes. I wouldn't want to risk leaving you behind."

Robert thought he'd have a look out while the doors were open. A man hurried up to where Mrs. Hackworth stood near the steps to the train. She threw her arms around him. *Oh, no! Kissing,* Robert shuddered. It was one of those long, slobbery kisses too.

He was about to leave in disgust when he heard the man say. "When this beastly war is over, Darling."

"I know, I know, Rolf," replied Mrs. Hackworth. "It is so hard to wait. I do so love you. I don't know how much longer I can take it." She handed him one of her white gloves.

"I'll carry it over my heart," he said, putting the glove inside his suit jacket.

They started kissing again. Robert had as much as he could take. *If she wants to kiss somebody, she should be kissing Mr. Hackworth.* As he turned to leave, Mr. Raymond appeared at the door. Seeing Mrs. Hackworth and the man, still kissing, he looked at Robert and shook his head. "Sometimes a person can see things he'd rather not see. Probably a good idea to say nothing about it. We might ruin Mr. Hackworth's breakfast."

"Okay," said Robert, grinning sheepishly.

Mr. Raymond stepped off the train, "All aboard!"

Robert hurried on his way before Mrs. Hackworth boarded.

"Did you see Old Shep?" Grace wanted to know immediately.

"No," said Robert, "but I found my notebook." Looking out he could see the man who had been kissing Mrs. Hackworth hurrying to a car in the station parking lot.

"I want to draw the patch for the 442nd." He flopped into a chair and began digging in his knapsack for drawing pencils, all the time wondering if he should tell the others what he had seen. "I wish I knew more about the 442nd."

"The patch looked like a hand holding a torch," said J.D.

"Go for broke, that's their motto." It was Dolly More, just entering the car. "Mind if I join you?"

She moved a chair over. "The 442nd is an infantry regiment made up almost entirely of second generation Japanese Americans. They have the reputation of being one of the strongest infantry units in the Army. I see you have a collection of patches. Did you draw these yourself, Robert? It is Robert, isn't it?"

"Yes ma'am," said Robert. "I hadn't seen the 442nd before."

"Do you have the patch for the Army Air Force Training Command?"

"I do," nodded Robert, flipping through his notebook until he found it. "Star, flame, and wings." He proudly showed her.

"That's quite a collection," said Dolly. "Can you recognize the patches when you see a soldier? That isn't always as easy as seeing them in a picture."

"Sure," said Robert. "I'm good at it."

"How come you know our names?" asked Grace.

Dolly laughed. "I asked. People have been treating you like royalty since you got to the station in

Kansas City. I wish I'd asked sooner, though. I'd have spoken to your mother. I met her and your Uncle James when I was a little girl. My Auntie Myrtle had a house in Sage, Oklahoma, not far from your Grandpa and Grandma Matthias' farm. She taught school in Sage when your Uncle was a boy. We used to go to her house in the summer. We always visited your grandparents, too. How are Mr. and Mrs. Matthias? It's been years since I've seen them."

"They're good," said Mary Carol. "We go there every summer for a whole month."

"Except this summer," said Robert.

"I know," sighed Dolly. "This war has everything turned upside down. May I see your sketches, Robert?"

He proudly showed her his drawings. Dolly took time to look at every one and comment on them.

"Wonder when we'll see the mountains?" asked Mary Carol.

"I was wondering the same thing myself," said Dolly.

"You got the wrong magazine," said Grace.

Dolly looked at her, hand closing over the magazine in her lap. She had a curious expression on her face.

"When that man ran into you. He gave you the wrong magazine," Grace explained, adding, "at the train station."

Dolly laughed. "I think I got the best end of that deal. I hope he likes my *Ladies Home Journal* as much as I'm enjoying his copy of *The Saturday Evening Post*. I'd read my magazine from cover to cover by the time we boarded.

"What were you saying about the mountains, Mary Carol?" Dolly, changed the subject.

"Mr. Elijah said that we'd probably see them before we get to La Junta," said Mary Carol. "He said they look close, but then they seem to shift position and look far away again."

Grace didn't say any more about the magazine. But she wondered. The magazine the man took looked just like the one Dolly had with her.

"I guess that's like a mirage on the desert," said Dolly. She looked out the windows on both sides. Standing suddenly, she said, "I'll bet the porter has our beds put away. I'm going to check on mine, if you'll excuse me." She hurried out the opposite end of the car.

"The sun is too bright on that side, Laverne. I can't see a thing. Let's sit over here," said Mrs. Hackworth as they entered the observation car.

Chapter 4

"I wanted to book the Super Chief. I don't know why you're in such a gall danged hurry, Irma. They'll think I'm too eager," Mr. Hackworth whined.

Robert supposed he meant Lockheed. *At least he didn't blast it out over the whole car,* he thought.

"Laverne, darling, you're getting tiresome. But you're right about one thing. I don't think anybody interesting takes the Chief anymore." Mrs. Hackworth sat down not far away. "Although I heard there is a famous singer aboard."

She gets around in a hurry, thought Robert. He'd decided not to say anything to the others. *It's none of my business anyway.*

"Let's go back to our seats," J.D. said in a low voice. "I'd just as soon leave before they notice us. The minute we make a sound they'll be complaining."

"Do you think Dolly saw them, too?" asked Mary Carol. She couldn't erase the image of Dolly climbing down from the top berth in the night.

"She left in a big hurry," said J.D. as they gathered their things, "and in the opposite direction from her car."

Chapter 5

An Unexpected Assignment

When they got back to their seats there was a smartly dressed lady with white hair sitting where Mr. and Mrs. Hackworth had been. She was dressed in navy-blue except for the white bow on her hat. Grace noticed her shiny navy-blue lace-up pumps. The lady looked over the top of the book she'd been reading and smiled at them.

Sergeant Nakamura sat next to her. He was reading a newspaper.

"Did you trade places?" asked Grace.

"Don't disturb them, Gracie," said Mary Carol, adding in a whisper, "Remember what Mr. Raymond said. Besides, it's rude to ask personal questions."

"Oh that's all right," said the woman. "As a matter of fact, I did trade places. Mr. Moses promised that I'd have good neighbors. I see that he wasn't mistaken."

Sergeant Nakamura put down his paper and smiled at them, nodding. He gave the impression of bowing without actually doing so. "That goes for me, too. I see that everybody is up and about after that long wait in Kansas City."

"Yes, sir," said J.D. "We sure appreciated your help."

Grace looked at them, puzzled.

"He carried you down the stairs to the train, Gracie," said Robert. "Yeah, you were like a rubber duck, except about fifty pounds heavier."

"He did?" Grace looked completely flummoxed.

"Excuse me, Sergeant Nakamura," Robert began, "Would you mind autographing my notebook? I'm drawing Army patches that I've seen. I'm not sure if I have the 442nd right."

"Not at all," Sergeant Nakamura smiled. "May I see the book?"

Robert proudly handed it over.

"The 442nd looks good." The Sergeant leafed through the notebook. "An impressive collection, young man. You don't have autographs with all of the patches, do you?"

"No, sir, sometimes I don't have a chance to ask."

The sergeant signed the book next to the 442nd patch, passing it back to Robert.

"Ta-da-shi Nakamura," read Robert, trying to make sure he said it correctly.

"It isn't in Japanese!" Grace sounded disappointed.

Sergeant Nakamura smiled ruefully. "Japanese writing isn't in favor right now."

"Well, it should be," said Grace. "Mamma says we should learn as many languages as possible. She didn't get to learn German because of that other war."

"Your Mamma sounds like a very wise person," said the woman.

"I see you've met Miss Spright." It was Mr. Raymond. Lowering his voice to a whisper, he added, "Except for yourselves, she is my favorite passenger. Sergeant Nakamura is on my favorites list now, too. They were kind enough to trade places with the passengers seated here.

"I thought you children might want to go up to the observation car so you can have a good view of Dodge City. It's coming up soon."

"We don't mean to be rude, Mr. Raymond," said J.D., trying to be tactful, "but we just came from there. It was starting to get crowded. . ." his voice trailed off.

"It so happens just about everybody up there has moved to the bar," said Mr. Raymond. "Apparently there is a famous singer aboard who happens to be in the bar. Word gets around."

"*The* Dodge City?" said Mary Carol. "Was it really so bad in the old days?"

"Hard to say," said Mr. Raymond. "It was on the old Santa Fe Trail. Later it was a stop when they drove cattle from Texas to Montana. I reckon it was lawless in the way a lot of places were until they got organized."

They were between cars when they met Dolly. "Quick, over here. I was looking for you." Putting a finger to her lips to silence them, she motioned them to a luggage area away from possible traffic. She spoke calmly and quietly, "This is very important. I need your help. I have to get off the train. Robert, put this in your knapsack and keep it hidden." She handed him her magazine. "There's someone on the train who'd like to have it. If they get it, some very bad things could happen to our troops. Give it to an Army Air Force Training Command Staff Sergeant at the station in La Junta. You'll recognize the patch on his uniform, just like in your book. Don't try to find him. About 10 minutes before time for the train to board he'll sit somewhere at the back of the waiting room and read *The Saturday Evening Post*—it will be exactly like this one, woman with the umbrella, April 8. When the Station Master announces boarding for the Chief, he'll get up, leaving his magazine on the seat. You be there to pick it up."

"Wait a minute," said J.D. "Begging your pardon, but we don't really know you. I promised to look out for everyone. I can't let Rob do something dangerous." He spoke quietly, firmly, and politely, but inside, J.D. was shaking. Dolly seemed nice enough. She knew a lot about them—but what if she'd found out the same way she found out about their names? *What if she is an enemy spy?*

"You're right, J.D. We've only just met. You're right to be suspicious," said Dolly, brow furrowed. "Okay, what will convince you? I haven't much time."

"What was Uncle James' dog named?" asked Grace before J.D. could get in a word.

"Old Shep," said Dolly, putting her finger to her lips again to remind them to speak softly.

"What did Uncle James collect when he was a boy?" asked Robert.

"He had a moth collection. His prize was a Luna

moth." Dolly looked around anxiously.

"I'm convinced," said Mary Carol. "I was anyway." The others nodded agreement. "You wouldn't know about the moth collection if you hadn't been to the Matthias farm. It's still there."

Dolly quickly repeated her directions, adding. "The Staff Sergeant will walk up to the ticket window after he leaves the magazine. Go up to him and say, 'The lady in the gray suit couldn't come. She told me to ask, "How is your dog doing?"' If he says 'Cowher is fine, how is your dog?' you say, 'Old Shep is doing great. I think you left this magazine.' Give him this one. Keep the one that he left. You can throw it away when you get to your Uncle's house, but not before."

"Old Shep!" Grace clapped her hands.

Dolly asked hurriedly, "Can you do this, Robert?"

Wide-eyed, Robert nodded "yes." He took off his knapsack, carefully putting the magazine in the back while Dolly made him repeat the directions and exactly what he was supposed to say. "If the Staff Sergeant doesn't say those exact things, give him the magazine he left behind and keep this one. Give it to your Uncle James and ask him to destroy it."

She looked at them searchingly. "Can I count

on all of you? You'll be safe as long as you don't talk about it to anyone. Keep the magazine in the knapsack until you need it, Robert. I'm so sorry to have to ask this. It's not safe for me to stay on the train and I don't know anyone else I can turn to. Besides, there are some things only a child can do. Now go quickly. I hope we meet another time."

"Me too," said Grace, throwing her arms around Dolly.

"Go now, please!" said Dolly. "You'll be safe. Nobody has any reason to put us together. And don't say anything about me getting off the train."

The children hurried up to the observation car just as the train came to a halt. They could see passengers getting off, but Dolly wasn't among them. They kept their eyes fastened on the platform below, too worried to look out over the city. The train was pulling away when they saw her, suitcase in hand, hurrying to the station.

"Oh good," said Grace. "Old Shep is with her." She could see Old Shep trotting along right next to Dolly. The others looked at each other quietly shaking their heads, but nobody said anything.

They watched Dolly to see if anybody followed her, but it appeared as if she got off at the last possible minute. They stared out the window, afraid to talk about what they wanted to talk about and not having anything else to say. J.D. wondered if he should take on the assignment of switching magazines, but Dolly asked Robert. *She must have had her reasons. But if anything happens to Rob, I'll never forgive myself.* Nor could he help wondering about what to do if Grace kept insisting she saw Old Shep. He was starting to worry about her.

Mary Carol tried to plan out the logistics. She imagined Robert walking up to the officer. *Maybe we should provide a distraction, but what?* She wasn't worried about Grace. *She's such a little girl. It's hard for her to be away from home.* There was something else, too, though Mary Carol wasn't prepared to discuss it with the others. Old Shep just might be magic. *Maybe we can't see Old Shep because we don't believe he's there.*

Grace wondered who the people after Dolly were and what she'd do if she met one of them. She hadn't seen anybody who looked that mean. *What if they catch Robbie? Old Shep was there to help Dolly. Will he be here to help Robbie?*

Except for Robert, they spent a miserable hour before lunch, worrying and trying to occupy themselves with the activities they had brought along for the trip. Robert wasn't worried. He calmly wrote notes to himself in his own adaptation of pig Latin so he wouldn't forget exactly what to say. If enemy spies happened to get his notebook they wouldn't be able to make sense of it.

He'd done a lot of stuff that nobody ever suspected him of doing, like putting a water balloon on top of a door at school and having it splash all over the biggest bully in his class. The boy deserved it, too. He always gave that door a shove when he came through, just like he always gave Robert a shove when he walked past. *The thing about being small for your age is that nobody thinks you can do anything,* he thought. *Which means you can get away with a lot.*

When Mr. Raymond came to get them for lunch, it was almost noon. "Miss Spright said you hadn't returned to your seats. How did you like the looks of Dodge City?"

"It was very different than we expected," said J.D. truthfully.

"Didn't see any gun fights, then?" said Mr. Raymond, giving them a mischievous look.

"Spright, that's another name for fairy," said Mary Carol, changing the subject as they made their way through the car.

"Is she really a fairy?" asked Grace. There was something about Miss Spright, something mysterious that seemed to simmer below the surface.

Mr. Raymond gave her a big, conspiratorial smile. "I wouldn't be the one to say. You never know whom you'll meet on the Santa Fe Chief."

"Anyway, fairies are much smaller," concluded Grace matter-of-factly. "And I think they have wings."

"Are we getting close to the Rocky Mountains?" Robert asked. In all the excitement he'd almost forgotten. Seeing the Rockies was one of the things he most looked forward to on the trip.

"We'll see the Sangre de Cristos any time now. They're part of the Rockies that come up from the South," said Mr. Raymond. "You might catch a glimpse of Pike's Peak before we turn south out of La Junta. You'll probably get a good view from the dining car after while. It's a nice, clear day."

They were in the dining car when the train stopped in Syracuse, Kansas. Nobody said anything about looking for a black and white dog, but their eyes searched the platform. "Old Shep. There he is again," Grace said, pressing her face to the window by their table. "I guess that means. . ." she checked herself. "means everything is okay. I wonder if he is going to be at every station?" She knew the others didn't believe her, but she also knew what she saw.

By the time Mr. Elijah brought lunch, a long line of snow-capped mountains appeared on the horizon to the left of the train. They looked as if giant fingers had crimped them like the edge of a piecrust, then dusted them with powdered sugar. On their side of the dining car, they saw the dark purple silhouette of Pike's Peak rising above the lavender-colored shadows around it.

"That must be the tallest mountain in the the whole United States of America!" exclaimed Grace.

"No, that would be Mt. Whitney in California," said Mr. Elijah, setting down their dessert.

"Not if you count Alaska Territory," said Robert.

"You're right about that, young man," said Mr. Elijah. "The tallest mountain would be Mt. McKinley. That's one mountain I'd love to see."

"Mt. Everest is the tallest in the world. Mt. McKinley is the third tallest," said Robert. "Its ancient name was Denali."

"I suppose you read that somewhere," said Mary Carol, rolling her eyes.

"Mountains are very pretty, but I don't ever want to be a mountain climber," said Grace. "It would be too cold and too scary."

"Don't worry, Gracie," said J.D. "We aren't going to be doing any mountain climbing on this trip."

Chapter 6

The La Junta Station

As frightening as the possibilities ahead of them were, the children were eager to get out and stretch at La Junta when they finally arrived shortly after noon. "There will be an hour and a half lay-over," a conductor announced. "They are making some track adjustments along the Raton Pass. One and a half hours."

The children looked at each other. They hadn't dared to say a word about what would happen in La Junta.

"We usually have a much shorter layover," Mr. Raymond explained when the train came to a stop. "We've been asked to give the cleanup crew a little more time on the Pass. How about you stand here on the platform with me until everybody is off?"

"Do train stations have a dog mascot like fire

stations do?" asked J.D., looking up and down the platform to see if he could catch a glimpse of a black and white dog. "You know, you always think of Dalmatians at a fire station." He had to allow for the fact that Grace might actually have seen a black and white dog at the other stations and they just happened to miss it.

"Not to my knowledge, why?" asked Mr. Raymond.

"Just wondering," said J.D.

Stepping out of their car, a man handed Mr. Raymond his briefcase. "I don't want to leave this unattended. Look after it, will you, George?"

"I don't see George, Mr. Phelps," said Mr. Raymond in a pleasant voice. "My name is Raymond Lincoln Moses. I will be glad to take care of your briefcase." Then, turning to the children, he said, "Don't run off exploring. Stick together. Wouldn't want anybody to miss the train. We're adding a private car at the end. You might like to watch them hook it up. Just stand back on the platform."

"How will we know when it's time to board?" asked Mary Carol pensively.

"They'll announce the train inside the waiting room," said Mr. Raymond. "I'll come get you if you are in any danger of being late."

"I'd like to know about 10 minutes before hand,"

said Mary Carol.

"There's a big clock in the station lounge. You won't need to worry about keeping track of the time." Mr. Raymond saw the last of the passengers out of the car.

The air felt cool and fresh. Along the platform vendor carts were selling gifts and snacks. There was a hotel and restaurant connected to the station where you could get a proper meal if you were on a train that didn't have meal service.

"Any money burning a hole in your pockets? Take a look at what the vendors have for sale," said Mr. Raymond. "There's an exhibit in the station lounge that you may find interesting. La Junta's a famous spot. Back in pioneer days, the Oregon Trail and the Santa Fe Trail parted ways here. By the time you get all that done, it will be time to board."

"What's a private car?" Robert asked.

Mr. Raymond explained. "Sometimes rich folk buy or lease their own railroad car. They have it furnished the way they want. There's plenty of space for a sitting room, dining room, bedrooms, and a private bath. Some of them have servants' quarters and a kitchen area. The railroad has a private car for the higher-ups in the company to use as an office. It has bedrooms and a sitting room, too. Sometimes your Uncle James travels in an office car."

"Does that one belong to a movie star?" Mary Carol asked hopefully.

"Could be. It isn't an office car," said Mr. Raymond. "It came down on the train from Denver yesterday. It's had a long wait, too. We usually pick up several passengers from Denver when we get to La Junta. Now off you go. Enjoy the fresh air."

They walked to the far end of the platform where nobody could hear them, pretending to watch the private car. "Golly, Robert, do you think Dolly is a spy?" asked Mary Carol.

"Maybe she just overheard something that put her in danger," said J.D.

"But she was going all the way to L.A.," said Mary Carol.

"If she is a spy, she's a good spy," said Grace.

"She watched everything that was going on when we were in Kansas City," said Robert.

"No she didn't, she was asleep at least half the time," said J.D.

"No, she was pretending to be asleep," said Robert. "I think she's a spy."

"Well, she was very kind to me when that awful Mrs. Hackworth yelled at me for bumping into her in the Ladies Room," Mary Carol said. Then she had to tell them what happened. "And the other thing. I saw her climbing out of the top berth where Mr. and Mrs. Hackworth slept last night. It was when we stopped in Emporia."

"Gee!" Robert whistled.

"Wonder what she was doing?" asked J.D.

"Mr. Hackworth was talking about having a proposal to make to the aircraft company, but he was stuck to that briefcase like glue," said Robert.

"But he said he felt like he'd been drugged," said Mary Carol.

"What about the magazine?" asked Grace.

"Right," said J.D. "Maybe it had a secret message that an agent was passing along to her."

"It was the same magazine," said Grace. Seeing their puzzled look, she explained. "At the station in Kansas City. The magaine she dropped and the magazine the man gave her were the same. It wasn't *The Ladies Home Journal.*"

"Wait a minute," said Robert abruptly. "I just remembered something I read. Sometimes it takes heat to read a secret code written in invisible ink. Dolly asked the porter to fill her hot water bottle with boiling water right after we got on the train. Maybe there was a message in the magazine and she needed the hot water bottle to read it."

"Or something the Hackworths had," added Mary Carol, "otherwise, why would Dolly be climbing up into their berth in the wee hours of the morning? Maybe she was stealing something."

"Hmm," said Robert. "Dolly was drinking something hot before she boarded the train. . . ."

"And so were the Hackworths," Mary Carol added.

Robert put words to what they were both thinking, "You don't suppose she could have put something in their cocoa, do you?"

"There's no way we'll ever find that out," said J.D., returning to the practical. "Obviously we can't ask Mr. and Mrs. Hackworth. We'd better plan a strategy for looking as normal as possible and doing what Dolly asked us to do. The fact is, nobody said, 'Old Shep,' anywhere near her. She didn't pick it up from us. She's using Old Shep as a code. And she could answer our questions without so much as a pause. So I don't think she's an enemy agent. She has to be one of ours. I think she got trapped somehow and had to get off the train. Since she knows Uncle James, she knew she could trust us."

"*If* she knows Uncle James," said Robert.

"We're just going to have to trust that she does," said Mary Carol. "She seemed trustworthy to me."

"But if you were a really good spy, you'd want to seem trustworthy, wouldn't you?" asked Robert.

"I trust her," said Grace, "even if she didn't tell the truth about the magazine."

"Actually, I do, too," said J.D. "She admitted that she learned our connection to Uncle James by asking a porter, that she didn't begin to figure it out until we were all on board. And Old Shep—you wouldn't just pull that out of the air. Who would know about that moth collection? Nobody, unless they'd been to the farm. I think we made the right decision. Now we have to follow through."

Mary Carol took a deep breath, bracing herself. "Okay, everybody, we have some time. We'd better start acting normal right now. Maybe we should look at the vendors, like we would if this hadn't happened."

"And we can look for Old Shep," said Grace. "Maybe Old Shep is at the station. Maybe he knew we'd need him."

"Then we can go into the station and find a place to sit near the back," said J.D. "Mamma gave me Chutes and Ladders for the trip. We can play that and keep our eyes open. Another thing, we can look around to see if there is a dog that looks like Old Shep, but let's not use his name since it's the code name Dolly gave Robert. We should be careful."

"What about a distraction?" Mary Carol asked.

"I don't think so," said J.D. "Nobody pays much attention to kids anyway, unless they're acting out."

"Yeah," agreed Robert. "I probably have a better chance if we just keep quiet—but not too quiet. That would look suspicious."

"We can't talk about it any more until we are absolutely alone," said J.D. "But we can talk about other stuff. Remember, Gracie, we won't say Old Shep, even if we see him."

"No, we'll just go hug him," said Grace.

They agreed that it was the best plan, or at least the best one they could think of. So they moved on to the vendors. Everyone spent some of the money Mamma gave them for the trip. J.D. found a water bag. "Does this thing really hold water?"

"You bet," said the man minding the cart. "It's the best kind of water holder for desert conditions: lightweight and efficient. Planning on doing some desert exploration?" He handed J.D. his change.

"No, guess not," J.D. grinned. "But I like this water bag."

Mr. and Mrs. Hackworth made their way through the vendors, passing by the children as if they weren't even there. Sergeant Nakamura was buying a newspaper nearby.

"Makes me sick to my stomach to see 'em in uniform," said Mr. Hackworth.

"Well, he is, Laverne," said Mrs. Hackworth. "You're going to have to deal with it. That's the way it is."

"What a mean thing to say!" Mary Carol exclaimed. She didn't care if they did hear her. "And after he traded places with them."

"Do you think they give a fig?" asked Robert.

"No," said J.D., "unfortunately, they probably don't."

Grace bought a tiny music box carousel. The usually practical Robert bought a kaleidoscope. Mary Carol looked at Indian blankets, worrying about the time.

The man who handed Mr. Raymond the briefcase rushed past them and into the lounge. "Wonder why people keep calling Mr. Raymond, George?" asked Grace.

"He doesn't look like somebody named George, does he?" J.D. wondered. "Somebody famous?"

Miss Spright was looking at curios at a nearby vendor. Turning to them, she said, "Excuse me. I couldn't help overhearing. 'George' is a very rude way of addressing a porter. It goes all the way back to slave days when slaves were called by their master's name. The man who built the first sleeper car was named George Pullman. So there are rude people who want to call Pullman car porters George, as if they didn't have a name of their own. There's no excuse for it. That's your history lesson for the day." She smiled at them kindly.

"Well, that's just not right," said Grace indignantly.

"Unfortunately, it isn't a very nice history," said Miss Spright. "So we have to do our bit to set it right."

"That's why you traded places," said J.D.

"Partly," said Miss Spright. "I was glad to do it for Mr. Moses. And just think, if I hadn't, I wouldn't have met you four. Are you looking for a blanket, Mary Carol?" She took them to a vendor where she knew the lady selling blankets. Mary Carol got a discount, but even so, she spent all of her trip money to buy it. She wasn't sorry, though. It was a beautiful blanket, full of possibilities.

"It can be a tent, or a cloak, or just about any-thing," she explained. "You just have to use your imagination."

"That's the spirit, Mary Carol!" Miss Spright smiled, eyes sparkling. "Imagination can take you all kinds of interesting places."

After that they sat on the floor in an out-of-the-way corner of the station waiting room where they had a good view. There were a few soldiers in the station, but none of them were officers and none wore the Army Training patch. They began playing Chutes and Ladders. Grace, who wasn't involved in the game, was busy noticing how much you could see, sitting on the floor. Unfortunately, she hadn't seen Old Shep, but she was hopeful. She watched as a lizard scurried from bench to bench.

Suddenly Mary Carol exclaimed, "She must be a movie star!"

The most beautiful woman they'd ever seen swept through the station. Just about everybody in the waiting room stopped what they were doing and stared. The woman held her head high as if she were indifferent to the world around. Grace thought she enjoyed being looked at, though. There was something about the haughty way she walked. She wore high-heeled shoes that matched her purse, handbag, veiled hat, and pencil-slim black skirt. She was wearing silk stockings, too. There was a dark mink fur around the shoulders of her fitted, red jacket. Grace could hardly bear to look at the little head and feet that dangled from the fur.

The woman held on the arm of a man who looked

like a movie star, too. He also had a haughty look about him—haughty and vain.

"I'll bet they're going to that private car," said J.D.

"Guess that will make Mrs. Hackworth happy," said Robert. "She is keen to see somebody famous."

"Uncle James said lots of famous people and movie stars still take the Chief," said Mary Carol. None of them knew enough about famous people or movie stars to know for sure.

"I don't like her," said Grace.

"What? You don't even know her," said Robert. He started to tousle her hair. Grace dodged.

"Maybe he's the movie star," said Mary Carol, glancing at the clock. Ordinarily she'd have been completely star-struck, but now she was too worried about Robert.

"I just don't like her," Grace repeated. She didn't know why, but it was more than the fur the lady wore that troubled her.

"It's almost ten minutes until time to board. He should be here by now," breathed Mary Carol.

J.D. whispered, "Whatever you do, don't anybody gawk or nudge each other when he comes. Why don't you go over and buy a candy bar or something from the newsstand, Rob. That way you'll be on your feet when he does appear and you won't look so conspicuous."

"If he appears," breathed Mary Carol restlessly.

"We're not supposed to be talking about it," said Grace primly. The others let it pass; they were too nervous to start a fuss. Besides, she was right.

Chapter 7

Robert's Big Moment

"I'm out," said Robert as if they were playing an ordinary game and the only thing he had to worry about was boarding the train. "You two finish." He stood and stretched, opened his knapsack and looked inside. Carelessly putting it over one shoulder, he walked across the back of the lounge as if he didn't have a care in the world. At the newsstand, he bought a candy bar. Just as he was paying for it, a soldier entered the station. Looking around casually, the soldier took a seat near the back of the lounge. Robert immediately noticed his Army Air Force Training Command patch. Below was the insignia with three chevron stripes for sergeant with one rocker, indicating a staff sergeant.

The others could see a soldier, but they were too far away to tell if he was the right person. J.D. took a deep breath, trying to look absorbed in the game. Grace put her head in Mary Carol's lap, afraid to look. Mary Carol felt frozen. When the soldier sat down and began reading a magazine, she thought her heart would stop beating. Robert casually made his way back around the lounge, pausing to look at one of the exhibits not far from where the Staff Sergeant was seated.

"All aboard the Santa Fe Chief stopping in Albuquerque, New Mexico; Ash Fork, Arizona; and Los Angeles, California." The Station Master's droning call rang out. Startled, Mary Carol resisted the nearly overwhelming impulse to gawk. She figured it was okay to look Robert's way, after all, they'd be boarding together. It would be perfectly normal for her to look for him and worry. Passengers hurried to gather their things. Nobody seemed to pay them any attention.

Robert watched from where he stood, pretending to be absorbed in one of the displays. The Staff Sergeant got up, left his magazine, and walked up to the newsstand by the ticket counter.

Robert walked over to the bench where he had been sitting, picking up the magazine. It was *The Saturday Evening Post,* April 8, 1944, woman under an umbrella on the cover. Without looking around he put it in his knapsack, right at the front. He walked straight up to the sergeant. Pulling out his notebook with the army patches, he said. "Excuse me, Sir, could I have your autograph?"

The officer looked a bit put off at first, but smiled kindly. "Sure, Son," he said, quickly scrawling his name next to the Training Command patch. He looked around the station searchingly as he handed it back to Robert.

"The lady in the Gray Suit couldn't come," said Robert quietly, hoping that his voice didn't sound as shaky as he felt. "She told me to ask, 'How is your dog doing?'"

"She did, did she?" The sergeant looked at him directly with stern eyes.

"Yes, Sir." Swallowing, Robert didn't drop his gaze.

"Tell her Cowher is doing fine. How is your dog?"

"Old Shep is great. And I think you left your magazine, Sir," said Robert. His hand shook as he reached into his knapsack. He was careful to pull the one from the back where it had been since Dolly gave it to him.

"So I did. Thank you, young man," said the Staff Sergeant.

Robert turned without looking back. He met the others who were waiting at the door of the station.

Before Mary Carol could stop her, Grace said, "That was a very nice thing you did, Robbie." She used her charming little girl voice and smiled sweetly.

Somehow it seemed like exactly the right thing to say. It broke their heavy silence and made things seem almost natural. *You may be small, but you're a brick, Gracie,* J.D. thought.

Mr. Raymond stood by their car, greeting passengers by name. Mary Carol asked about the beautiful woman. "Sorry I missed seeing a pretty lady. Like I said, you never can tell who'll be on the Chief. But, like my Mamma always used to tell me, you can't judge a book by its cover." He motioned for them to stand with him. "Better stand out here with me and enjoy the last bit of cool, fresh air while we can. Looks like we may have some rain going through the mountains. But it will be a long haul through the desert before we get to L.A."

The sky to the south was clouded over, but the children were too keyed up notice or to appreciate the fresh air. They stood quietly by Mr. Raymond, unable to think of anything to say. Grace kept hoping to see Old Shep. But he wasn't there.

A very tall man with silver-gray hair and a short, neatly trimmed beard came toward them, an old canvas messenger bag slung over one shoulder. Grace recognized him immediately from his shoes.

The others had seen him, too, a man slouched in a chair not far from where they sat, broad brimmed hat pulled down over his face, feet propped up on his canvas bag. He must have been fast asleep. He was probably the only one in the lounge who didn't sit up and take notice when the beautiful lady walked through.

"Now, this is somebody famous," said Mr. Raymond.

"Maybe to you and three or four other people. How are you Ray?" The man shook Mr. Raymond's hand. "What he means is that sometimes I ride his train." He sounded gruff. But there was a twinkle in his eyes.

"This is Mr. Nichols," said Mr. Raymond. "He's the archeologist responsible for collecting many of the fossils in the Denver Museum of Natural History."

J.D. suddenly felt the tension leave him. "Gee! I've never met an archeologist before."

"Did he say that I collect old fossils or that I *am* an old fossil?" Mr. Nichols asked. "Both would be correct."

He turned to Mr. Raymond, "These four were having a grand time sitting on the floor in the lounge playing Chutes and Ladders. Maybe I should say these three. The youngest was lizard-watching. They don't know me, but I know them."

Shaking J.D.'s hand, he said, "You have to be J.D., the eldest. I can see why your mother put you in charge. You show all the signs of a good leader."

Turning to Mary Carol, he said, "You are a lot like your mother was at your age, Mary Carol. She was always looking out for others, too—and smart, just like you."

"Robert, the one who's always prepared—very sensible. Take good care of that knapsack." He shook Robert's hand.

"And Grace, the youngest. You see more than people think you do."

Dumbfounded, Grace suddenly felt too shy to speak.

"Your Uncle James told on you." Mr. Nichols laughed a comfortable, jolly laugh. "He told me you'd be on this train. I've known him since he was younger than you are now, Grace."

"So that's how come you know so much about us," said J.D., relieved that it didn't have anything to do with Dolly.

"He said I should avoid you four at all costs." Mr. Nichols sounded very serious. "He said you're frightfully boring and he dreads having to spend an entire summer with you." He paused for a moment, stroking his short silver-gray beard. "Or was it the other way around? Maybe he said that I'm frightfully boring and he'd hate to have to spend a summer with me. He'd be right, of course. I'm a dreadful bore."

Mr. Nichols was anything but boring. He had them all completely distracted from their worries. They felt as if they'd known him forever. He seemed like the kind of person you could tell a secret to without ever worrying that he'd give it away.

With the last boarding call, Mr. Raymond hurried them onto the train. Once they were on board, Mr. Nichols disappeared among the other passengers. "Do you think we'll see him again?" said J.D.

"I hope so," said Mary Carol. "He isn't at all like Uncle James."

"I think he's really old and not old at all," Grace said thoughtfully.

Robert looked at her curiously. "That's a funny thing to say."

Once they were back on the train, the thought of what Robert had just done came back with full force. They were all loose nerve endings, scared, cross, desperately needing to talk about it, and afraid to talk about it. Grace was at her worst. She was tired, frightened that there might be somebody bad loose on the train, missing Mama, worried about Daddy, upset about what had happened to Dolly, and disappointed that Old Shep wasn't at the station.

She began playing her music box. It was tiny, but loud enough to be terribly annoying. She played it over and over until other passengers looked their way, frowning. Even Miss Spright gave them a questioning look. The others begged her to please stop. She wouldn't until Mary Carol passed out bubble gum, threatening to leave her out.

J.D. suggested they go to one of the lounges to have lemonade with oatmeal cookies Mamma sent along for the trip.

"Maybe you'd like to play Old Man?" said Miss Spright. She began rummaging in her purse.

"Old Man?" asked Mary Carol.

Miss Spright handed them a set of playing cards. The words "Old Maid" on the box had been crossed out. Below them was written "Old Man" in black ink. The picture of the Old Maid had been altered, too, with a mustache and beard. "I don't think it entirely fair to always make an unmarried woman the object of ridicule, now do you? They are my own set, but you may keep them. I can make another set easy as not."

Sergeant Nakamura looked over the top of the magazine he was reading, an amused look on his face.

Once they were in the lounge they had a good laugh over the cards. "Miss Spright is a character, that's for sure," said Mary Carol. "But she has a point."

"I like her," said J.D. "She isn't afraid to be different. So is everybody ready to play?"

"No," said Grace. "I'm worried."

"I think we're all feeling a bit let down," J.D. said. "We can't do any more and it isn't likely that anybody will ever tell us anything more than we know. That is going to make it even harder."

Grace looked ready to burst into tears at any moment. "We'll never know what happened to …?"

"Shhh," scolded Mary Carol.

"Maybe we will. If she knows Grandpa and Grandma Matthias," J.D. tried to reassure her.

"But we've done the right thing," whispered Mary Carol as she dealt out Old Man cards. "We have to keep looking like nothing happened."

"We can't talk about it," whispered Robert, looking around to make sure nobody had been listening.

Chapter 7

Outside the sky was a heavy gray, as gray as they all felt inside. Splashes of rain began to fall against the windows.

"I'll get us a lemonade," said J.D., trying to lighten the mood. He still had some spending money left. But the porter in the lounge car wouldn't hear to it.

"Four lemonades coming up, courtesy of the Atchison, Topeka, and Santa Fe Railroad," he said, a broad smile on his face. "I wouldn't want your uncle to think we aren't looking out for you."

It wasn't long before they started to fuss. Robert, who was tired and shaken from his experience, but wouldn't admit it, slammed his cards on the table after the second game. "Why do we always have to let Gracie win?"

"Quit picking on her," Mary Carol scolded.

"Nobody's letting anybody win, Rob," said J.D. calmly.

"She's old enough to play fair," whined Robert.

"I am playing fair," said Grace, giving him an infuriatingly sweet smile.

"No you're not. Everybody helps you because if you don't win, you go into a pout. Then you put on that charming little girl act you always use to get yourself off the hook. I'm tired of this dumb game.

And I'm sick of this stupid old train. I'm going back to our seats."

"We're supposed to stick together, Rob," said J.D., trying not to lose his temper. "It's more important now than ever."

"Think you're big enough to make me?" Robert stood in a huff, knocking over his lemonade.

Mary Carol's temper flared. "Now see what you've done! Smarty pants! Think you're so smart because she gave you the responsibility!"

"Hold it everybody," said J.D. quietly, but firmly. "This isn't something to be fussing about out here in front of the whole train."

Robert stormed out, leaving the mess behind. *Everybody always blames me for everything. You'd think they'd have some appreciation.* Giving the magazine to the sergeant was the bravest thing he had ever done in his whole life. He may have acted cool and calm, but he was scared to death. Muttering to himself and too angry to realize what he was doing, he went past their seats, past the bedroom cars, all the way to the end of the train, and right into the private car.

Chapter 8

The Private Car

Robert thought he was in a bedroom car at first. A corridor ran along the side to the left by the windows. To his right were three rooms, two small and one larger. The window curtain on the door was open in the middle bedroom. It looked unoccupied.

Then he heard voices. That's when he knew he'd made a big mistake.

Ahead the corridor opened into a large paneled room with a polished wood table and chairs. Two people, backs to him, were studying a paper spread out on the table. The woman wore pink satin pajamas. She held a long jeweled cigarette holder in her left hand. The man was in his shirtsleeves, trousers held up with striped braces, sports jacket draped over a chair. He covered his mouth to suppress an enormous yawn.

Robert began to ease backward, hoping to get out before they noticed him. Just then, someone knocked on the door. He darted into the empty bedroom. Afraid to close the door completely for fear of making a sound, he held it almost shut, hunkering down out of sight.

"I'll get that, Darling," said the man.

"Your coffee, Sir," said a porter. As soon as they passed him, Robert stood up. It was so dark outside now that looking out the bedroom window, he could see everything reflected in the windows across the corridor. The man was with the beautiful woman they saw at the La Junta station.

"We're honored to have you on the Chief, Madam," the porter said politely. "Please let me know if there's anything I can do. . . ."

"Take it from him, Gary. You can set it on the end of the table out of the way." The woman interrupted without looking up. She spoke as if the porter wasn't even there.

The porter handed his tray to the man. Robert ducked again as the man saw the porter out. "When I return to collect the coffee service, I will get your dinner order, Mr. Lawton. I left a menu on the tray," the porter said.

"Thank you. We do prefer to dine in," said the

man—Mr. Lawton—handing the porter a tip. "It's nearly dark as night out there. Must be a doozey of a storm we're moving into," he said as he closed the door. Turning, he looked at his reflection in the corridor windows, running his fingers through his hair. Robert ducked down out of sight just in time.

As soon as it looked safe to do so, Robert quietly slipped out of the bedroom. He intended to leave immediately.

"The puzzle is what to do about these drawings." The woman bent down, looking closely at the paper.

Robert caught his breath. *Are these people working for the Axis powers? Was this why Dolly had to get off the train?*

"Here you have the condor, sacred to American Indians." The woman traced the edge of the paper with her forefinger. "Notice everything along here: various reptiles, small animals, and birds. I don't know if it's just border decoration or they mean something."

Robert had heard about the possibility of enemy invasion of the continental United States. If they were planning an invasion, he needed to know about it. Listening intently, he hardly dared breath.

"Here's Coyote, trickster in the old legends. I wonder what role he has to play? He's all over—

down here, over there." She pointed to different places on the paper. "So he's not to be ignored."

"It looks like it was meant to be a decorative map." Yawning again, Mr. Lawton poured their coffee. "Here, Darling."

The woman took the cup. "Oh, no. That's what the boy thought. This is far more than a decorative map if it's what I think it is. The boy didn't know what he had. I doubt that his mother knew what she was drawing when she made it for him. It was the paper she used."

"Paper? Boy and his mother?" Mr. Lawton sounded baffled. "I thought this was about an antique map that was supposed to be yours." He drained his cup of coffee. "M-mm, good coffee. Let's try these cookies."

"The boy and his mother were interfering in matters they had no business getting into. They are of no consequence to you." She took a sip of her coffee.

"Here's Raven, a trickster like Coyote. He's up here in the border." She tapped on the paper with the end of her cigarette holder. "Snowy Owl, sacred to some. . . . Mountain range. Here's the ocean."

"If that's the Pacific Ocean, the coastline isn't right," said Mr. Lawton, pouring himself another cup of coffee. "Do you want one of these cookies? They're excellent, homemade, big enough to get your teeth into."

"This isn't a 1940s coastline," she said, ignoring the cookies. "I'm not entirely certain of the time period—prehistoric. Sometime after the Ice Age. The map isn't exactly true to period, but it is true enough. Everything seems to move us north, but where?" She finished her coffee and handed the cup to Mr. Lawton.

Utterly baffled, Robert couldn't bring himself to leave.

"It can't be that old," said Mr. Lawton, finishing off his cookie. He took her cup, poured more coffee for both of them, and took a bite out of another cookie. "I mean, it's parchment. If it were ancient, wouldn't it be on vellum or papyrus or something like that?"

"It's old," said the woman. "That's not what I'm talking about. I'm talking about what the map is showing us."

"What about these flowers and the sea shells?" Mr. Lawton asked, gesturing with a half-eaten cookie.

"Now those are decoration. I can't see any use for them. All of this along the border has to be decoration." Pausing, the woman straightened up. "This is infuriating. It is *his* mischief at work! I should have done more to untangle this when I first heard about a map. The boy offered me a map. I didn't take him seriously." She stamped her foot angrily.

"What boy?" said Mr. Lawton, mouth full. "I do better with information."

"Don't talk with your mouth full, Gary. Never mind. It is as it is." Sighing again, she pointed to another part of the paper. "Up here you see Seagull, the Sun, Grizzly Bear, and Fire. Thunderbird—he's sacred to people of the north. But which ones of these are the important ones? Or, are all of them important? Maybe none are important. Maybe they are all just decoration. Confound him! He's made an infuriating puzzle of this."

"I don't get it. Why do you think the map is moving you north?" asked Mr. Lawton. Finishing off his cookie, he offered one to the woman, who ignored it. He took a bite.

The woman almost growled. "Because north is where the activity is. Aren't you following this? Or are you just stuffing yourself. See, there is practically nothing here at the bottom and nothing much over there by the mountains to the east. Nice little drawings, not entirely accurate, but accurate enough. That's why I think she made the map for the boy. They were mapping the West—the boy's parents. She must have been making guesses about what the land was like. His father was a geologist and cartographer. He would have had some ideas about what the land was like before. That's what makes me think it is supposed to be sometime following the Ice Age, well before this part of the country was populated. There are some lakes still scattered across the landscape, left over from when the glaciers receded. Lake Bonneville is still there where we now have the Great Salt Lake, though greatly reduced in size. It isn't marked as swamp land so it has to be well after the glaciers withdrew."

"I told you we should have had a full meal at the hotel," said Mr. Lawton. He poured himself another cup of coffee and took the last cookie. "I don't see how you can follow a post Ice Age map and get anywhere."

"*I* don't intend to," the woman said firmly.

Robert knew he should go back, but he was frightfully curious. If they weren't working for the enemy, did they have a map to some ancient buried treasure? Or was it all a terrible enemy plan written in code?

Flattening himself against the wall by the bedrooms, Robert watched the reflection in the corridor windows and listened. He could feel his heart beating rapidly. It was frightening, but terribly exciting at the same time.

"No hidden runes." The woman held the map up to the light. "Another confusing thing, where does it start and where does it end? The start to this thing is as critical as the end, if my guess is right. That's how *he* thinks." She laid the map down again. "But then, he didn't do all of this himself. That's another argument for the boy's mother. I think he took her map from the boy and added to it. There was more than one hand in this. I have to keep that in mind, not to mention the magic. He wouldn't call it magic, but it amounts to the same thing."

"He who?" asked Mr. Lawton gathering the crumbs from the cookie plate and licking them off his fingers. "None of this makes any sense to me. You're talking about people and things I've never heard of before."

The woman ignored him. "Then there is the writing," she said. "The boy's mother couldn't have done that."

"What writing?" asked Mr. Lawton.

"On the back," she said, turning the map over. There was a long pause. "It's in the ancient language. There isn't a good way to translate. It's a poem, a bit of sentimental slush not worth repeating. And there's a riddle. The writing is much older than the map itself. It is hard to explain. The best I can do is to say that he must have taken the map back in time where the writing was added, then brought it back. Or maybe the writing was there before the map was ever made—but then she, the boy's mother, would have seen the writing. Has to be some magic at work. This is the first time I've actually seen the map. I didn't know it existed for certain, though I had my suspicions after I met the boy. The little sneak would have given it to me. I should have taken it then."

Mr. Lawton yawned again. "So you said. You still haven't said what boy." Having finished off the cookies, he tried to pour more coffee. The pot was empty. He reached for a box of chocolates at the end of the table.

"James, the boy was James Matthias," the woman muttered.

James Matthias? Uncle James? Robert was bewildered. *But Uncle James isn't a boy.* He waited, hardly daring to breath lest he make some noise.

Chapter 9

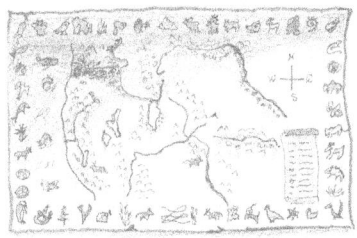

The Mysterious Map

After what seemed a very long time, the woman looked up at Gary Lawton and smiled. "You did good work getting this map, darling." She took a puff on her cigarette holder, and frowned.

Mr. Lawton produced a lighter from his pocket and held it for her. Blowing the smoke straight up, she traced something with her free hand. "I'm beginning to think some of these figures are clues. I'm not at all certain about the riddle. It says something like:

Fresh as the day the earth was made,
Water from the rock of a thousand lights,
for the healing of Mother Earth.

"Well, that's rubbish! Mother Earth can heal herself." The woman studied the paper for what seemed a very long time. Mr. Lawton studied the menu the waiter had left, popping a chocolate in his mouth. Robert was so anxious he was sweating.

"This part's illegible." She continued at last, "I can't read it at all, and I don't remember the poem very well. It's ancient. Anyway, below it says, *the one who may claim it,* or it could read *for the child who may claim it.* Yes, of course. It has to be *the child.* He added this last bit about the child. He must have. If it was ever a part of the riddle, I don't remember it."

She sounded bitter. "It's rightfully mine. He used a child to take it from me. So he'll use a child when he needs it. That's how his mind works."

Mr. Lawton quickly put down the menu before she could look up. "What? Take what? The map?"

"No. Hush a minute while I think. He's put a lock on the map. It's to keep me out." She began reading again. Mr. Lawton picked up the menu and reached for another chocolate.

"Another illegible bit, then it says:

Neither by asking nor by taking,
but the Keeper must be paid what is due.

"Ha! That part couldn't be changed, even by *him.* I don't know who this Keeper is, probably somebody he has put in charge of the crystal. It doesn't matter. The Keeper will have to obey the magic. There isn't any way around that." The woman laughed a wicked laugh. "As far as I know, the writing on this map is the only reference to the crystal that exists. The riddle doesn't appear in any of the old books. That's good. Otherwise, some fool of a wizard or magician would have been after the crystal long before now. I know at least one who'd give a large fortune to get his hands on it. There were seven crystals in the beginning. This is the last one. I must have it back."

The way she said it made a chill creep up Robert's spine.

"The 'rock of a thousand lights' is a crystal?" asked Mr. Lawton absently as he studied the menu.

"Yes." The woman bent over the map, tracing something with her forefinger. "The important thing about this map is that it shows how to find the Last Crystal—if you can read it." Straightening up, she said in a very angry voice, "I can promise you it was never meant for my eyes. He's used some magic that I don't understand yet to hide the full meaning and to control who can read the map. I assume that no mere child could figure it out—it would have to be a child in cahoots with him. The girl was in it with him or he'd never have figured out how to take my crystal."

"He who?" Mr. Lawton quickly put the menu behind his back.

Robert began inching back toward the door. The way she said "a child" terrified him. He was even more frightened than he had been at the station in La Junta.

"If another child had ever come for the crystal before now, I'd have known," the woman said. "It doesn't matter where he hid it. I'll know if anybody so much as touches it. I made sure of that when it was mine. I had it a long time ago when I didn't need it."

"How long ago?" Mr. Lawton asked. Yawning again, he covered his mouth with the menu and reached for another chocolate.

"Don't ask stupid questions!" she scoffed, slapping his hand before he could reach the other chocolates. Then adding, almost to herself, "I can't wait around for it indefinitely. I paid a very high price for those crystals. He will not cheat me of this last one."

"He who?"

"Hush your he who-ing. You sound like a donkey," she scolded. "And put away that menu. Keep eating everything in sight, and you won't be fit to be seen with."

Terrified, yet fascinated, Robert took a few silent steps backward, keeping his eyes on the woman's reflection in the corridor mirror.

She studied the paper, taking another long puff

on her cigarette holder, slowly blowing the smoke upward. "It must be somewhere in this area along what's now the Canadian border. I'm confident you'd have to start in the right place and work your way through these clues—the drawings—in some order that isn't clear at the moment. Certainly not in the order in which they appear, that would be too obvious."

As Robert eased his way back, she exclaimed, "They're more than clues! They must be like tokens. Maybe tokens you'd have to collect."

"And you cash them in for the crystal?" Mr. Lawton sounded bored.

The woman sighed impatiently. "Why do I waste my time with dullards? Haven't you heard anything I've said? I'm trying to think this through. They're clues, maybe. Tokens, maybe. Maybe they give you the right to see the crystal. Maybe you interact with them to unlock the map bit by bit. Maybe you have to give them to someone. Maybe just the Keeper, I don't know. That's the point. I DON'T KNOW!" She was practically shrieking now. "I need time. What I don't have is time. Why did I let this go on so long? How could I have been so utterly stupid?"

"Maybe they're the Keeper's due? It says the child must pay…," Mr. Lawton began.

"Oh, no," she cut in, laughing wickedly. "It will

require a great deal more than some simple tokens, or whatever they are, to claim the crystal, Keeper or no Keeper. At least that part of my work remains untouched. He couldn't change everything. A child may have deceived me and taken it, but the golden box holding the Last Crystal has not been opened. That's crucial and *he* knows it."

"What box? Who?" asked Mr. Lawton. Now he sounded cross.

She thought for a moment. "Unless there are five of them. Yes! Of course. That must be it. Five tokens. That would bring it to six. Six is important. He is obviously trying to interfere, but he hasn't figured out that part after all. That's good."

"What would bring it to six?" Mr. Lawton asked impatiently.

The woman ignored him. "But which ones of these things are the crucial tokens? I'm going to need some time to study this. I used to be very good with all this lore, but I haven't kept up. I didn't suppose I'd ever need it. I'm not even sure why he put all this writing on it. I can't see a purpose."

Robert silently stepped backward. He wanted out.

"There has to be a key to the map, something missing that allows you to interpret it." The woman's words were wrapped in hard fury. "Otherwise you couldn't expect a mere child to understand it, magic or no magic. Are you sure there wasn't anything else with the map?"

Curiosity overcame fear. Robert froze, listening intently.

"My dearest darling, Celeste, the map was the only thing in that locked box, in the *locked* cabinet, in the *locked* storage room, in the *locked basement* of the Denver Museum of Natural History. I know what I'm doing."

"I shouldn't have expected it to be as simple as stealing it," said the woman.

"I wouldn't call what I did a cakewalk." Mr. Lawton sounded angry.

"I'm talking about the big picture. We have to find the key before I can set this in motion. And it has to be before he wants it. With this silly war going on he could try something 'For the healing of Mother Earth,'" she said sarcastically. "I can't let him out maneuver me."

"I can't imagine anyone out maneuvering you," retorted Mr. Lawton.

She still ignored him. "I suspect that he's set it up as a quest—something heroic. That sounds like him. The writing must be there as part of the enchantment, inviting me in and locking me out. To understand it fully requires going backward. I know that much. He knows I can only go forward. My part will come at the end when the magic I set in place takes over. Someone must do this for me. You can manage the tokens. But I shall require a child to deal with the Keeper and to claim the crystal for me, at the very least."

"Don't ask me to go looking for your crystal," said Mr. Lawton. "I'm no Boy Scout. And I can't follow some prehistoric map with writing on it that I can't even read."

"No, perhaps not. But you're possibly the best thief I've ever known. Why do you think I took up with you?" The woman was so fierce she sent another wave of chills up Robert's spine. Suddenly, her tone changed. "I'm being very hard on you, Darling, I've enjoyed every minute of corrupting you."

"Sometimes I wonder," Mr. Lawton said.

"Anyway, you'll have to do this for me. There's no one else I can rely on to do it right," she said sweetly. Turning to him, she put her arms around his neck and gave him a kiss on the cheek. "Don't worry about reading the map. I suspect that the right child will be able to read it." She pushed a lock of hair out of his face.

If they started kissing, Robert figured he could

dart out unnoticed. He had been steadily easing backward through the corridor. He was almost at the door to the car when suddenly the train lurched, throwing him against the corridor wall. The bedroom door had never shut properly. It flew wide open, slamming shut with a loud bang before he could catch it, leaving him sprawling on the floor. Whipping around, the woman shrieked, "Who are you and why are you in my car?"

"Excuse me," Robert gulped, looking up. "I didn't know. I was exploring the train. I thought this was another bedroom car. It was open, like the others. So I just came in. I do beg your pardon." He stood, stepping back, hoping they'd think it was the door to the private car that slammed shut.

The woman towered over him in an instant. She was even taller than she looked standing at the table. "How dare you! Can't you read? It says 'Private Car' on the door. Leave immediately."

"Wait, darling," Mr. Lawton put his hand firmly on Robert's shoulder, keeping him from making a run for it. "Here we have a child. What could be more convenient?"

"You bobblehead. I am not in want of a *boy*," she hissed. "It can't be just any child who happens to walk into my private car uninvited, either. It has to be a particular sort of child. A child like the first child. There's a lot to be done before we can even think about that part." Turning back to Robert, she demanded, "How long have you been here?"

"The train lurched. It threw me on the floor," said Robert, trying to avoid telling an out-and-out lie.

"She took a long puff on her cigarette holder. Blowing the smoke upward, just over his head, she surveyed Robert with a calculating look. "Let go of him, Gary."

"This car looks like all the others," said Robert, glad to be free of the grip on his shoulder. He was pretty sure it would be better if they didn't know the whole truth. The woman looked at him as if she were a snake swaying in front of her prey. Once at school he'd watched a filmstrip showing how the hooded cobra hypnotizes its prey. She had the same glinting look in her eyes as she studied him. For one horrible moment, Robert thought she was a cobra.

In his worst nightmares for years afterward, Robert relived that moment, wondering what might have happened next if things had gone differently. But at that very instant, the door to the car flew open.

Chapter 10

In the Nick of Time

"Oh! Beg your pardon." It was Mary Carol. Right behind her were J.D. and Grace. "We didn't mean to. . ." Words failed her.

"We're looking for our brother," said J.D.

"Now we have the whole nursery," Mr. Lawton said sarcastically. "Darling, shall we send for tea and cakes?"

For just a moment the woman stood frozen, staring at Grace. Then her whole manner changed. "So this is your brother," she said sweetly. "I thought there was a sign that says *Private Car*. Perhaps I am mistaken—you'll have to take care of that, Gary. Though I am surprised your parents allow you to go wandering about the train unsupervised."

"Our parents aren't with us," said Grace. Catching Mary Carol's disapproving look, she stopped short.

Mary Carol didn't like the way the woman was looking at Grace. She quickly changed the subject. "Are you a movie star, Miss?"

"What makes you ask?" The woman's eyes glinted.

Sensing the woman's vanity, J.D. jumped in, "Because you're so beautiful, Ma'am, and you never know whom you'll see on the Santa Fe Chief."

"Oh really?" The woman smiled a satisfied smile. "I seldom find children to be so observant."

Using his best manners, Robert said, "Again, I apologize for my mistake. We'll be on our way now."

Mr. Lawton gave them one of those silly, pouting looks adults who know nothing about children use when talking to them. "What? No tea and cakes?"

"Thank you, but no," said Robert firmly, before anyone could accept. "Mr. Raymond is expecting us."

"Mr. Raymond?" The woman raised her eyebrows ever so slightly.

"I shall be more careful in the future, Miss." Robert hurried on, afraid Grace would say Mr. Raymond was a porter. He didn't like the way the woman was looking at her, either. There was something cold and calculating going on behind her smiles. It gave him the chills.

"I'll say this for your brother," she said, looking at Robert. "He has impeccable manners." As they left the car, she added softly, "Even if he is a little liar." Robert, last to go, knew she meant for him to hear. He was nearly overwhelmed with relief when the door closed behind them.

"My knapsack!" Robert started. "I've left my knapsack."

"It's okay, Rob," said J.D. "I have it. You left it in the lounge."

All the way back the others chattered about the woman and man and the private car. It was a relief to have something to talk about besides the mystery surrounding Dolly. For his part, Robert shouldered his knapsack and said nothing.

"Still," J.D. said, voice lowered, when they got to their seats, "I didn't like the way she looked when Gracie said our parents weren't with us. Anybody else notice?"

"Maybe she's just interested," said Mary Carol. "And the man was very nice. He offered to send for tea and cakes."

"He was being sarcastic," said J.D. "Keep your voices down."

The train slowed as it pulled into a station, coming to a stop. "Let's see if the dog is at the station," said Mary Carol. They all hurried to the lounge at the end of the car where they could see out to the other side of the train. A sign read Trinidad, Colorado. There wasn't much activity and there was no black and white sheep dog sitting on the platform. Not even Grace saw one.

"I wish a dog was there and it was. . . ," Grace started to say Old Shep, but checked herself. She was more disappointed than she could say.

"I know," said Mary Carol. "It would be nice to think he is watching over us."

"I felt like somebody was watching over us back there in that private car," Robert spoke at last. "I say we got out of there just in the nick of time."

Grace brightened. "Maybe it was, you know who, but we couldn't see him!"

Mary Carol and J.D. pelted Robert with questions. J.D. gave a low whistle—all thought of espionage and spies was gone from his mind for the moment. "You think it's a map to buried treasure?" He looked around for fear someone had heard. Thankfully, Miss Spright and Mr. Nakamura were absorbed in reading and the other people who sat in their compartment were asleep. "Reckon we could get a look at that map?" he asked.

"No, not buried treasure," declared Grace. She'd been so quiet, they hadn't realized she was listening.

"Okay, what are you thinking, Gracie?" asked Mary Carol.

"Well, she was talking about finding things, and where the map is leading to. It almost sounds like the special route is as important as the crystal."

"Maybe you're right, Gracie," said J.D. "Rob, can you remember details? I mean, things on the map, like the condor."

"I'll write everything down," said Mary Carol, getting her little notebook.

Robert was so unnerved he found it hard to remember.

"You said Grizzly bear," prompted Grace.

"Just a minute," said Robert. "I'm trying to go in order. Coyote, Seagull, Sun, Snowy Owl, Grizzly bear, and Thunderbird—there are too many to remember. Oh, and Raven."

"It would help to see that map," said J.D.

"They mentioned flowers and sea shells—she didn't think they were important," added Robert.

"That doesn't mean they aren't important," Grace said.

"Okay, I'm adding them," Mary Carol put down her pencil. "Maybe we should make friends."

"She's not the kind you can make friends with. She gives me the heebie-jeebies," said Robert.

"But she was very nice to us when we barged in on her," Mary Carol said.

"You weren't there when she found me," said Robert. "I'm not sure what she'd have done if you hadn't come. She was furious. She looked at me like she was a snake hypnotizing its prey. I thought she was going to turn into a snake! Honestly. I was scared. I wouldn't look her straight in the eye. I was afraid to. Then you all came. Suddenly, she's sweet as honey. You didn't hear, but on the way out she called me a liar. I didn't lie to her. I just didn't tell her all the truth. I don't trust her."

Mary Carol still wanted to think good of her. "If you were looking at a secret treasure map, you might be suspicious of everybody, too, and pretty mad if you were interrupted."

"You couldn't get me to go back there with a team of wild horses," said Robert. "She's the kind of person who'd stuff you in a trunk and throw you off the train as soon as look at you."

"Robert James Harrison! What an awful thing to say," Mary Carol exclaimed.

"I mean it. She scares me. I don't want to ever see her again."

"Throw you off the train?" Grace was alarmed.

"He was exaggerating to make a point, Gracie," said J.D., trying to reassure her.

"I don't think so," said Grace. "She could be a very bad person, even if she is beautiful. You know, like Snow White's stepmother. If Robbie doesn't trust her, I don't either, no matter how beautiful she is. Besides, I didn't like her when she walked through the train station."

"Don't be unfair, Gracie," said Mary Carol. "Just because she's beautiful doesn't mean she belongs in some fairy tale where beautiful step-mothers are the meanies."

"What about the man?" asked J.D. "Maybe he's the meanie."

"He was just her side-kick," said Robert. "He didn't know what she was talking about half the time. He was too busy eating snacks, when he wasn't admiring himself."

"You don't think it could have something to do with the war, do you?" asked J.D. "I mean you hear about secret codes and all that."

"I did at first," said Robert. "But I don't think so. It is something very different, like something from fairy tales or from outer space—I'm serious."

Discussion ended when Mr. Raymond called them for dinner. "We'll be coming up to the famous S curves shortly. You can see the whole train at once, front and back. You'll get a good view from the dining car. You've probably noticed the train is going slow through the mountains. This is where they had the storm that held us up yesterday."

Chapter 11

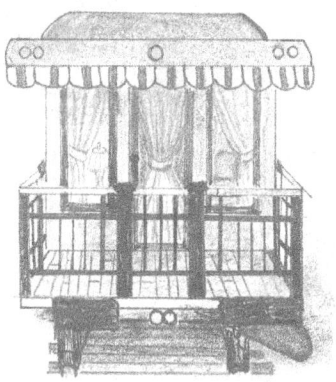

The End of the Train

They were leaving the rain behind. The mountainous landscape of northeastern New Mexico spread out before them as they looked out of the dining car. Neither of the things most on their minds could be discussed with so many people around. The train stopped in Raton, New Mexico. There was no black and white dog on the platform. Grace looked crestfallen. "I miss him," she said, without naming Old Shep. "And I miss Mamma and Daddy." She looked as if she could burst into tears.

Mr. Elijah brought their dinner. "Look out the window. We're on an S curve. You can see the whole train from here." Seeing the end of the train and the private car sent a chill through Robert.

"I think I know four people who are getting very tired," said Mr. Elijah "You all are awfully quiet this evening. I hope you'll be awake long enough to go up to the observation car and watch the sunset. It will be mighty pretty. First one to spot a star gets to make a wish."

They were just starting to think about dessert when a porter brought them an envelope addressed, "To: J.D., Mary Carol, Robert, and Grace," it read:

I want to apologize for being such a meanie to Robert this afternoon. I was very busy and not at my best, I fear. May I be allowed to make it up to all of you? Mr. Lawton and I want you to come for dessert after dinner, about six thirty. We'd love to let you explore our car. There's a platform on the end. It's like a little balcony. When you step outside you can feel what it's like to be out in the mountains. Maybe we'll be able to see the stars come out.

Yours sincerely,

Celeste

"Madame has asked me to deliver a reply," said the porter. "What shall I say?"

Mary Carol was for it. J.D. said they should ask Mr. Raymond. Grace wondered how she knew their names. Robert said he wouldn't go.

"What? No dessert?" asked Mr. Elijah, when they excused themselves to go find Mr. Raymond. "You all *must* be tired."

"I don't see why not," Mr. Raymond said, when they found him. "Keep it to an hour. I'll come looking if you're there too long. Wouldn't want to delay your bedtime too much."

It was almost six thirty by then. J.D. said they might get a look at the map if they went. He didn't say so, but he hoped it would help him determine if Robert was in danger. He still wondered if the map was somehow related to the war. *It could be a trap if they think Rob heard their plans.*

Grace said they ought to try and find out what the woman was up to. That seemed like a good idea to everyone, even Robert. That and curiosity won him over. He was as eager to explore the private car as the others. Plus, he didn't like the idea of being left behind. They'd promised Mamma to stick together. He didn't need reminding that he'd broken the promise.

Robert cautioned, "Be careful what you say to her. I don't care what her note says. I'm telling you, she's up to no good. Don't anybody look her straight in the eyes, either. There's something spooky about her eyes. It's like she could hypnotize you. I read somewhere that you can't be hypnotized unless you want to be, but don't take any chances. That woman is dangerous."

117

Chapter 11

Outside the private car a sign read, "Private Car, No Entry." All smiles, the woman let them in. "My dears, please call me Celeste. I'm not your auntie or a neighbor. I'm your friend." She sounded very sincere, she was even nice to Robert.

Gary Lawton brought up the rear as she led them on a tour. The first three rooms were service rooms: pantry, the servant's bedroom where Robert had hidden, a kitchen, and a toilet for servants. "We don't have help with us on this trip," Celeste explained. "Just us two. One of the porters is available if we need him."

Beyond the dining room, with its polished wood table, chairs, and built-in cupboards, were two bedrooms with a small study and a bathroom between. A yellowed paper was rolled up on the study desk. Robert nudged J.D. The two boys quietly agreed on a plan and passed the word along to the girls. Celeste, who was absorbed in talking about the features of the car, didn't seem to notice. Mr. Lawton seemed bored with it all.

At the end of a comfortable lounge, a door opened to an observation platform with a rail around it. "Come," said Celeste, stepping outside. "Isn't this a spectacular view? It will be even more dramatic when the stars begin to come out." They were still in the mountains, but now the land around them was cut through with red-dirt canyons that ran parallel to the tracks. The sun had not yet begun its final drop over the vast horizon. Robert occupied Mr. Lawton and Celeste with questions about the mountains and desert they'd be going through, while J.D. slipped away. If Celeste or Mr. Lawton missed him, Robert would say he'd gone to the toilet. Grace stood by the rail smiling her best "charming little girl" smile. Celeste seemed especially anxious to please Grace.

Mary Carol hung back next to Mr. Lawton. If Robert and Grace didn't keep Celeste busy, she could deflect attention from J.D.'s absence.

It went smoothly. J.D. got away without any problem. He tried to stay calm and unhurried. It wasn't easy. Hands shaking, he spread out the map. He was pretty sure it was of the U.S., but only the western part. There were rivers, mountains, and plains, but the shape of the coastline was off. There were no state or territory boundaries. All around and scattered over the map were small drawings of plants, animals, and birds colored in with watercolor. He'd stuck a pencil and paper in his pocket, hoping to make notes. He made a few hasty notes of animals Robert hadn't mentioned: bison, antelope or deer of some kind, vulture, rattlesnake, something that looked like a cross between a mouse and a rabbit. There were too many animals to get them all down without being gone too long. There was nothing else to be learned without taking the map. He didn't dare do that. He held it up to the light. There wasn't anything more to be seen. On the back he could see the strange writing that he couldn't read.

Meanwhile, the others watched the sun begin to gradually drop, turning the sky to pink and gold. Robert spotted the first star. "What did you wish for, Robbie?" asked Grace, not forgetting to be cute and sweet. She'd hoped to be the first one to see a star. *I would have wished for Daddy to get well,* she thought, disappointed. Mary Carol thought the same thing. Despite the excitement of the day and the fun of the train ride, their father was always on their minds. They carried their worry in their hearts like a heavy weight.

"Can't tell or it won't come true," said Robert, who had wished exactly what Grace and Mary Carol would have wished. "Miss Celeste, Mr. Lawton, do either of you know anything about the elevation here?" he asked, keeping up the chatter. "I read somewhere that Trinidad, Colorado, is the highest point on the rail line. That is 5,990 feet above sea level. We must be lower than that now. Do you know when we actually make our descent out of the mountains?"

Mr. Lawton suddenly took an interest. "Sounds like you studied up before making the trip, young man. Good for you. Actually, we stay on a high plateau all the way to Albuquerque. The elevation there is a little over 4,900 feet."

"But that's a thousand feet difference," said Robert.

Mary Carol could see that Celeste wasn't interested in elevation and was glancing toward the door. "It must have been something building this railroad through the mountains," she said hoping to divert her attention.

"Oh! It must have been such very hard work!" Grace was her most charming. Any other time, Mary Carol would have wanted to slap her. Now she was grateful that Grace knew how to hog the attention. It kept J.D.'s absence from being noticed.

Celeste beamed at Grace. "You children are certainly well informed."

"Can you see the Big Dipper anywhere?" asked Grace sweetly. "I think it should be right up there." She deliberately pointed in the wrong direction. Everybody looked up.

"Over there to the right, Sweetheart," said Celeste, pointing up to the Big Dipper.

"Silly me!" said Grace. "So that must be the Little Dipper."

"Yes, and do you see the North Star?" asked Celeste.

"And Caseopia's Chair, closer to the horizon and over to the right," added Mary Carol. Celeste ignored her.

Back in the study, J.D. was discouraged. Rolling up the map, he put it back where he found it. Before leaving, he hurriedly had a look at what was on the shelves. There wasn't anything that would lead the untrained eye to be suspicious. *If Celeste is a spy, there's no way for me to tell.* He gave up and returned to the platform. He had no trouble slipping behind Mr. Lawton. They were still gazing at the sky. Robert had just asked something about meteors and their effect on the landscape of the mountains. Mary Carol followed by asking if they knew anything about the legend of coyote hanging the stars.

"What a lot of questions you children have!" exclaimed Celeste. Mr. Lawton had a stab at the meteor question, but neither of them had anything to say about the legends.

Celeste was delighted. The children were warming to her. It was going exactly as she had planned. "Our dessert is waiting. I think we should go back inside," she said.

"Yes, Ma'am," said Robert, seeing J.D. "Maybe we should go in."

Noticing J.D., Mr. Lawton apologized. "Sorry, I've been blocking your view."

"No, sir," said J.D. truthfully. "You can see all around from here."

"You've been awfully quiet," said Celeste, eyeing him as they returned to the lounge.

"Yes, Ma'am. Everybody had so many good questions there wasn't much left for me to say." He hoped that would satisfy her. "I was taught that if you don't have anything to contribute, it is better to keep your mouth shut."

"Good advice," laughed Mr. Lawton, giving him a pat on the back. He pulled the door to the platform balcony closed behind them.

Over chocolate teacakes with pink frosting, Celeste asked about the family. Mary Carol started blabbing. J.D. stepped on her foot under the table. Before he could shut her up, she'd told about their father being wounded, and that they were going to L.A. to stay with Uncle James.

"Uncle *James*, you say? And the family name?" Celeste asked.

"Harrison," said Mary Carol, thinking Celeste meant their family name.

J.D. stepped on her foot again. "You wouldn't like him; he's really boring," he said.

"I knew a James, not Harrison. James Matthias.

Hm-m-m." Celeste seemed to be caught up in thought for a moment.

They all flinched. Nobody offered to tell her James Matthias was their uncle.

"Tell me, is this Mr. Raymond a friend of the family?" Celeste asked.

"Yes, our uncle's friend," said Robert, hurriedly. He was worried. Celeste knew nearly everything about them now and they didn't know a thing about her.

"Gary, darling, why don't you take the children to the lounge." It was more like a command than a question. "I'll put away the cakes. The children might like to take them for later."

"We have to go soon," said Robert. "Mr. Raymond's coming for us."

"Then Mr. Raymond will just have to join us." Celeste smiled at him, an unpleasant glint in her eyes.

"I challenge everyone to a game of Chinese checkers," Mr. Lawton said, leading the way to the lounge. "Board and marbles this way."

"There's something I want to show you," Celeste whispered to Grace. "Shhh. It's a surprise."

She was suspicious, but it occurred to Grace that

she might learn something important if she stayed behind with Celeste. She couldn't help thinking how wonderful it would feel to be the one finding out things. "I love surprises!" she said, turning on her charming little girl voice and clapping her hands.

Grace Hears Alarm Bells

Celeste showed no interest in putting away the cakes. Instead, she opened one of the cupboard doors, removing a miniature trunk. It was about fourteen inches tall and wider than Grace's hands put together. "Look," she whispered, opening it. On one side, tied in place with satin ribbons, was a beautiful doll with a porcelain head. She was dressed in an old-fashioned dress, cloak, and hat. A whole wardrobe of dresses hung on the other side of the trunk, with changes of shoes below. A drawer held stockings, handkerchiefs, and underwear. It was any little girl's dream come true.

Grace clapped her hands again. "It's beautiful!" She wasn't putting on an act either. But for good measure, she deliberately added in her most delightful tone of voice, "I've never seen anything so lovely in my whole, entire life."

It seemed to work. Smiling, Celeste let her choose a dress to put on the doll. Then together, they laid out all her pretty things.

"Grace, dear," Celeste said. "If you could make a wish right now, what would you wish for?"

Grace didn't hesitate. "For Daddy to be well."

"Oh." Celeste seemed taken aback. "Oh. I wasn't thinking of that. I was thinking you might like to have this doll." She seemed to consider for a minute. "Of course she would be worried about her father," she muttered to herself, oblivious to the fact that Grace could hear her. "Still, I believe it could work."

She began gathering up the doll's things. "Anyway, the doll isn't something I could give away. But, if you want to play with her, you may come any time. I'll tell Mr. Raymond."

"May Mary Carol come, too?" asked Grace sweetly. "She so loves dolls."

"No, this would be just for you. It would have to be our secret."

"But that would be unfair," protested Grace, pouting her lips prettily.

"Do you think so? Then I shall have to think of something special for Mary Carol, too, won't I!" With that, Celeste returned the doll to her trunk, leaving it open for Grace to see. "There may be a way to help your daddy, too. I'll think on it."

Thrown off guard by Celeste's comment, Grace abandoned her charming little girl act. "Mamma says the best thing we can do for Daddy is to all work together."

"That's it!" Celeste sounded very pleased. "Your mother is exactly right. You and I can work together. But there's also magic. Do you believe in magic?"

"I believe in Santa Claus and the fairies," Grace said cautiously, afraid to admit to too much.

"Fairies?"

"They leave a present under your pillow on your birthday."

"Hmm," Celeste paused. "I suppose such creatures do still exist. They can be quite troublesome. I was thinking of a different kind of magic, though, a very powerful magic. It could make your daddy well. But it would come at a cost. You can't have this kind of magic for free."

Make Daddy well? The thought was almost overwhelming to Grace. "What would it cost?" she asked cautiously.

"We'd have to work together to do something—something very hard. You'd help Mr. Lawton get something for me, something that is hidden." She looked at Grace very intently. "I couldn't go with you to get it. That's how the magic works."

She spoke softly, looking into Grace's eyes. "It will be like a game. There are clues for you along the way and a map telling you exactly where to go." Celeste's voice was soothing. She talked as if Grace were in complete agreement. "It will be a short side trip that will hardly take any time away from the others. They won't even miss you. Think of how wonderful it will be to see your father well again! And you'll have the doll to keep as your very own, forever." Her eyes glinted.

Grace suddenly felt like little alarm bells were going off in her head. She wanted to run away, anywhere to get away from Celeste's demanding eyes. "Do you mean that all I have to do is go with Mr. Lawton?" She was determined to find out what Celeste was up to. Maybe it was something she could do.

"Yes, because if you weren't there, you wouldn't be able to use the magic for your father. If it were only for me, I could just send Mr. Lawton." Celeste paused. "Look at me, dear. I need to see your eyes. That way I know you're listening. This is very, very important."

Celeste's eyes were such big, commanding eyes.

Chapter 12

"I don't understand what you're talking about," Grace said slowly, trying to keep her wits about her. "What do you want me to find? Why is it hidden?"

"I'm going to tell you a secret. None of the others must ever, *ever* know," Celeste whispered soothingly. "There's a crystal as old as the earth. Inside is water from the Dawn of Time. I need you to get that crystal for me—and your daddy," she added hastily. "That water can make him well. But you see, the crystal is hidden because a little girl like you stole it from me. The magic requires that a little girl just like you find it and claim it for me. That's why I need you to help me. And the best part is that we can use the water inside the crystal to make your daddy well."

Celeste's eyes were like two big pools of water you could fall into. Grace didn't want to fall. Every word was a struggle now. "What. . . about. . . J.D. and. . . Mary Carol and Robert? Will they come, too?" She let out a big sigh. "If we're all working together?" Wrenching herself away from Celeste's stare, she looked toward the lounge hoping to see the others. If only one of them would come back and rescue her!

Celeste spoke softly and gently. "Oh, no, the others can't come. Too many would spoil the magic. It has to be our secret. I'll come for you when it's time. The others have no idea that you're big enough to do such an important thing. Imagine their surprise. Think how proud they'll be—and envious!" Celeste gently took Grace's chin. "Grace, dear, you must relax and look at me. It's so important that you hear what I'm saying so you'll remember."

There was no escape from Celeste's soft, soothing voice, "Nobody knows where to find the crystal except the Keeper. And nobody is sure how to find the Keeper."

Grace struggled to think about Mamma and Daddy while she looked at Celeste. But the eyes were still there.

"The only way to find the Keeper is to follow the map," Celeste continued. "You must find some tokens for the Keeper, too—five of them I think. It could be more. You have to figure out what they are and how many, but there will be clues. You can't ask for them or just take them either. That's why it will be so much fun. The others couldn't do this. It has to be someone as clever as the little girl who stole it. You're the only one that clever. When you find the Keeper, you must tell him that you've been sent for the crystal and give him the tokens. Then the magic goes to work. You'll be home again and the water will make your daddy well." Celeste quietly shut the doll's trunk, still looking into Grace's eyes.

Grace recalled how sad but determined Daddy

looked when he left for the war. She remembered how worried Mamma looked after the telegram. She was determined, too, determined to keep Celeste from trapping her. But there was something else pulling at her. It wasn't Celeste. It was like a little voice inside calling to her. She wanted to find that crystal and make their daddy well. She knew the others thought she was a little brat—their dear baby sister, somebody they loved and had to protect, but still a little brat. If she could find the crystal, it would all be different. *We would have Daddy back and they'd know I can do things, too.*

"Grace, are you listening?" Celeste asked.

The little selfish voice made her want to go along with Celeste. "So it is like a game," Grace said slowly, considering. Her tongue felt thick, "except it's magic, and it will make Daddy well. And I get to do it without the others."

"Exactly," said Celeste, eyes glinting. In that terrible, terrifying moment she looked like a snake to Grace.

The cobra! Robbie told us about the cobra. Celeste is the cobra. I'm her prey. That alarming thought was like a blast of cold air in her face. *Robert said you can't be hypnotized if you don't want to be.* When Grace tried to pull her eyes away from Celeste's eyes, it was nearly impossible. *Robert said a cobra paralyzes its prey like that.* With a great deal of effort she moved her eyes to the doll's trunk, trying to stall. If she could just make Celeste think she was already completely under her spell, maybe she wouldn't have to look into those eyes again. She couldn't hold out much longer. She wanted to tell the little voice inside her to shut up, but she knew it was still there, urging her to go along with Celeste.

Grace was deliberate. "If I help you find the crystal, do I get the doll, too?" It wasn't the doll that tempted her. But she tried to sound as if she were a greedy little thing who wanted the doll most, even more than for her daddy to be well.

Grace's strategy worked. Celeste laughed in cruel delight. "Why yes, darling, you are clever. I like that." A triumphant look was on her face, as if she'd won a game. "As I said, you shall have the doll. But if you tell a soul, it won't work—none of it. The doll can only be yours when I have the crystal. And your daddy will be well then, but *only* when I have the crystal."

The crisis passed. "Why can't I have it now?" Grace whined. She knew Celeste thought she was in her wicked power. But she was thinking her own thoughts. She kept looking at the doll case as if she were enchanted. "When... can... we... go?" She asked slowly, as if she were nearly asleep.

"Soon, dear, when I'm ready. But it is entirely up

to you whether or not you go."

"I do want to go!" said Grace petulantly. "I want the doll."

"Now Grace, be yourself again." Celeste waved her hand in front of Grace's face, cutting her off from staring at the trunk. "You'll remember everything I've said. You won't tell anyone. I will come for you this summer while you're with your Uncle."

Grace knew that she was already herself. She had been from the moment she chose to over-ride the part of her that wanted to go along with Celeste. "And I can have the doll!" she exclaimed, adding very prettily, "Oh, and help Daddy to be well, of course."

"But of course." Celeste was all smiles.

Grace smiled back at her sweetly. "May I play with the doll now?"

Meanwhile, Robert was worried. He pretended to look at a book while the others played checkers. "Where's Gracie?" he asked when he could stand it no longer.

"Oh, she's fine," said Mr. Lawton. "She's helping Celeste put away the cakes."

"It's taking a lot of time to put away cakes." Robert started for the dining area.

Mr. Lawton stood, blocking his way, "You just stay right here," he said.

Thinking quickly, J.D. upset the Chinese checkerboard, sending marbles rolling in front of Mr. Lawton. Robert wiggled past. Trying to grab Robert, Mr. Lawton slipped on the marbles, tottered, and fell flat on the floor, letting out a string of curses. J.D. and Mary Carol rushed past him, avoiding the marbles.

Robert got to Grace just as she was asking if she could play with the doll. "What doll?" he asked.

Ignoring him, Celeste closed the door to the cabinet. "How about tomorrow morning, Grace, dear?" She gave Robert a self-satisfied smile.

J.D. and Mary Carol were close on Robert's heels. A limping Gary Lawton brought up the rear, swearing.

"Language, Gary, darling! We must watch our language," said Celeste. "Whatever have you been playing with these children? I thought I could trust you with Chinese checkers. Have you lost your marbles?" She was in high spirits, laughing heartily at her own joke.

"We'll pick them up, Miss Celeste," J.D. said. "Then we have to go. Mr. Raymond is expecting us."

"Oh, you needn't bother. Mr. Lawton can pick

up his own marbles." She handed a plate to Grace. "Here are the cakes I promised. You must come back and see me." She gave Grace a knowing smile. Grace gave her a charming little girl smile in return.

"Sorry. We'll get to L.A. tomorrow," Robert snapped.

"Will we? I'd quite forgotten about time," said Celeste, giving him a snake look.

Break Down

They met Mr. Raymond coming for them. "How did you all like the private car?"

"Impressive," said J.D.

"The cakes were lovely," said Mary Carol, offering him one.

"Thanks, but I already had my dessert," said Mr. Raymond. "I'm glad you had a good time. If you want to go to the observation car, you'll get a good view of the stars. I'll get your beds made up. Remember, girls up top tonight."

As soon as they found a place to themselves in the observation car, they began talking in whispers. Everyone wanted to know if J.D. found anything on the map. He hated to disappoint them.

Grace was reluctant to say what happened to her at first. "Celeste said I couldn't tell or nothing would work. But if she's a wicked person, we shouldn't have anything to do with her. So I think it's right to tell." She couldn't bring herself to tell them about wanting to go along with Celeste, though. It was too painful to admit that she came so close to betraying them all.

"Good work, Gracie," said Robert.

"Rob, you were right. I'll be the first to say it," said J.D. "Celeste is up to no good."

"I was wrong, too, Robbie," said Mary Carol. "She'd keep the crystal for herself once you found it, Gracie. I wonder why she wants it? Do you think she has some dread disease?"

"What about Mr. Lawton?" asked Grace. "He didn't act very nice either."

"No, he's not nice, not if he is stealing things for her," said Robert. "I'm not sure how he fits in, but I don't trust either one of them."

"All this magic stuff—do we really believe it?" J.D. asked.

"Not me," said Robert. "She's a wicked person. That's what I believe. Whatever she really wants— maybe the crystal, maybe something else—it's something she can't get on her own. Do you remember how she stared at Gracie? She wants you and Mr. Lawton to do the dirty work, Gracie."

"Maybe there's something about Gracie," said Mary Carol. They didn't get to finish the conversation. The observation car was becoming too crowded as people stopped in after supper. Besides, it was getting late.

As they started back to their car, the train slowed to a stop. "Lamy. Lamy, New Mexico," called a conductor.

It was a short stop. By the time they were back to their seats, the train was moving again. A few compartments were already made up, including their beds. Miss Spright looked up from her book. "Sergeant Nakamura said to tell you, 'Good-bye.' You just missed him. He got off in Lamy."

"Lamy?" J.D. asked, "What's in Lamy?"

"I believe there is a bus station," said Miss Spright. "I expect he'll be taking a bus to Santa Fe. He didn't say so, but I rather imagine he is going to the Santa Fe internment camp. He is from Hawaii. I suspect that like many young Japanese-American servicemen from Hawaii, he has a father who is imprisoned in Santa Fe."

"His father's in an internment camp when he's in the army?" J.D. was incredulous. "Why would they do that?"

"The truth of it is, there are a lot of loyal

Americans imprisoned," said Miss Spright grimly. "People think that because they're Japanese, their first loyalty is to a country they left generations ago."

"Well, that's just wrong!" exclaimed Grace.

"Yes, it is wrong," said Miss Spright. "I wish it weren't so. Unfortunately people get scared and they quit thinking sensibly, even people in our government who are supposed to be looking out for everybody."

"That's what Mamma says," said Mary Carol.

"Quite frankly, I think our government should be reassuring people rather than putting the blame for Pearl Harbor on innocent people who happen to be Japanese in origin." Miss Spright sighed. "I admire young men and women like Sergeant Nakamura who stand up for their country when their country isn't standing up for them. But I think you came back to get ready for bed, not to hear a sermon. I do have a tendency to go on and on."

After everybody got ready for bed, they decided to gather in the upper berth. In quiet voices they wondered about Dolly and why she had to get off the train.

"Were you scared, Robbie?" asked Grace.

"Yeah, I was afraid I wouldn't be able to switch

magazines without somebody noticing. That's why I decided I could just ask for his autograph. If he didn't say Cowher when I asked about the dog, then I would have an excuse to be talking to him."

"Good thinking, Rob," said J.D.

"So do you think the people Dolly was getting away from are still on board?" asked Mary Carol.

Robert shrugged.

"You have to wonder what was in that magazine. Bound to be something in code," said J.D., "Somebody left information for her when she was getting on the train in Kansas City. . . ."

"And she was to leave information for somebody in La Junta," Robert completed his thought.

"But she must have stumbled onto something she didn't expect," said J.D. "because she got off the train in such a hurry. I think she decided sometime after she left us in the observation car and before Mr. Raymond came to get us so we could see Dodge City."

"Or before," said Robert. "What about those cakes, Gracie? I'm ready for a snack."

"They're below," said Grace, scrambling down the ladder to get them.

"Do you think we dare eat them?" Mary Carol

wondered. "I mean, what if she poisoned them?"

"We ate them earlier," said J.D. "Nobody's dropped dead. Let's have a look at that magazine."

"*The Saturday Evening Post*, April 8, 1944," Robert read, smoothing the cover as J.D. took the plate of cakes from Grace.

They went through the magazine. The only thing they found was a *Li'l Abner* cartoon clipped from a newspaper. In the cartoon, Ma and Pa Yokum were complaining of the toxic smell coming from Skonk Hollow. *Li'l Abner* was a popular cartoon. They couldn't make anything of the clipping.

"It has to be a clue, but what?" said Robert.

"They could have used invisible ink," said Mary Carol, licking pink frosting from her fingers. "Should we get a hot water bottle?"

"All that would do is attract attention to us if whoever was after Dolly is still on the train," said J.D. "Besides, any messages would be in code even if they're written in invisible ink."

"And I don't think Celeste and Mr. Lawton have anything to do with it," said Robert. "They're after this hidden crystal."

"But what about 'fox-hole radios'?" asked J.D. "The Germans can detect regular radio signals, but they can't detect old-fashioned transmission from a crystal radio. So some of the soldiers near enemy lines rig up their own crystal radios."

"Yeah, but they don't have actual crystals." Robert corrected him. "That's why they use pencil lead, safety pins, and razor blades. I read an article about it. Actually, I should have brought stuff to make a crystal radio. If we were stranded, it would help to have a radio."

Mary Carol rolled her eyes.

"She doesn't want the crystal. She wants the water in the crystal," said Grace. "She said it could make Daddy well."

"If we can believe her," said Mary Carol. She was thoroughly disillusioned with Celeste. They gave up trying to sort things out and went to bed.

Grace sat up abruptly, wakened by a dream. In the dream she was crying. Daddy and Mamma were there. She reached out her arms to them, but they couldn't see her. Then that awful Celeste came after her. Behind Celeste were the terrible people who were after Dolly. She ran and ran, but she couldn't get anywhere. Then Old Shep came bounding to her. She threw her arms around him. *Old Shep, I almost let Celeste trap me. What if I'd done what she told me to do?* "But you didn't." He didn't actually say it, but Grace understood. He licked her face, like he did sometimes, comforting her. It felt so real, she half expected to be able to reach out and touch him next to Mary Carol.

Mary Carol opened her eyes. "Are you okay, Gracie?"

"I dreamed about Old Shep, and I miss him and I miss Mamma and Daddy and I want to go home, and Celeste was chasing me," she sobbed.

"I know," said Mary Carol. She took Grace in her arms and held her, rocking her back and forth like a baby.

"I wish it had been Old Shep at all those train stations," she sobbed.

"Me, too," said Mary Carol.

"Except I really did see him, Mary Carol. Why doesn't anybody believe me?"

At last Grace fell asleep. *Poor dear,* Mary Carol thought, *it is harder for her than for any of us. And she was so brave this afternoon.*

All of a sudden, the train came to an abrupt halt. It wasn't a scheduled stop. Mary Carol looked out. People in the car began to murmur. Robert and J.D. were looking out from below. Mr. Raymond made his way through the car reassuring passengers who were awake. "Looks like we have some technical problems. We should be moving shortly."

"Technical problems!" said Robert as he flopped back into bed. "Do you think it is, well, you know..." he asked in a whisper, "enemy subversives trying to disrupt the trains?"

A Short Desert Walk

The next morning the train was still not moving. When Mr. Raymond made the breakfast call he announced that there was a problem with the engine. "Our people are working on it. We'll keep you informed. Meanwhile, enjoy your breakfast and please stay on board. We don't know how long it will take and we wouldn't want to leave anybody behind. We're in the middle of the desert. Please keep your windows closed. We want to keep it nice in here as long as we can. We should be ready to leave soon."

"Let's go find a table where we can spread out and work," J.D. suggested as they finished breakfast. "Maybe I can come up with a sketch of that map."

When they were settled, J.D. looked at Grace, "You're special to us, Gracie. But why to Celeste?

If we can figure that out, maybe we can stop her."

"It was on the map," said Robert. "The poem said something about a child. Celeste said it meant girl."

"We're the only children on the train," said Mary Carol.

"Then why not you?" asked Robert. "I mean, if it has to be a girl."

"I don't know why, but she said it had to be me," said Grace. "She said that a girl like me stole the crystal from her so it has to be a girl like me to get it for her."

"That sounds like a bunch of phony baloney," said Robert.

"But it explains why she kept staring at Gracie," said Mary Carol.

"We have to keep you two away from her," said J.D. He spread out a sheet of paper and began making a sketch. "I think she knows you heard more than you admitted to, Rob. If this train hadn't come to a stop, we'd be in L.A. before she could do anything. She may have said she'd get you this summer, Gracie. But I don't trust that. We'd better not let anyone out of our sight. From now on, we stick together like glue."

Mary Carol was still trying to make connections.

147

"Gracie, you look more like Uncle James and Mamma than any of us. Maybe that's the connection. Celeste said she knew a James Matthias."

"Yeah, but our Uncle James?" said Robert. "He isn't exactly the adventurous type. There has to be another James Matthias."

J.D. shook his head in disbelief, "I can't imagine him having anything to do with the likes of Celeste. Thank goodness nobody told her his name; I mean, you never know."

J.D. put down his pencil. "Here's what the map looked like. There were the pictures—I couldn't get them all—and a compass showing direction."

"She couldn't figure it out," said Robert. "She said it was *his* doing. She kept talking about him, but she wouldn't tell Mr. Lawton who. And there's a missing something. She called it a key."

"Makes sense," said J.D. "You brought a map, didn't you, Rob?"

Robert fished in his knapsack, spreading out a U.S. map. "Okay, this is the key." J.D. pointed to the square at the bottom of the map that showed what all the symbols meant.

"That's the legend," said Mary Carol.

"But sometimes it's called the key," said J.D.

"There wasn't a key on her map."

"So the map didn't look anything like this one?" Robert wondered.

"Yes and no. We're here on this map," J.D. pointed to Robert's map. "The pictures of the Condor and Coyote and Salmon—did I say Salmon before? On her map all of those things were along the sides like they were decorations. Some of them looked like American Indian drawings. It didn't show anything like roads or highways. There were some rivers and lakes—I'm guessing just the big ones—and mountains. It was land here, mountains, then the ocean."

"She said it's the Pacific Ocean, right Robbie?" asked Mary Carol.

"Mr. Lawton said it didn't look anything like the Pacific coast line," said Robert.

"It wasn't like any other map, that's for sure," said J.D. "I know there are different kinds of maps. Like your map, Rob; it has train tracks and highways marked. But you couldn't use this map to get anywhere. There's not enough detail. How would we get from here to up here if we used your map?" J.D. pointed to their location on Robert's map, drawing an imaginary line to the top.

Robert looked intently at his map. "Well, we

couldn't go by train unless we transferred in L.A. Then we could go up the coast."

"No roads on her map, J.D.?" asked Gracie.

"That's my point," said J.D. "No train tracks or roads."

"How do you get anywhere if there aren't any roads?" asked Mary Carol.

"You'd need something with a four-wheel-drive." It was Mr. Nichols.

"What about on foot?" said J.D.

"Like the pioneers," Robert added hastily so as not to give anything away.

"Well, I think the pioneers stayed out of the desert when they could. At least those with good sense did." Mr. Nichols laughed a jolly laugh, eyes twinkling. "May I join you?" he asked. Not waiting for an answer, he pulled a chair up next to J.D. "The most sensible way to walk from here to the coast would be almost straight across. You could follow some natural pathways and animal trails through the mountains and come out just above Santa Barbara." He traced a line across Robert's map with his finger. "Depending on the time of year it might be doable or it might do you in. You can see that the elevation is high along here." He showed them how you can tell about elevation by looking at the legend and referring back to the map.

"High elevation means harsh winter cold," Mr. Nichols explained. "But in the spring it warms up during the day and there are more water sources than in the summer when it heats up. That would be true anywhere you find desert-like conditions and mountain terrain. I think that's why pioneers liked to get started early in the spring. You started from Kansas City about the time most wagon trains would have started. But you covered their route a whole lot quicker. Maybe the moral to that story is to take the train and not a covered wagon!" he laughed.

"I doubt you signed on for a geography lesson." Leaning back, Mr. Nichols sighed. "My only defense is that I can't resist a good map. But actually, I came to find you four. It appears that the train will be here for a while. I'm getting ready to take anybody who is interested for a walk out into the desert before it gets too hot. That's why I'm dressed like this." He looked as if he were headed out for a safari in Africa, except he still had his broad-brimmed canvas hat. "I thought you all might like to come along. We won't go more than a few steps from the train. I've got my collection bag. We'll pick up a few bits and bobs to talk about later. And, since you're interested in desert conditions, we'll talk about survival in the desert. What about that, Robert?"

"He's got you pegged, Robbie," said Mary Carol.

151

Chapter 14

Robert grinned.

Just then a conductor asked for everyone's attention. He announced that they'd had to send to L.A. for parts. "We should be moving again sometime before noon." Then he added, "One of our passengers is a naturalist. Anybody who would like may join him for a short walk into the desert before it gets too hot. He asked me to tell you to wear long sleeved shirts, jackets, sweaters, or blouses, if you have them and to bring a hat for protection from the sun. If you have a thermos or canteen with you, fill it with water and bring it along, too. Anyone interested, please meet at either entrance to the observation car in ten minutes." The children hurried to get their hats. The boys were wearing long sleeved shirts, but the girls had on short-sleeved dresses, so they put on their cardigans. J.D. filled his water bag. Robert didn't have to fill his canteen; he was always prepared.

When they got off the train, a small group had collected. "Got your hats?" Mr. Nichols asked. "That goes for everybody." While a few passengers went back for hats, Mr. Nichols turned to the children. "I want you to stay close to me. I'll need some good assistants. Here, Mary Carol and Grace. I noticed you don't have your own water supply. You can keep these. You'd better go fill them." He gave Grace and Mary Carol each a small water bag that read, "Denver Museum of Natural History." The bag had a strap so it could be worn across the shoulders.

"Gee, thanks," said Mary Carol. Grace nodded vigorously in agreement as they hurried back to fill their bags.

Once everyone had gathered, Mr. Nichols explained about plants and rocks and what to watch out for in the desert. People got to ask questions. And he talked about what you'd have to do to survive in the desert if you ever had to. It felt good to be outside. It was warm, but not terribly hot.

"There's a vulture." Miss Spright pointed to a large bird circling above. She had exchanged her little navy blue hat for a wide-brimmed straw hat that tied under the chin. She was carrying a canteen with her purse in one hand and a walking stick in the other.

"That's a California condor, Miss Spright," Mr. Nichols explained. "They're in the same family. You can tell it isn't a vulture by the size, for one thing. He's way up there or you could see. Condors have white spots under their wings. If he'll be kind enough to come closer, maybe we can get a better look. They glide on the air looking for food. They only eat the carcasses of dead animals."

"That's disgusting!" exclaimed one of the men.

"To you or me. But they're part of Mother Nature's clean up crew. They perform a valuable service." Mr. Nichols said. "After lunch, I will be in the observation car to talk about some of the things we see in more detail. It's getting too hot to stay out much longer. Anybody up for a walk around the whole train before we go in? It will give us a good stretch. I don't advise it unless you brought along water."

The children were eager to stay outside, along with a youngish looking man whose name was Bob, a middle-aged couple, and Miss Spright. She seemed as glad as they were to be out in the desert.

"First, everybody have a drink of water." Mr. Nichols took a drink from a canteen he had in his collection bag. "We'll keep a steady pace, but not fast. Anybody want to guess why?"

"To conserve our strength in the heat," Bob replied confidently.

"And body moisture," said Mr. Nichols. "That's why I harped on proper clothing when we were talking about desert survival. If we were stranded out here without the train to go back to, I'd say to keep your mouth shut, too. In fact, if you have a handkerchief you could put it over your nose and mouth to conserve moisture. The next thing would be to look for shade and hunker down until past the heat of the day." He reached into his bag and pulled out a handful of bandanas. "Anybody need a handkerchief? Here. Tie one of these on and see if it doesn't make a difference.

"Come to think of it, you boys might want to put a bandana under your caps so you have a flap to protect the back of your neck."

"It's better to travel at night in the desert," said Bob, as he tied on his pocket handkerchief.

Robert was prepared, too. Everybody else took a bandana from Mr. Nichols.

"If you are equipped," said Mr. Nichols, patiently. "But it gets very cold—think winter—so unless you have your winter coats and there's enough moonlight to see your way, you're better off taking shelter until before sunrise when it begins to warm and there's more light."

The middle-aged man started to pull off his jacket, "It's warm enough now."

"Not a good idea," said Bob with authority. "You could be dead in three hours in this sun without the right covering."

"You'd be at risk," said Mr. Nichols. "Covering is important. Your body wastes a lot of energy trying to keep you cool if you aren't covered. If you're preparing for desert conditions, that's one thing. You can plan ahead. But if you're caught by surprise, you are better off staying covered and under cover in the nearest shade if you can find it, rather than thrashing around trying to find water or help. Plus, you run the risk of sunburn. That can hurt."

"And conserve your water," said Bob, who seemed to consider himself an expert. "Just drink sips of water."

"Actually, your body is a good water tank," said Mr. Nichols. "If you are thirsty, you are better off drinking water as long as you have any. Eat less, not more, even if you have plenty of food. Why do you think a person should do that, Robert?"

Robert, who knew quite a lot about survival skills, was stumped. "You might get a stomach ache in the heat?"

"There is that," Mr. Nichols agreed, "but also, digestion requires work and uses body fluids, so you are better off eating just enough to stave off starvation or not eating at all."

"You can survive longer without food than water," Bob added in his authoritative way.

By this time they were rounding the front of the train. The red war-bonnet engine gleamed in the hot sun, radiating baking-hot waves of heat. Mr. Nichols waved at the engineers. "You can take your bandana off if you want to. We won't be out that long and we wouldn't want our friends to think we're going to rob the train." Everybody laughed. They did look a bit like cowboy bandits.

"If it was me and I ran out of water, I'd cut one of those big barrel cactuses and get water that way," said Bob.

Robert wasn't in the habit of contradicting adults. Mamma and Daddy were very firm about showing respect to elders. But Bob was really annoying and he was wrong about cacti. He said, as politely as he could, "I read somewhere that the pulp can make you sick."

"Yes," Mr. Nichols injected. "The only problem with a barrel cactus is that there isn't any water inside except in the pulp. You could eat the pulp, but it is likely to cause vomiting or diarrhea—you'd end up losing more body fluid in the long run. So you're better off going without. But you're right, Bob. You do need to think about other sources of water—like right now, lemonade sounds good!" Mr. Nichols laughed his jolly laugh. "What do you think, Mary Carol?"

"If lemon trees grew in the desert!" she laughed.

"I'd look for a dry streambed where there are some plants growing and try to dig a hole down to water," said Robert.

"Some times of the year that would be a very good idea," said Mr. Nichols. "But you have to be careful not to expend too much energy unless you're pretty sure you will find water. Morning or evening would be best times to dig. That brings up another danger in the desert that has to do with dry streambeds. Anybody know?"

J.D. was about to say, "Flash floods," but Bob answered before anybody else had a chance.

"Especially during July in this country," said Mr. Nichols. "Don't ever camp in a dry streambed and be sure you know a fast way out when you are in one. You could find more water than you can deal with and without any warning."

"What about snakes?" the middle-aged lady asked fearfully.

"Wildlife prefers to stay away from you. If you're going to hunker down in a natural shelter like a cave, you want to check to make sure it isn't occupied. Animals like coyotes and bobcats know about staying out of the sun, too. Snakes, spiders, and scorpions will usually get out of your way if you give them time. You'd want to check the area where you find shade—for one thing, you wouldn't want to lean up against the rocks until well after sunset. Anybody know why?"

"Well, snakes and things," the lady said hurriedly

before Bob could answer.

"And rocks will be much warmer than the shade. They'll hold heat well into the evening," Mr. Nichols explained. "If you want to keep your body cool, don't make it work harder. Enjoy the shade they cast. When you start to feel cool is the time to lean up against the rocks, after you've checked for occupants and tapped on the rocks to chase away any critters."

"I'd think a good stick would be helpful in checking out rocks," said Miss Spright, tapping her walking stick. "It helps to keep your footing on this dry turf, too."

"Nothing like a good stick," said Mr. Nichols.

Miss Spright, Grace, and Mary Carol were in the lead as they rounded the end of the train. Celeste and Mr. Lawton were sitting out on their observation platform having coffee. Celeste waved, calling to Grace, "I thought you were coming to see me this. . . ." She stopped short, staring at Mr. Nichols. Her expression was one of astonishment and pure hatred.

Mr. Nichols tipped his broad-brimmed hat. "We meet again," he said.

Celeste stood, turned her back on all of them, and swept into her car. Mr. Lawton followed.

"Do you know *her*?" Robert asked in astonishment.

"Oh, yes," said Mr. Nichols, rather grimly. "I've known her for more years than you can possibly imagine."

It was getting hot. As they got back on board, the middle-aged couple handed Mr. Nichols their bandanas. "No, they're yours to keep. I always give them out when I'm leading desert walks. You never know when you might need one." He advised everyone to have a long drink of water. Robert opened his canteen. Mr. Nichols shook his head in disapproval. "First rule of the desert: Don't waste your resources. Let's get a head start on lunch. They'll be serving in a few minutes, and it is sure to be crowded. Care to join us, Miss Spright? We'll ask them to put a couple of tables together. We'll start with some big glasses of lemonade. How about it, that is if you kids don't mind being in the company of an old fuddy-duddy? Anyway, I don't want your Uncle James to accuse me of neglecting you."

"You aren't a fuddy-duddy, Mr. Nichols," said Grace.

"I'm not?" said Mr. Nichols in mock disbelief. "How do you know?"

"Uncle James wouldn't have a fuddy-duddy for a friend!" Grace exclaimed.

Mary Carol, Robert, and J.D. exchanged glances. They thought that Uncle James probably would have a fuddy-duddy friend. But that didn't explain Mr. Nichols. He was no fussy, old-fashioned, stick-in-the-mud like Uncle James.

Some Curious Magic

Mr. Elijah couldn't have been more helpful. "I'm glad you came early. We'll put you up here at the far end where it won't disturb traffic." In less time than it takes to tell, they were seated with glasses of lemonade in front of them.

"We were talking about pioneers earlier," Mr. Nichols explained to Miss Spright as they settled at their table. "The early pioneers had some real challenges. They didn't have good maps, either. The ones who survived were the ones who knew how to read the signs that Mother Nature gave them from the land around. That included the night sky. Let's be glad that all we have to deal with is a little train delay." He paused while Mr. Elijah took their orders.

"Mr. Bradford, I shall also require some table salt and sugar, if you please. I don't want to deplete the sugar bowl and salt shaker," said Mr. Nichols.

"Now, does anybody here believe in magic?"

"I do!" Grace didn't hesitate.

"Well, then Grace, as soon as Mr. Bradford returns with the necessary supplies, I am going to show you a magic trick. The pioneers would have had better luck in the desert if they'd known this one."

Mr. Nichols tore six sheets of paper from a note pad, spreading them on the table. Mr. Elijah brought a dish with sugar and another with salt. "Now don't get these two mixed up, you hear?" he advised.

Mr. Nichols put two heaping teaspoons of sugar and a generous pinch of salt on each piece of paper. Folding one so the salt and sugar couldn't escape, he said, "If the pioneers had known this one trick, it would have saved some lives. When you're in extreme heat, your body sweats—here, everybody fold one. You can become dehydrated. One of these packets in a glass of water helps replace salt and sugar. It helps your body hold on to water, too." He showed them how to fold their papers to make a packet. "So here's some Mr. Nichols magic for you."

"Keen!" said J.D. "It isn't really magic, but it works like magic."

"You might say that," laughed Mr. Nichols. "I believe in practical, everyday magic! Put those somewhere you won't lose them."

"May I make one?" asked Grace.

"Why not?" Mr. Nichols gave them all another paper from his note pad.

When they each had a neat little packet, Miss Spright said, "Here, Grace. You take mine. You never know when they might come in handy." Mr. Nichols gave his to her as well. She put them in her purse as if they were great treasures.

Later, while they ate their lunch, Miss Spright said, "If I remember my school studies correctly, this wasn't always desert."

Mr. Nichols nodded in agreement. "If you went back into time, long before pioneer days—say 10 to 12,000 years ago—this whole area would be grassland. Now, if you were caught out in the grasslands, you'd have some of the same challenges as you find in the desert."

"You mean like needing water and shelter," said J.D.

"Exactly," said Mr. Nichols. "So any of that ice cream today?"

Mr. Elijah was clearing their plates. "Shall I make that six ice creams?" Ice cream sounded really good after being outside. Everybody agreed.

"But wasn't it a vast inland sea at one time?" Miss Spright asked.

"Yes, the Western Interior Seaway stretched from Mexico up into Canada. It split North America into two landmasses. That would have been back about 150 million years ago. It reached from the Rockies all the way to the Appalachian Mountains."

"What happened to it?" asked Grace, eyes filled with wonder.

"Well, the mountains started pushing up and land shifted—that is an oversimplification. But eventually it was replaced by grasslands."

"What about dinosaurs?" asked Robert.

"Depends on when you're talking about. Dinosaurs ruled the day for several million years. Many died during the Ice Age."

"That must have been something when everything was covered with ice!" J.D. said.

"Some scientists think there were pockets of land that weren't ever covered," said Mr. Nichols. "Some of the early Americans came along pathways that weren't iced over. The dinosaurs were gone by then. It would have been a great time to find dinosaur bones, though."

Despite the fun of their walk, Mary Carol was

still worrying about Grace. "Do you think Uncle James will know about us? I mean, that the train's broken down?"

"He'll know what's going on," said Mr. Nichols. "As a railroad officer, he's concerned about the whole train. He knows you're in good hands with Mr. Raymond. You've got me to keep an eye on you, too." Mr. Nichols pushed away his empty ice cream dish. "Now, look at that landscape. Did you ever see anything more beautiful?" Bright blue sky painted a background for red-brown flat land covered with low gray-green shrubs and cactus as far as the eye could see.

"It has its own kind of stark beauty," said Miss Spright.

"At night, you can't beat the desert for star gazing. The most important star in our night sky is the North Star, anybody know why?"

"It's like a compass," said Robert.

"Right, Mother Nature's compass."

"Now here's a question I've wondered about, Mr. Nichols," said Miss Spright. "Has the night sky always been the same?"

"That's my kind of question," laughed Mr. Nichols. "Anybody have an idea about that?"

"The night sky is different in the summer than it is in the winter," said Mary Carol, eager to get in a word before Robert had the answer. He usually did have the answer. She couldn't resist giving him a quick superior look when Mr. Nichols said she was right.

Robert rolled his eyes. "It changes over the course of a night, too."

"Yes, and the night sky also changes over time," said Mr. Nichols. "We think of the North Star as being due north. But the ancient Phonecian mariners actually used the Little Dipper constellation as their guiding point because the whole constellation was more or less centered over the North Pole. It wasn't until about the fifth century that Polaris, our North Star, was used for navigation. It was called the 'ship-star' then."

"And before that?" asked Miss Spright.

"Before that, well, I suppose that depends on when you're talking about. The ancient Egyptians used Thuban as their polar star. Before that it would have been Vega. Study of the stars is fascinating. Maybe one of you youngsters will be an astronomer one day and work out how to travel to the moon and into outer space.

"I could go on and on," he said, "but I think we'd better move on and let some other people have these tables." Patting his pockets, he said, "I need to get rid of some stuff. Could you use an arrowhead, Robert?"

"Golly! Is it real?" Robert asked.

"You bet." He gave Robert a small, arrowhead worked in a shiny, red-brown stone and hanging from a leather cord. "You never know when an arrowhead will come in handy. All you'd need to do is notch a nice straight stick for it and you'd have a first rate spear for fishing. That's how the first Americans did it. You don't need a bow to make an arrowhead work for you.

"Let's see what else is in here." He fished in his pockets. "This little critter is an owl. Since you are the eldest, J.D., it seems fitting that you should wear this. It was made a long time ago by the first Americans. The person who wears it is supposed to show wisdom." He hung a silver owl tied to a leather cord around J.D.'s neck. The owl was no larger than a penny, but it was so finely worked they could see feathers and tiny claws.

"Thank you," said J.D. "I don't think I'm very wise, but I'll do my best."

"I'll wager you're wiser than a lot of folk twice your age." Standing, Mr. Nichols patted him on the shoulder. "People who know the limits of their wisdom are wiser than most of us."

He gave Mary Carol a lump of polished turquoise held by a silver chain. "Native people thought of turquoise as an amulet—that is, something that could protect them from harm."

"It's beautiful!" exclaimed Mary Carol.

"You're a real care-giver, Mary Carol. That is a good thing if you don't forget to take care of yourself," said Mr. Nichols, fastening it around her neck. "Just remember that, every time you see this bit of turquoise."

"Now, Grace," he said, unbuttoning a shirt pocket. "You're the only one who'd admit to believing in magic. What's more magical than a magnifying glass? Anyway, you may need it more than I do." He handed Grace a little magnifying glass that looked as if it were made of crystal. It was set in a golden frame and hung from a long gold chain. He put it over her head without even having to unfasten the chain. "It might be a good idea to keep it tucked inside your dress when you aren't using it. We wouldn't want it to fall into the wrong hands."

Grace gave him a hug. "This is for you. Her name is Kitty," she said, spontaneously handing him the little plush kitten she carried in her purse.

"Oh, she's far too valuable for me to keep," Mr. Nichols said. "Suppose we consider her mine and she stays with you? I'm due for a visit with your

Uncle James. I'll visit her when I see you."

Grace laughed. "Okay."

"So how's about we go up to the observation car? I promised to give a talk about the desert. We'll get the best seats." Mr. Nichols led the way.

"Something about him reminds me of Celeste," Grace whispered to Mary Carol. "Except he's nice and she's not."

"Where do you come up with these ideas, Gracie?" asked Mary Carol.

Chapter 16

Mary Carol Disappears

They hadn't been in the observation car very long when they heard the porter make an announcement. A famous singer who was on board would be giving a concert in the bar. In the observation car, Mr. Nichols would be talking about the desert. "The parts have arrived from L.A. It will take some time to make repairs, but we expect to be moving again sometime well before evening."

The children sat at a table with Mr. Nichols as a small crowd began collecting in the observation car. He stood so everybody could see and hear. One of the rocks was a flint rock. Mr. Nichols explained how to identify rock hard enough to create sparks if you want to make a fire. "And don't think you don't need fire in the desert at night."

While she was listening, Grace amused herself by rearranging the things Mr. Nichols placed on the table. She felt a tap on her shoulder. She thought it was Mary Carol warning her to quit playing with them. She was just about to say, "You're not the boss of me," when she saw it was a porter with a note. It read:

> *I'm waiting for you, my dear.*
> *Come at once, <u>alone</u>.*
> *There's still time to play with the doll.*
> *Your friend,*
> *Celeste*

Grace showed the note to J.D. and Robert. That's when they realized Mary Carol wasn't there. "We'd better find out where she's gone," said J.D., grabbing his things.

They met Miss Spright coming their way. "If you're looking for Mary Carol, I was just coming to tell you that man who was sitting on the platform at the end of the train came for her. He said you three were waiting. She seemed to know him. But it didn't feel quite right to me. He told me he is her uncle."

"Uncle?" said Robert.

"I didn't think you knew him well enough to be calling him *uncle*."

"We don't," said Robert, heading toward the private car.

"I have a bad feeling about this," said J.D.,

following Robert at a trot.

"Shouldn't we tell Mr. Nichols?" asked Grace.

"I'll take care of that," said Miss Spright. "You'd better catch up with the others. Your sister may need you."

Mr. Lawton let them in the private car. Celeste sat at the polished table sipping coffee, holding her long jeweled cigarette holder in one hand. "Oh dear, Grace, this will not do. I asked you to come alone." She took a sip of coffee, looking at Grace with snake eyes. "I'm afraid you can't have the doll. You've broken your word. But, still, there is your father, if *he* is of any concern."

She looked coldly at J.D. and Robert. "I did rather suspect everyone would insist on coming." She extinguished her cigarette and stood. "Come, Gary darling, I've changed my plans. I would prefer to wait, but obviously *he* is on the move. I have to act before he does. You're very resourceful. I'm sure you and Grace will be able to figure it out. I've packed your haversack with some necessary things. You'll need it." She led them into the lounge where Mary Carol, face tear-streaked, sat tied to a chair, a gag in her mouth.

"I'm so sorry," said Celeste in a voice that didn't sound at all sorry. "Your sister has been quite a lot of trouble. She's staying here with me. Mr. Lawton is taking you three on a little excursion. As long as you stick to business, Grace, your sister will be fine. The boys will be a nuisance, Gary, but I can't risk having them here with me. Should you forget your promises, perhaps you'll remember that Mary Carol is counting on you to return, not to mention your dear, dear father?"

Several things happened all at once. Screaming, "Let her go!" J.D. jumped at Celeste, throwing his shoulder into her stomach. It knocked the breath out of her and would have knocked her to the floor if a sofa hadn't been in the way. Grace ran to Mary Carol, throwing her arms around her. Robert heaved a lamp at Mr. Lawton, who dodged it. The lamp smashed to the floor behind him.

Celeste grabbed wildly at J.D., catching him by the hair as she steadied herself. "Stop!" she gasped, still panting. "Stop them, Gary."

"Yes. This has to stop." Mr. Lawton's voice was like steel. To their astonishment, he started untying Mary Carol. "Grace, take the gag out of your sister's mouth," he ordered.

Finding her voice, Celeste shrieked, "Have you gone mad?" She let go of J.D.'s hair. Giving him a mighty shove that threw him backward onto the sofa, she started for Mr. Lawton.

"Run, J.D.! Get them out of here as fast as

you can," Mr. Lawton ordered. "Go, Mary Carol, please!"

Mary Carol jumped up, finding it hard to stand after being tied to the chair. Celeste flew at Mr. Lawton, clawing him. He grabbed her by the arms, flipping her around so she couldn't move. "Run for your lives!" he yelled.

Robert and Grace steadied Mary Carol, steering her out of the way as fast as they could. Catching his breath, J.D. dodged furniture upset in the struggle. Celeste broke free from Mr. Lawton. With lightening-speed, she put herself between the children and the corridor that led back into the other train cars. They stopped short, backing away from her.

"Now, my dears," she said breathlessly. "Let's stop all this violence. I so hate violence. We need to be reasonable." She spoke in a sweet, soft, reasonable voice. "Come, Grace dear, look at me. You have something very important to do. Remember?"

The effect of her voice was remarkable. Robert froze, panic stricken. J.D. wondered if they could reason with her. Grace felt confused and a bit dizzy. Mary Carol shook with fright. Nobody seemed able to move.

"Back! The other way—get off the train." Mr. Lawton shouted. "Get back on at another car."

Chapter 16

"Why, Gary darling, what has you so upset?" Celeste crooned. "You mustn't disobey your Celeste."

"Don't listen to her! And quit looking at her. She'll try to hypnotize you." He stepped between Celeste and the children. "Quickly, out the end of the car while you can!"

"Did I hear you correctly, Gary?" Celeste was deadly calm. Terrifyingly so. "Do you dare go against my wishes?"

"They're children, Celeste, CHILDREN. What you want is unthinkable," said Mr. Lawton.

"Excuse me, Darling?" Celeste hissed. "You will do as I say."

"I will not," Mr. Lawton retorted. "I have lied for you. I have cheated for you. I have stolen for you. But I *will not* do this. It's cruel and wicked. It's certain death, even if I'm with them. I will not go. And I will not take this child or her brothers. On my life, you cannot make me."

The minute Mr. Lawton cut off Celeste's awful stare, J.D.'s head cleared. He understood what Mr. Lawton was saying. "Quick, run out the back!" he cried. "We'll jump."

The others were jarred into action. J.D. held open the back door to the lounge until they were all on the platform balcony. By this time Robert had the gate to the balcony open. "Go, Rob, get to the next car so you can help the others get on. Don't wait for me," he yelled, helping Mary Carol to follow Robert. She held out her arms for Grace. "Find Mr. Raymond. I'll be right behind you," J.D. urged, as he lowered Grace off the platform.

Celeste broke free of Mr. Lawton's grip before J.D. could jump. Hurling herself out the back door to the platform, she grabbed him by the shoulders, pinning him against the railing. Her fingernails dug into his right shoulder. J.D. bit her arm, hard. She shrieked in pain, let go, and he jumped.

At that very instant, the train lurched abruptly and began moving forward slowly. Celeste lost her balance. Before she could right herself, Mr. Lawton, who was coming from behind, fell into her, knocking them both to the platform floor. Grabbing the rail, she tried to pull herself up. "Fools! There's only one way back. You'll never find it now," she screamed after the children.

The last thing J.D. heard as he ran after the others was Celeste shrieking, "Go then and die, fools! Go and die!"—and some strange words in a language he couldn't understand.

Running as hard as they could, the children caught up to the next car. Robert, ahead of the others, reached for the steps so he could pull them on after him before the train picked up speed, but as he grasped the handrail, there was nothing to hold. The train vanished into thin air.

They were alone in the heat of the day. Everything was silent except for the wind gently blowing through tall grass that stood all around them. Something fluttered to the ground where the tracks should have been.

Robert reached down to pick it up. It was the map.

Chapter 17

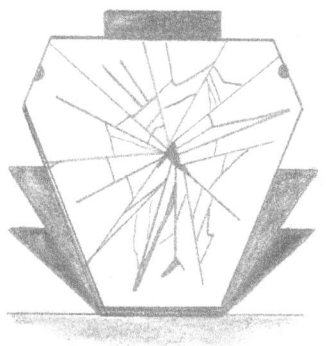

An Uninvited Guest

When Celeste commanded Gary Lawton to tie up Mary Carol, something in him snapped. It was as if somebody lifted blinders from his eyes. He saw Celeste as she was, instead of the way he hoped she was. When the children leapt from the train, he tried to block her way to the platform. She got ahead of him, but he was right on her heels. As Celeste shrieked at them, Mr. Lawton pulled himself up from where he'd landed and threw the map, wanting rid of it. He hadn't the least idea that the children had vanished or that the map would reach them.

Just then, a loud knock came at the door of the car. Someone came in uninvited. They could hear footsteps making their way through the corridor, past the dining room, and into the lounge. Standing at the platform door was Mr. Nichols.

Celeste straightened herself, patting her rumpled hair. "I might have known it would be you. Gary, darling, disappear until I send for you."

Gary Lawton snapped into action. "Don't bother to send for me, Celeste. I'll get my things. I'm leaving. I won't be back."

"Suit yourself," said Celeste, smoothing her dress. "You're getting to be tedious. I can't think why I've kept you so long."

Mr. Nichols waited. Gary grabbed his suitcases. He walked out without saying good-bye or looking back. "Lost another one, Celeste?" Mr. Nichols asked dryly.

Celeste ignored him. "Come to beg me to repent and change my ways? You're a little ahead of schedule. I used to get at least five hundred years between lectures. It's not even fifty years since the last series. Your lectures haven't worked yet. But you will persist."

"I came for the children, Celeste. I see they've gone overboard. It isn't too late. You could call them back. I'm asking you to do it." He spoke calmly, quietly.

"*My dear,*" Celeste's voice was dripping with sarcasm. "You know I can't do that. Besides, I didn't throw them off the train, they jumped, the little fools. Can I help it if there was a thin place where they'd fall through? I haven't had anything to do with thin places for centuries. You know well enough that I have very limited powers. I gave my powers up centuries ago."

"Celeste, they're children. I would not have thought that even you could stoop to this." Mr. Nichols wearily sat down in one of the lounge chairs. "Need I remind you that you do have powers related to the crystal? Otherwise, how did you imagine you could send Gary Lawton and that little girl off to find it for you?"

"Suppose I did say a few words to help those brats on the way once I saw what was happening? I have no way of knowing where they've gone, now, do I?" Celeste smirked. "You thought you were so clever with that map. How did you get it away from the boy—that James Matthias?" Without waiting for a reply, she went on. "Did you really suppose you could hide it from me? And in the Denver Museum of Natural History? How unimaginative. Finding it was child's play." She lit a cigarette in her long jeweled holder. "Do you think you can keep me from this last of the crystals? All of your stupid tricks are for nothing." She paced back and forth.

"The map was not intended for you." Mr. Nichols sighed. "I daresay it has not been what you hoped for."

"The limp words of a defeated man," she said. "It wasn't *intended* that I have the crystals to myself, but I have had them, haven't I? I will have this last one, too."

"My dear, Celeste, I hear the desperate stand of a weary woman who wants to buy a few thousand more years of youth."

Celeste flinched at his words. But she said nothing.

"Your time is running out," Mr. Nichols continued. "The moment you chose to take the first crystal and use it to stay young and beautiful, the clock began ticking. It's counting the years before you will fade and die like every other mortal who has walked this earth."

"But what years they've been!" Celeste was defiant. "Look at you. You're an old man, while I'm still young and beautiful. Do you think I would trade places with you? Who wants to live forever as a wizened old fool?" Celeste scoffed.

"Ah, Celeste, old is a matter of the heart, not the color of your hair," Mr. Nichols sighed. "The price you paid to stay young wasn't yours to pay. You sold the health of the planet to buy a few hundred thousand years of beauty. But time is catching up with you. You've squandered all the crystals but this last one. Your clock is running faster now. I'm old, but so are you, my beloved sister, older than me."

"C'lestin, my *darling twin brother*. You were born just after me in the morning of the world," she sneered. "What are you calling yourself these days? Still Mr. Nichols? Dearest C'lestin—Mr. Nichols, Mr. Whoever—don't try to appeal to my sentiment. I haven't any."

"Seven crystals set aside for mending the world. 'Waters they held in rainbow lights, Fresh from the Dawn of Time; Immortal twins, oh guard them well, Till Mother Earth has need,'" quoted C'lestin. "What happened, Celeste? How could you let yourself be so deceived? I shall never understand."

"Do you think I care if you understand? And don't quote that soppy poetry to me. I'm not interested in all your words about duty and honor and caring for the world. The world has been doomed from the first. Why should the seven crystals be wasted on healing a world that can't last? You may be eternal, but the Earth isn't. This sun won't shine forever. So where will your precious Earth be when there is no longer a sun?"

"These are not your words, Celeste. In your heart, you know it," said C'lestin. "I fail to see how you could have fallen for such an argument."

Celeste began pacing again. "I'm selfish. I make no apologies. Why shouldn't I look after myself? I'm the only one who matters to me. Don't tell me you care for the world. Don't tell me how it breaks your heart every time a forest is cut down or a species destroyed. People tear up the Earth. They always have. They always will. There is nothing you can do that will make a difference. The only thing that matters is right now. It is all we have. The past is over and done. The future is always out ahead someplace where you can't see it. But when I look in the mirror, *that* is real. That is now."

Celeste ran her fingers through her hair. "I am the most beautiful woman who has ever lived. Women model themselves after me. I've been courted by emperors and kings. Knights and soldiers have fought for my favor. Do you think I could possibly give that up to add a few hundred thousand years to the life of a world that is doomed?"

"No, Celeste, I don't expect you to give up the life you chose for yourself," sighed C'lestin. "Yet I will ask. Love never quits trying."

"What a bunch of driveling sentimentality. Love! What do you know about love? And don't ask me to feel sorry for those brats. Gary was supposed to go with the girl. But he's too weak. They forced my hand and left before I was ready. YOU forced my hand. I knew you were up to something when I saw you strutting around the train with them. They'll die out there now. Stupid children. I shall have to find another way. And I will." She threw herself into a chair across from him, took a long drag on her cigarette, slowly exhaling the smoke.

"Don't be too sure, Celeste," said C'lestin. "I think there's more to those four children than you are capable of imagining. They have an impossible task and little enough to go on. But mark my word. They will put you to shame."

At this Celeste let out a shrill laugh. "Suppose they do figure it out? The Keeper will demand payment. I don't care if you put him in place. He has to march to my tune. You can't get around that! He has to answer to the magic. And it's my magic."

"How twisted your mind has become, Celeste. You imagine everyone to be as wicked as you have chosen to be."

"But the magic, C'lestin! You, of all people, cannot deny the magic. My mortality prevents me from going back to claim the crystal for myself. But I wrapped each of those crystals in magic before I gave up my powers. You have to admit, I was always much more powerful than you. You were only clever enough to get your hands on this one."

"Yes, but I'm the one who has hidden the crystal this time, Celeste. The magic you used was never yours. It was borrowed. That might be something to think about."

"You have made my task more difficult, but you have not stopped me," Celeste retorted. "You were so clever. The magic, *my* magic, said that neither Angel, Immortal, Man, nor Beast could undo the spell that bound my crystals. You found the loophole. You had a girl take the Last Crystal from where I hid it. Now a girl has to claim it. But I can send a girl as well as you can. I know my magic better than you do. You will not stop me."

"There you are wrong, Celeste. I didn't find the loophole. The girl—Grace Willis—figured out how to open the black alabaster box that held the crystal. She was very much like you were when that 'soppy poetry,' as you call it, was written: smart, brave, clever. She bested you and the magic. Now you are responsible for four children thrown back into time with nothing but their wits to see them through. Just so they can buy you another few thousand years of beauty? Celeste, you've outdone yourself." He shook his head in disbelief. "But you don't have the crystal yet. I don't think the children will be defeated either. I may be honor bound to live within the rules, unlike you who apparently have no honor left, and I may be hampered by the magic you have wrapped around that crystal. But I have found a way. Unlike you, I can go back. And unlike you, I am not mortal.

"You will die, Celeste. Maybe not this year, maybe not a thousand years from now, but you will die, even if you get the Last Crystal. I wish it were not so. But that is an absolute fact. The question is, how do you wish to face it? You still have the opportunity to die with dignity and honor. There are far worse things than death."

With that, C'lestin—or Mr. Nichols as the children knew him—stood. "It's not yet too late to call them back. If you do, you will have to give up the Last Crystal. You'll become old, but you will save yourself and them. And you might just learn that there are rewards to being old."

"Not in a hundred thousand years, brother dearest," scoffed Celeste.

"You don't have a hundred thousand years. Not this time." Mr. Nichols nodded his head to her. "I take my leave." With that he walked out of the private car. He closed the door behind him without looking back. Had she been able to see him, Celeste would have noticed that her twin brother's eyes were filled with tears.

She stood on the back platform of her private car leaning on the rail and looking out at the desert as the train sped toward L.A. She stood there for a long time, seething with red-hot anger. Then she went into her bedroom and looked in the mirror that hung above her dressing table. There was an unmistakable wrinkle showing on her forehead. She grabbed a vase from the dressing table and smashed the mirror. It fell, knocking over a beautiful vial that held water from the sixth crystal. Celeste threw herself at it, trying to catch the vial before it hit the floor.

Chapter 18

The Grim Truth

What happened the next few days is almost too painful to tell. At first, the children didn't know what to think. Robert said they'd flag down a train traveling the same route to California. Mary Carol said they should look for the tracks. Grace said Uncle James would come looking for them.

J.D. said nothing. He knew they wouldn't find the tracks. They were surrounded by land, covered with gray-green grass and scrubby bushes. It wasn't at all like the desert where they'd been with Mr. Nichols that morning. It looked more like prairie land. There were no stark sandstone formations peppering the landscape like those they could see from the train. Nor was there any sign of civilization—no roads, no electric or telegraph lines, no train tracks, no houses, no livestock pens anywhere in sight. The only similarity was the heat. It was really hot.

Furthermore, the train didn't gradually fade into the distance as it should have. It vanished. In the instant it vanished, everything changed.

He wasn't prepared to explain it. In a way, where they were and how they got there was irrelevant. Their first job was to survive. They had to find shade and a water source. Then they could have the luxury of trying to figure things out.

The others wanted to walk in the direction the train had gone. J.D. wouldn't let them. "Didn't you hear anything Mr. Nichols told us? It's too hot out here. We have to find shade and water. It won't matter if a train comes past if we're dead!" He was so fierce that he alarmed the others. "We're better off searching this evening. Besides, if a train comes within twenty miles, we'll see or hear it in this flat country. Then we can make for the tracks and stop the next one. There'll be plenty of trains after that long break-down." He knew it wouldn't happen, but he had to reassure them. They'd get the picture soon enough.

Reluctantly, they agreed. J.D. set their course toward an outcropping of rock and trees, the nearest spot that promised shelter. They'd taken no more than a few steps when Mary Carol said, "My blanket!" It lay on the grass, rolled up and tied with a blue cord. "Did you bring it, Robert?"

"No, there wasn't time." He looked questioningly at the others.

"The last I knew it was folded up on my seat where I left it when we went out to walk in the desert with Mr. Nichols," said Mary Carol.

"Then somebody must have known we'd need it," said J.D. grimly. He picked it up and threw it over his shoulder.

The outcropping of rock and trees looked closer than it was. The longer they walked, the farther away it seemed. The sun was blistering hot. Except for Mary Carol, they had hats. Hers had been lost, probably somewhere in Celeste's car.

"What am I thinking?" J.D. paused reaching in his pocket. He always carried a square of parachute cloth Daddy gave him when he was in training to be an Army pilot. "Here, put this over your head, Mary Carol. You have to have something. You can tie it on with your bandana."

"We should cover our faces and necks like this morning," said Robert.

"What about Mary Carol?" asked Grace.

Mary Carol produced a long hair ribbon from her purse, tying it around the parachute cloth.

"Now you look like one of the shepherds in the

Christmas pageant," J.D. said, trying to lighten their spirits. They all had a good long drink from J.D.'s water bag since it was the heaviest and hardest to carry. He knew it wouldn't be heavy for long, but he didn't say so. "Let's tie on our bandanas now," he said. "Mary Carol, you'll look like a shepherd bandit."

There was no path. Prairie grass was nearly waist high in places. The boys had on trousers, but grass lashed Mary Carol and Grace's legs. "Rob, let's go first," said J.D. "We can trample the grass down. Maybe that will help." Even so, the girls' legs were itching, scratched, sunburned, and bleeding in places, when they finally reached the rock formation. They were all thirsty, hot, and hungry. J.D.'s shoulder ached. Celeste's fingernails had drawn blood.

On the near side, their shelter looked as if a giant child had been playing with stone blocks and left them on the floor. Nestled behind was a small grove of trees and brush that made a perfect campsite. Exhausted, they threw themselves down.

They all had another long drink. The water bags Mr. Nichols had given the girls only held about a quart of water each. Robert's canteen and J.D.'s water bag carried more, though they'd taken down almost all of J.D.'s supply.

Nobody wanted to say it, but in all this time, they

hadn't heard or seen any sign of a train.

Gradually, after they'd caught their breath, they began to make some decisions about what to do. "Okay, let's take stock," said J.D. "Rob, what do you have in your knapsack?"

Now that he had recovered from the shock of having the train disappear from his grasp, Robert was thinking like himself again. He began digging in his knapsack, placing its contents on the ground beside him and explaining why each item was essential. "I took my books out yesterday so it wouldn't be so heavy." He had a compact cooking tin with a cup, fork, and spoon that folded up together. There was his map of the U.S., a large bag of dried fruit and nuts, a small jar of peanut butter, and four packages of beef jerky, each holding six sticks of jerky. He even had first aid supplies: a bottle of Mercurochrome, a roll of adhesive tape, and a few rolls of white bandage cloth. In one pocket were a writing tablet and two pencils, as well as his notebook. The side pockets held a magnifying glass, a compass, the matches, and a length of rope.

"Daddy said this is *nylon* rope. It's a new synthetic invented for the war. We'll need it if we have to scale any steep banks before we find the train tracks. I have my jackknife and a ball of string in my trousers pockets," he added, returning things to his knapsack. "Oh, and my two salt and sugar packets. We should have put them into our water bags."

"Robbie, I'll never complain about you over-stuffing that knapsack again!" Mary Carol smoothed her dress, grateful that it still looked pretty. "All I have is two handkerchiefs, a brush, mirror, nail file, and the old Maid—I mean Old Man cards, and lip salve—I should have remembered that. Here, everybody put some on." She handed it around. "Mamma gave me a bag of hard candy for the trip. I stuck that in when we went with Mr. Nichols. I was going to share, but I got so interested I forgot."

"We may need that extra sugar," said J.D.

"That hard candy will help keep our throats from getting so dry," said Robert. "Especially if we run short of water before we find the next train."

"And I brought Sugar Daddy suckers for everyone," Mary Carol said. "I bought them with my own money. That's all the food. Oh, and a sewing packet. I forgot. Mamma put that in."

"Let me have that mirror," said Robert. "I'll signal S.O.S. before the sun goes down. Maybe one of the trains will pick up the signal, or if there are any cowboys or anybody like that around." He climbed to the top of the rocks. Grace followed. He explained how it worked. Holding the mirror up to his temple, he positioned it right next to his eye. "I have to be able to see where I'm sending the light. I'll angle the mirror so the light will hit my hand." Keeping the mirror next to his right eye, he stretched out his left arm.

Grace watched as he moved the mirror gradually, walking the light beam along his arm. "Now I'm going to send the beam through my two fingers." Robert made a V with two fingers, left arm still outstretched in the direction they had come from. "It's like using the sight on a gun, Gracie."

He sent the light beam through the V and began to signal. "Flash, flash, flash, f-l-a-s-h, f-l-a-s-h, f-l-a-s-h, flash, flash, flash. That's Morse Code for SOS," he explained. "Three dots, three dashes, and three dots." After a pause, he repeated the signal twice more.

"Can I do it?" asked Grace.

"Sure, we're going to turn slightly so we're sending it in a different direction now. You'll have to take off your hat so nothing interferes with the sun." He turned Grace slightly to the left. Helping her hold the mirror next to her eye, "Stretch your arm out straight ahead where we want to send the signal—aim it over the tops of the trees below."

Grace marched the light beam up her arm and made a V with her fingers. She let Robert help her send the signal. She did it three times. By this time

J.D. and Mary Carol joined them.

"Can they try, too?" Gracie asked.

"May they try," Mary Carol corrected her.

"Everybody *may* try," said Robert. "But we need to keep watch in case somebody returns the signal from one of the places we've sent it." They all kept watch for each other, gradually turning so the signal was sent out in every direction before the sun was too low to give them a good clear beam. But there were no signals in return.

When they climbed back down, Grace emptied her purse. "I don't think I have anything that will help us," she said. Her purse was bright red with a kewpie doll face. It was her favorite. Uncle James gave it to her for Christmas. She pulled out the little black plush kitten with a white spot on its nose, a lace-edged handkerchief, a string of bright gold glass beads, a package of sugar-coated peanuts, two very squashed oatmeal cookies left from their snack—wrapped in another handkerchief—a little box of colored pencils that came with its own writing pad, and the tiny carousel music box.

"The sugar-coated peanuts will help," said Mary Carol. "We may get pretty hungry before we're rescued. But Mr. Nichols said it is better to be hungry if you're caught in the desert."

Grace brushed off bits of chaff that clung to her dress. "It doesn't look so awfully not pretty does it?" she asked...

"You still look as good as new," said Mary Carol.

Robert rolled his eyes. "What else have you got in there?" he asked.

Grace turned her purse upside down and gave it a shake. A long length of what looked like hose fell out.

"What are you doing with that old bicycle inner tube?" asked Robert.

"Daddy said it wasn't any good except for scrap," Grace defended. "I was going to make a lead for Kitty."

"Maybe you won't mind if I take some of it," said J.D. "If we can find a good, sturdy forked stick, I could use it to make a slingshot. I didn't think to bring mine. I'm not sure I could shoot any animals for us to eat, but I could sure scare them away if I had to." He emptied his pockets, adding a package of lifesavers and a very squishy chocolate bar to their supplies. He also had his pocketknife, a nickel, and two pennies. "I'd of had a flint rock if I hadn't had to wear my good trousers," he apologized.

"We'll put that parachute cloth and our handkerchiefs and bandanas out on the grass tonight to catch the dew," said Robert. "We can also get dew off the grass in the morning. My supplies won't last us too long. We have to find water since we don't know how long it will be before we're rescued."

Suddenly, Mary Carol understood the grim truth. "We aren't ever going to find the train tracks, no matter what direction we go in, are we."

"No," said J.D. "We aren't going to find the train."

Part 2

Into the Unknown

Chapter 19

Right Where She Wants Us

The children sat in silence pondering the awful realization that they were completely, utterly lost.

"So we aren't going to find the train," said Robert at last. "What makes you so sure?"

J.D. let out a big sigh. "Come on, Rob, you're the one good at surveillance. Look where we are. It doesn't even look the same. This is grassland, not desert. I can't explain what happened, but it's happened. We're nowhere near where we were when we walked around the train this morning. You, more than anybody, should be able to see that."

"We aren't going to ever find the train?" Grace's eyes welled up with tears. "How will we get home?"

J.D. was sorry the others were beginning to understand their peril. He grasped at ways to reassure them, even though he didn't feel hopeful. They were on the Santa Fe Chief, broken down in the desert. They'd just rescued Mary Carol, who had been kidnapped and was held in Celeste's private car at the end of the train. They escaped from the platform balcony. But before they could board again at another car, the train vanished. Celeste's words, "Go then and die, fools!" kept ringing in J.D.'s ears along with the other words, words that sounded like a curse in a language he couldn't understand.

He was wise enough to know that hope was one of their strongest allies. He couldn't let them give up hope. "Don't forget. Celeste didn't throw us off the train. We jumped. I'm not sure how, but I think that makes a difference. A big difference." J.D. figured that the only way to keep the others from falling into despair was to keep them busy doing things they needed to do to survive. "We need to start acting sensibly," he said. "I was hoping we'd find a stream with all these trees. But at least there is plenty of firewood. We should gather some of these sticks and branches before it starts to cool off. We'll want to keep a good fire going tonight. This may not be desert, but I'll bet it gets cold out here."

"Tell you what," said Robert. "I'll start a fire now before the sun goes down so I can use my magnifying glass. It will be a lot faster than rubbing sticks together. We'd better save the matches." While the others collected wood, Robert gathered dry grass for tinder. He aimed light from his magnifying glass so it made a fine, bright point on the grass. It began smoldering within seconds. He gently blew on it until he had a flame, building it up with more paper torn from his tablet and dry grass. When a good blaze was going, he added the wood the others brought.

"We found a few mesquite pods," said Mary Carol. "Grandpa Matthias says you're supposed to be able to eat them and the pith on the inside."

Robert pried one open with his jackknife. "It's still early for mesquite pods, but this tastes okay. We can eat the pith. I've read that it tastes a bit like brown sugar."

"The seeds are good, too," said J.D., "if we can smash them. They're nearly impossible to break unless you have the right tools. We could try one of those big rocks." He pulled the bark from a sturdy Y-shaped piece of wood and began making a slingshot as he talked.

Robert and Mary Carol tried smashing mesquite seeds, but with no luck. "We're wasting our time," said Robert, "all we're doing is breaking the rocks."

"Maybe it isn't a complete waste," said Mary Carol, picking up a piece of rock. "Isn't this flint rock?"

Robert took a look. "It is! Well spotted. We can use that."

"And there won't be any critters left in the rocks," said Grace hopefully. "You've scared them all away."

Robert grinned. "Good point, Gracie."

Again and again, they went over what happened. While Mr. Nichols was talking to people in the observation car, Mary Carol went to the toilet. It was too crowded near the observation car, so she went back to their car. When she stepped out of the lounge, she could see Mr. Lawton waiting by their seats. "So I thought he must be looking for us. He said, 'Good, I found you. The others are waiting.' All I could think about was sticking together. So like a dummy, I went with him. Then all of a sudden Celeste was stuffing a gag in my mouth and he was tying me up!"

"So why did Mr. Lawton let you go?" wondered J.D.

"He didn't want to tie me up. But Celeste said, 'It's the only way now that she's refused to come.' She meant you, Gracie. She was really upset when she saw us walking around the train. I don't think she likes Mr. Nichols. She was furious that we were with him. She was expecting Gracie to come play with the doll. She said they'd have to take hostages now or you'd never go. She blamed Mr. Nichols for some reason. She kept saying, 'Now that he's in it.'"

"Jeepers, Gracie. She really was going to send you out here with Mr. Lawton!" exclaimed Robert.

"Mr. Lawton argued with her all the time he tied me up," said Mary Carol. "He said she was trying to do something wicked."

"Yeah, I'd say it was pretty wicked," said J.D.

"She said he was becoming soppy and she was going to go have a cup of coffee. She just walked away. That's when he told me he was tying me up with knots that would come right out. He said I should try not to be afraid because he was going to help me escape. I wonder why she didn't push him off the train with us, since she planned for him to go with Gracie all along?" Nobody could answer that question.

"I'll bet we landed exactly where she wanted Mr. Lawton to take Gracie," said Robert. "She was planning this from the minute she set eyes on you, Gracie."

"Right where she wants us," said Mary Carol, looking around at the vast unknown grasslands surrounding the rock formation where they had found shelter. "I think we'd better strategize; I mean not just about food and water."

"Okay, let's think this through," said Robert. "Gracie, Celeste said that as soon as you find the crystal, you'll be back. That must mean the only way we'll get back from wherever we are now is to collect her tokens and get that crystal."

"Maybe the crystal really will heal Daddy," said Grace. "What if it could?"

"Do you honestly think somebody like her gives two cents for our daddy?" asked Mary Carol. "We'll do the work and she'll keep it for herself."

"If we can find it." Robert said. "She couldn't figure out the clues on the map. I wonder if we could? Let's have a look at that map."

"Wait a minute. Can she see us?" Mary Carol asked. "She said she would know what Gracie was doing."

"Yes, but we don't know what that meant. Maybe it was just a threat." J.D. said, trying to reassure her.

"If she can put us here, she might be able to see what we're doing." Mary Carol was worried.

"I'm not so sure she put us here," said J.D. "maybe it just happened. We can't do anything about it if she can watch us, anyway." Then, just to make everybody feel a little better, he stretched his mouth out, stuck out his tongue and crossed his eyes. "So there, Celeste. That's what we think of you!"

Grace pulled a face, too. Then Mary Carol and Robert. They all laughed. Somehow, it helped.

"The way I see it, our first job is to find water and make sure we can survive. Then we just have to get on with the clues," said J.D. "There is something at work here that we can't explain. All we can go on is the information that we have. So I'm with Rob. We have to find the crystal. Celeste can do whatever she wants with it after that."

"Anyway, she can't come here," Grace said. "That's why she wanted me to get it for her. Remember, she told me. If she can't come here, I don't think she can see us."

It was a comforting thought. At least they wouldn't be running from Celeste.

Looking at the old map was no good. There was no way to tell their location for sure even though north, south, east, and west were marked. The map was very much as J.D. remembered it from his brief look. It was hand drawn and painted with watercolors, with rivers and deserts, mountains, plains, and the ocean. Tiny pictures of plants, animals, and objects made a border around the map and appeared here and there on it.

"Let's compare this with your map, Rob," J.D. suggested.

Chapter 19

When they spread out the two side-by-side, they were able to make some guesses based on what Celeste had said about the ocean. There wasn't much resemblance between the two maps, though, except for the ocean and some of the mountains. "Seems like the mountains are closer to the coast on this map than on yours, Rob," said J.D.

"We might as well be on another planet," said Mary Carol.

"Are we?" Grace was alarmed.

"Does it matter?" asked Robert. "Wherever we are, we've got the same problem. We have to figure out the clues, find the tokens—whatever they are, and stay alive until we get home."

"Especially stay alive until we get home!" said Mary Carol.

"Let's have that compass, Rob," said J.D. "Which way is north?" He bent over Rob's map, drawing a line with his finger. "Assuming we're somewhere around here where the train was, we should be able to find a river if we head northwest. That's probably our best bet. Anyway, remember when Mr. Nichols looked at your map, Rob? He drew a path toward the ocean that went more or less along here. It would be here on the old map." *Give or take a few hundred miles one way or another*. He couldn't say it out loud, not if he wanted to keep the others encouraged.

"Well, I guess we can say for sure that the old map has nothing to do with a Nazi plot," said Robert.

"Just when you were getting the hang of being a spy," said Mary Carol.

"Gosh, that seems like a hundred years ago," said Robert.

As the sun dropped below the horizon, they were glad for the fire. After the stars began to come out, they looked for familiar constellations. "That's the Big Dipper," said J.D. It was further west and a great deal closer to the horizon than last night, but it was there.

"At least we know we're still on Earth!" said Robert.

"I've never seen stars look so close," said Mary Carol, marveling at the night sky, "not even at Grandpa and Grandma's farm."

"That's probably why the sky looks so different," said Robert. "The stars out here are so bright and thick you can't make sense of things."

Everyone was famished. But they agreed that they'd better ration food. "Okay, let's figure that we have to make this last three or four days," said J.D. He didn't want to say so, but if they hadn't found water and another food source by then, it wouldn't matter.

"Water is the most serious problem," said J.D. "I hope we capture some on the cloths tonight. We have about a day's supply among us."

They sat staring into the fire after they ate their meager supper: a piece of beef jerky, a blob of peanut butter, a few nuts and half a cookie each. Grace cuddled Kitty and began to play her music box. They'd been sick of hearing it when they were on the train. Now, the sound of the Welsh folk song it played was comforting. Mary Carol sang:

> *Sleep my child and peace attend thee,*
> *All through the night*
> *Guardian angels God will send thee,*
> *All through the night.*

Their mother had sung it to them from the time they were infants. It was one small comfort to hold on to.

"If we all squish together, we can put the blanket over us," said Mary Carol. She hadn't really looked at the blanket until then. Now, as she untied the cord binding it, she let out an exclamation. "These are navy blue shoelaces. Miss Spright had navy blue lace-up pumps. Wonder how she knew we'd need the blanket?"

"Maybe she really is a fairy," said Grace.

"Like I said, there's more going on here than I

can explain," said J.D.

They were so hungry that nobody would have been able to sleep if they hadn't been completely exhausted. J.D. sat up long after the others, studying the old map by the firelight, trying to make sense of it, attempting to compare it to Robert's map. His hand went to the silver owl Mr. Nichols had given him. He could almost hear Mr. Nichols saying, "The person who wears it is supposed to show wisdom." When they'd met Mr. Nichols he said, "You show all the signs of a good leader."

J.D. swallowed back a lump in his throat. *How can I do it? I'm no leader. I'm just a kid.* He blinked back tears as he tried to look at the map. The thought came to him, *Daddy said that sometimes we just do what has to be done, not because we know how it will turn out, but because it's the right thing to do. It's why he joined the Army Air Force.* Finally he gave up trying to make sense of things and crawled in the space under the blanket the others had left for him. As he was drifting off to sleep something else Mr. Nichols said came to him. "People who know the limits of their wisdom are wiser than most of us." *I'll do my best. That is all anybody can do*, he thought, and fell into an exhausted sleep.

Chapter 20

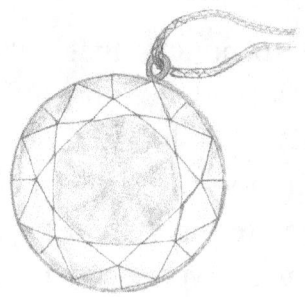

The Key

A pink snake coiled itself around Grace. She called for the others, but they couldn't hear. There was nobody to help. Then Old Shep came. He gave her a doggie kiss on the forehead. She could feel his warm breath. She struggled to sit up, but she couldn't. Old Shep stood over her, his feet on the blanket, but she couldn't feel his weight. He looked straight into her eyes. She understood. It was if he were saying, "You can do this. It won't be easy, but you can do it. You are stronger than you think you are."

She awoke expecting to see Old Shep. He wasn't there, nor was there a pink snake. Feeling Mary Carol on one side, and Robert on the other, was reassuring. She wasn't alone. They were in a terrifying situation, but at least they were together. They could take care of each other. Except for the worry about her father, it was the first time Grace had ever really thought about anything but being taken care of. She'd never seriously thought about the others needing care.

The fire was down to a few embers. Grace crawled out from under the blanket, shivering, trying not to disturb them. *Maybe Old Shep is right. I can't do very much, but I can do something.* She built up the fire, still wondering about the dream. The warm fire and approach of dawn helped.

The old map lay where J.D. had left it. Spreading it out, she studied it in the early morning light. The crystal magnifying glass Mr. Nichols gave her was still around her neck, tucked safely inside her dress. When she put it in the light, the crystal caught the first rays of dawn and light from the fire, throwing a prism of colors onto the map.

When she looked through the crystal, Grace made an extraordinary discovery. There was a map underneath the one she could see with the naked eye. It added more detail. Near the bottom was a legend with a red starburst and the words, "Child, I will show you the way." Next to the starburst was a dot labeled, "Safe Rocks". An arrow pointed from Safe Rocks toward the river; "3 Days Journey," it read. A line from Safe Rock led straight toward the river until it was almost there. Then it made a sharp turn to the left, approaching the river at an angle. There was a line going straight to the river, too, but there was an X over it. Try as she would, Grace could not find where the line took up again beyond the river. *At least it shows the way to water. Water can save us until help comes*, Grace thought. In spite of what the others said, she still hoped that Uncle James would send out a search party, when they didn't turn up at the station in L.A.

Robert sat up and stretched, suddenly realizing where they were. "Gosh. I thought I fell out of bed and was sleeping on the floor."

"Look, Robbie. Mr. Nichols said we need this." Grace eagerly handed him the crystal. "It shows where we are and the path to the river."

Robert looked through it. "What are you talking about? I can't see anything, Gracie. It's all fuzzy."

Awake now, J.D. looked, but he couldn't see anything more either. "Maybe it was a trick of the early light, Gracie." He didn't want to hurt her feelings. Grace could be a brat, but she wasn't likely to try and be cute about something so serious.

Grace looked again. It was all there. She read aloud and traced the path with her fingers so the others could see where it went.

Mary Carol awoke, stiff from sleeping on the ground, cold, hungry, scared, and grumpy. She looked through the crystal, too. Everything looked fuzzy. It was easier to read the map without the crystal. "This is just some of your make-believe! Like seeing Old Shep at the train stations. It's so unfair, Gracie. You shouldn't get our hopes up like that."

"But I did see Old Shep!" Grace was disappointed that the others couldn't see and crushed that they didn't believe her. Defensive and quarrelsome, she turned on Robert, "If you hadn't accused me of cheating at Old Man, we wouldn't have met Celeste and we wouldn't be lost."

"Making up things on the map is a pretty mean way to get even," Robert accused.

"Okay, you two, cut it out," J.D. said. Losing patience with both of them, he forgot all about being a wise leader. "You're both acting like brats."

It might have escalated into a mean-spirited squabble if Mary Carol hadn't suddenly remembered two things: Mamma hugging her at the train station in Kansas City and saying, "I'm counting on you," and Mr. Nichols saying, "You're a real care-giver, Mary Carol." She felt for the turquoise around her neck, a wave of guilt sweeping over her. "Okay everybody. I'm sorry I was so grumpy. Gracie, I apologize for saying that about Old Shep. Just because I couldn't see him doesn't mean you were making it up." To the others she said as kindly as she knew how, "I say that if Gracie says she can see things on the map that we can't, we ought to at least go along. After all, she's the one Celeste singled out. And, don't forget, Mr. Nichols gave her the glass. He could have given it to any of us. Another thing, when we first met him, he told Gracie, 'You see more than people think you do.'"

"I'm sorry, Gracie," said Robert, "you're right. It's all my fault. We wouldn't be here, if I hadn't been such a bad sport and lost my temper."

"No, it isn't." Grace suddenly remembered the little voice inside that wanted to go along with Celeste and outsmart the others. What if she had? It didn't bear thinking about. "I was a brat on the train. You were right, Robbie. I did cheat. It was my fault."

Astonished at Grace, Mary Carol breathed a silent sigh of relief. "It wasn't any one person's fault," she said. Then, changing the subject, she asked, "Do you think Mr. Nichols knew we'd need the things he gave us?"

"Maybe," said J.D. "I don't know."

"I wish he were here," she said. "I'd feel a lot safer."

"But he isn't here," said J. D., becoming practical again. "We're on our own, like it or not. Anyway, it makes sense to head toward the river. If you can find which way on the map, Gracie, I say all the better. We can figure out what to do next once we find water. We'd better get going before it gets hot."

"And before our breakfast melts!" said Mary Carol, eyeing J.D.'s chocolate bar.

Everybody set to work. There was quite a bit of dew on the bandanas and handkerchiefs they'd spread out. They wrung them out into Robert's cooking tin. He poured the water into J.D.'s waterbag. "We'd better save this. You can use your bandanas to draw dew off the grass. Then just suck it out."

Grace made a face, but she followed directions.

"It's like sopping up a spill," said Mary Carol, setting to work. When she sucked the water from her bandana it wasn't tasty, but it was wet enough to quench her thirst.

They made a quick end to J.D.'s chocolate bar. Everybody had a dollop of peanut butter with a little bit of dried fruit and nuts.

Both girls had raw places on their shoulders where their purses had rubbed. "I can fix that so you can wear them as a belt," said Robert, "but I'll have to cut the straps." He thought Grace might object, but her shoulder hurt too much. He put the hard candy in his knapsack, too, to lighten Mary Carol's load.

Chapter 20

"We have about enough water for a couple of days if we're lucky and we can keep collecting water at night," said Robert as he kicked dirt over the fire.

J.D. trusted Robert's judgment, but he wasn't so sure about the water supply. It would take a lot of extra water to keep them from using up their reservs. He suggested that they tie their wet bandanas over their noses. "We'll start out conserving body moisture. Let's head out in the direction Gracie suggested."

"The map suggested," Grace corrected him.

There seemed to be a natural path leading through the prairie grass in that direction, perhaps one made by animals. It made the going easier than it was yesterday.

As the sun rose, the landscape around them began to reflect beautiful colors that chased away the shadows. They began to work out the stiffness that they all felt from sleeping on the ground. Nobody said anything about food, but everybody was hungry and knew the others were too. They were terribly thirsty. The idea of running out of water made it worse. After they'd been walking about an hour, everybody took turns mixing a "magic" packet with water in Robert's cup. They drank another cup of water for good measure. Robert passed around some hard candy. It relieved their dry throats.

As far as the eye could see, it was desolate. The

dry, hot wind swept across the prairie grass, bowing it down in waves that looked like the tide coming in on an ocean beach.

Once, far in the distance, they saw a coyote watching them. It walked away in the direction of the river. They occasionally saw animal droppings along the path, possibly from deer or antelope. Otherwise, except for annoying insects, there wasn't another living thing, not even a bird flying overhead.

"Do coyotes eat people?" Mary Carol asked.

"I've never heard of it," said Robert. "Grandpa Matthias says coyotes are naturally shy of people, but they can be curious. Anyway, there are four of us."

They spent the heat of the day huddled under some scrubby oak with the blanket stretched over lower branches to provide more protection. They each had another magic packet with some water, but they didn't eat anything. "It's like he knew we'd need these," said Mary Carol.

"Save the paper for kindling," said Robert, sticking his in a pocket.

They talked little, napping most of the time. As the sun began to make its arc downward, they set out.

J.D. pointed out to the horizon. A herd of some

kind of animal was grazing. They were too far away to tell for sure, but they looked like antelope. As they got closer, the animals seemed untroubled. "Pronghorn," Robert said.

"Well, at least we aren't alone out here," said Mary Carol.

By nightfall they hadn't found shelter, so they made camp on the path. There weren't any shrubs or trees within walking distance and no wood along the path, but they were afraid to go without a fire. Besides the cold, they weren't sure what animals might be lurking about at night. Robert suggested pulling up grass to make a safe area for a fire. They tied the grass in sheaves so it would burn more slowly. They had to make quite a lot of sheaves to keep a smoky fire going. Mindful of saving energy, J.D. suggested that he and Robert cut more grass with pocket knives. It was a bit easier than pulling it up.

"Maybe if we make a big enough fire, someone will see it and rescue us," Grace said, hopefully.

Being seen wasn't altogether reassuring to J.D. He didn't say anything, but he wondered what they'd do if there were hostile people about. If their fire were to be seen by the wrong eyes, there wasn't anything they could do about it. There had been no evidence of people, though, not even so much as a patch of smoke on the horizon.

Robert wrote in his notebook: *Second night out. End of day 1 from the rock pile.* "I don't know if I should count yesterday. It was afternoon when the train vanished. This was our first full day."

"I think we should count full days," said Mary Carol.

As the stars came out, Robert checked his compass, "Either my compass is off or the North Star isn't in the right place. The compass is pointing in that direction, but Polaris is way over there."

"Maybe it's just the time of night," said J.D. "The constallations shift as the earth rotates. Anyway, we seemed to be headed in the right direction today, according to the sun." He tried to sound matter-of-fact, but he wondered what it could mean. He worried most about their water supply, but he didn't say anything. He tried to remember everything Grandpa Matthias had ever said about survival and all that Mr. Nichols told them. Their situation didn't look good.

As they settled down for the night their thoughts went back to family and worry over their father. Mary Carol asked if Grace would play her music box. They looked up at the vast starry sky and fell asleep before the music box quit playing, even J.D.

Chapter 21

The Spoiler

Celeste sat at her dressing table, looking at the cracked vial. She managed to save most of its contents. But at least a drop spilled onto a potted orange tree that stood in a beautiful ceramic pot next to the dressing table. The plant had been the decorator's idea. It had never done well in that spot. It was ugly. Celeste didn't like ugly things.

Now it suddenly began to grow at an alarming rate, its leaves richly glossy and green. It soon reached the height of her dressing table.

Celeste emptied a bottle of costly perfume, carefully pouring the precious water from the broken vial into it. Beside her, the tree shot up to the ceiling, spreading out like a graceful canopy overhead. Blossoms sprang forth. The bedroom smelled of costly perfume and the sweet citrusy fragrance of orange blossoms.

"I should have thought you would be more careful with our treasure." Standing under the orange blossoms at the door to her bedroom was an extraordinarily handsome man, fashionably turned out from the linen handkerchief in the breast pocket of his light blue suit to his immaculately shining black and white spectator shoes. He wore a white shirt. His brightly patterned red, white, and blue necktie sported a solid gold tie clip. He wore matching cufflinks. In one hand he held a straw hat with a blue band.

Celeste wheeled around to face him. "You! What do you mean, our treasure! And how did you get in here?"

"My dear Celeste, when did doors ever trouble me?" The man gave her a flashy smile. His dazzling white teeth were white enough for a billboard advertising toothpaste.

"More to the point, why are you here?" she demanded. "You never appear unless you want something."

"Why Celeste, you do me no credit," said the man in a hurt voice. "I am merely checking on my investment. Now that you mention it, I will trouble you for a drop."

"You have already had your drop from the sixth crystal as agreed," said Celeste firmly.

"My, my. Such a stickler for the rules. And I thought C'lestin was the rule-governed twin."

Celeste did not rise to the bait.

"The more important reason I'm here is because you are getting careless." His eyes moved from the perfume bottle and broken vial to the orange tree that was now growing oranges where the blossoms had been minutes before. "Tell me about these children you've sent after our last crystal. What kind of absurd lunacy is that?"

"You're the great Sandastros. You tell me," she said.

"In fact, it would be more accurate to say my treasure," Sandastros began. "The ignorant little Immortal you were when I found you didn't recognize the potential of those crystals. 'For the healing of Mother Earth,' you said. Poppycock. You couldn't have stolen them out from under your twin brother's nose without my guidance. Your capacity for magic was woefully undeveloped before you met me. I taught you everything you know about dark magic. Don't imagine for a minute that the student ever became greater than her master."

Celeste sat looking at him resentfully, saying

nothing while Sandastros had his say.

"The first mortals you met laughed you out of sight. They said you were the ugliest thing they'd ever seen. Fortunately, you didn't have the courage to challenge them. That goody-goody big brother of yours wasn't around. As I recall, you ran and hid. Poor little sweetheart. You wanted to be one of them, better than any of them, make them pay for laughing."

"I thank you to leave C'lestin out of this," said Celeste tartly. "If I choose to insult him, it is my business. I will not have it from you. And, for your information, I am the older twin."

Sandastros drew a cigar from inside his suit coat, bit off the tip and spat it on the floor. "As I look back on it, you were fortunate that I came along to rescue you. With my encouragement your desire for mortal beauty grew to an obsession. You gave up your immortality so you could outdo—be more beautiful than any of them. And you are. You have been through countless ages. My beauty." He lit the cigar, took a couple of puffs and offered it to Celeste. "A stupid choice my dear. I suppose you see that now that it's too late."

Waving away his offer with disdain, Celeste said, "You are becoming as dreary as C'lestin. Surely you have better things to do than deliver sermons."

Chapter 21

Sandastros seemed to delight in taunting her. "There is only one crystal left and when it goes, poof, there you'll go, out like a light." He took a long puff on the cigar and blew a ring of smoke into the air. "No more beautiful Celeste. Oh, dear. Shall we build a monument so we can remember her great beauty for all time? Never mind. Time will come to an end. So will the monument." He smiled at her, a beautiful smile, though there was neither warmth nor love in it. He took another puff, sending another smoke ring into the air where it followed the first. A third ring chased the first two and bumped into them, making a large ring that settled over Celeste's head like a halo. "My angel," he chortled. "I have decided to have the Last Crystal for myself and spare you the agony of another thousand years. It would be wasted on you. Why prolong a life that is doomed? Your fate was decided before you were born and you have no power to alter it. So let's get on with it."

"No power to alter it? That is complete rubbish." Celeste's eyes narrowed. "You may be the great and invincible Sandastros, roaming the earth and spoiling what he will. You may have been my teacher, but I have made my own choices. I will live by them."

"Or die," smirked Sandastros—all this while he had been leaning against the doorframe. Now he moved to one of the comfortable chairs in her bedroom and draped himself over it, legs sticking out over one arm and back leaning against the other.

Celeste watched him with disdain. "Need I remind you that it is my magic that bound the crystals? Yes, you were my teacher, but my magical powers were far greater than anything you've ever managed, for all your bravado. Big talker. If you were so great, you'd have had the crystals for yourself centuries ago. Don't you think I know that? You were so sly, preying upon a young Immortal. You made me think I had to forfeit my magical powers and my immortality to live among humans. It was only because you knew I was becoming more powerful than you. You wanted me out of the way." The seething anger in her voice could not be mistaken.

Sandastros puffed on his cigar indifferently. He sent smoke rings here and there.

"I may have been deceived into making an unfortunate choice, Sandastros, but I didn't forfeit those powers related to the crystals. That's all you ever wanted, to be rid of me and have the crystals. Do you imagine that I haven't seen how you've tried to get every one of them and failed? Even the great Sandastros has been powerless to get past the spells I used to bind them—bind them to me, in case your timeless memory fails you."

"But a child could," he said bitterly, swinging himself around to sit upright in the chair. "A child. How ironic that I, Sandastros the Immortal, Invincible, could be bested by a child—useless creatures, children. I can't think what these mortals see in them."

"No, to answer your question," said Celeste. "NO. You may not have the Last Crystal for yourself. If those four children survive the trip—and C'lestin thinks they will—I shall have it back. I will not share it with you either. Our terms are that you shall have a drop from each of the crystals. You said that is all you wanted out of the deal. I have kept my word. But you haven't. With every crystal, you have wanted more. Your nagging is becoming relentless. Frankly, I find it exceptionally boring."

Sandastros laughed a hearty, musical laugh. Standing up again he threw down his cigar, grinding it on the beautiful parquet floor of her bedroom with his foot to snuff it out. "Of course I haven't kept my promise. I make a point never to keep my word. But you believed me. That is so rich!" He plucked an orange from the tree that now bore a heavy crop of fruit and began peeling it, tossing the peel on the floor. "Yes, but for your selfishness, I could make use of the occasional drop from the crystals. I had much greater plans for those crystals than keeping you young and beautiful. I shall put the Last Crystal to much better use. There are thousands of people who would give nearly anything for one drop of that water. Your little mortal mind can't even imagine the fun I will have with it." He looked longingly at the crystal perfume bottle holding the remains of the sixth crystal.

Celeste followed his gaze. "You cannot touch the Last Crystal without me. You may go back on your word, but the magic doesn't go back on itself. And by the way, don't look longingly at that bottle. If you try to take it from me, there will be consequences that even the great Sandastros cannot escape. It is still bound to me. Touch it at your own peril."

"Perhaps," said Sandastros. "Now, about these children, my darling, you cannot see what they are up to. I can. And I can go back into time. You, my little mortal, are stuck in the here and now. I can do as I wish and you are powerless to stop me. If your little darlings get through that desert—and I'm inclined to think that they won't—I shall accompany them on their quest. Isn't that good of me?" he laughed his beautiful, musical laugh and popped an orange slice into his mouth. "I won't do anything to interfere until they do all the hard work, promise." He munched on orange slices, dropping the last of the peeling on the floor. "Lovely oranges, darling. I didn't know you had a green thumb."

"Your manners are atrocious," Celeste scowled.

"And a promise from you? What do you take me for?"

"Dear, dear. Don't frown so. One can get premature wrinkles," he smirked. "Now that you've spilled so much of the sixth crystal, you'd better be careful how often you use it. Once the wrinkles start, they set on fast. You'll never have your hands on the Last Crystal again. Mark my word. If your precious brother can use a child to get around the magic, so can I. If not the pretty little girl you sent out into the wilderness, then another. Oh, and by the bye, if someone else claims crystal number seven, I wouldn't count on what's left of the sixth crystal being any more bound to you than it is to me. You might not even be able to open that precious perfume bottle. And oh dear me, the wrinkles! Something to think about. Ta-ta." With that he swept out of the room, stepping over oranges that were falling from the tree and rolling out into the corridor and lounge.

As he opened the door to the platform, oranges rolled out, falling from the platform into the desert. Trees began springing up on either side of the railroad track. Sandastros put on his straw hat and tipped it to Celeste. Stepping off the platform, he vanished as the train sped on its way.

Chapter 22

Bad Decisions

If Robert hadn't been prepared, and if J.D. hadn't bought the water bag at the station in LaJunta, they'd never have made it so far. The children stuck with rationing food, but there was little to ration. By the end of their second full day going toward the river, they realized how small Robert's food supply actually was. Mr. Nichols said that if you are ever in the desert, it is better to eat as little as possible. Staying hungry to conserve body moisture was not their problem. Hunger gnawed at them constantly.

Most of all, they were thirsty. J.D.'s waterbag hung limp as did the small water bags the girls carried. "Dew-water," as they called the water they collected overnight and from the grass was enough to get them going the next day, but it wasn't adequate. Robert's canteen was empty by early afternoon. They shared equally. There was never any question about that.

They found shelter under some twisted trees that night, when it was too dark to walk safely. There was plenty of wood for a fire. Robert wrote in his journal, *Third night out. End of day 2 from the rock pile. Same flat grassland. Small shrubs. Water gone. Should reach river tomorrow.*

They were bruised and sunburned. J.D.'s shoulder hurt where Celeste had clawed him. Mary Carol looked at it when they were at the rock pile and thought they ought to use some of their water to clean it. J.D. wouldn't let her. The best she could do was wipe it off and put some Mercurochrome on it. He didn't let her look after that and he didn't talk about it. He struggled for ways to keep them encouraged. "This time tomorrow we'll be going for a swim!" He tried to sound cheerful.

They wearily crawled under the blanket, terribly thirsty. Grace played her music box, and they sang the lulluby, the sadness and fear in their voices barely disguised.

"We could use a guardian angel about now," said Robert.

"Could you tell us a story, Mary Carol?" Grace asked. Tired as she was, Mary Carol told one of their favorite stories. It was like having a bit of their mother with them. Mary Carol fell asleep before the story ended, but so did the others.

The third day they collected "dew water," but not enough to quench anybody's thirst. Their lips were parched and cracking, despite Mary Carol's lip balm. They had hollow, sunken-looking eyes, and they were all extremely tired. Grace's map, as they now called it, said three days from the rock pile to the river. They were counting on it. The thought of water and a bath before nightfall, kept them going.

A disagreement over the map led to angry feelings and a flareup before morning was over. They had been following the path Grace saw on the map without question. But when they came to the fork in the path as Grace predicted, she said, "This is where we turn left."

"It must be a mistake," said Robert. The path to the left was so overgrown it was barely visible. The other path was well worn. It went straight ahead and looked more inviting. "It must be an animal path to the river."

J.D. said, "We could probably cut several hours off our trip." Nobody had to say it. Several hours can make a great deal of difference when you're perishing for lack of water.

Grace was insistent. "The map shows two paths. The straight path has an X on it. We're not supposed to go on that path."

"Do you always have to have your own way?" Robert asked sourly.

Mary Carol tried reasoning. "Gracie, animals know the way to water. They wouldn't use it if it weren't a safe path. It might save us some time."

"It's the wrong path. The map says so." Grace wouldn't budge. "Besides, there aren't any fresh animal tracks on the path."

"And you know so much about tracking animals," muttered Robert.

"Maybe when your map was made it wasn't the right way, but now it is," J.D. reasoned, trying to keep things calm. "Couldn't we try it? We can't go on much longer without water. If it turns out the path is impassible, all we have to do is cut across to the way marked on the map. Or we'll back track if we have to."

"I agree with J.D.," said Mary Carol. "Besides, if we get to the river before dark, maybe we can find some food."

Grace wasn't convinced. There were more unkind words until J.D. reminded them, "Look, we're wasting time and energy that could be put to walking." It was three to one. They took the broad, direct path. Grace brought up the rear, sobbing, but without tears. She was too dehydrated for tears.

They made such good progress that even Grace was beginning to think they'd made the right choice when they began to smell a foul odor. It grew stronger as they went. Suddenly the path veered sharply and ended. A pool of water fed by a spring gurgled up out of the ground. The water bubbling up looked fresh enough. Only the foul smell held them back.

"It smells like a poison spring," said Robert. "Don't anybody touch that water until we have a look!" The far end of the pool was covered with scum. There were bleached bones everywhere along the bank.

As they looked closely into the water they could see the bones of an enormous animal lying at the bottom of the pool near the spring where the water was clear.

"Gee! You don't think it's. . . ." J.D. stopped short.

"A Coelophysis?" [see lo fiesis] asked Robert. "They'd have found it by now. It would be in the Denver Museum or someplace like that." But a Celophysis is exactly what it looked like. There was the unmistakable large skull with the long snout, elongated neck and tail, short forelimbs and narrow feet of a Coelophysis. There was no way to know how long it had been there. Nothing but bone remained. It gave them the creeps to think of all that flesh rotting off in the water.

Some of the bones that lay about were from large mammals, much larger than deer or antelope. There were tusks, too. But they were too scattered to identify and there were no fresh carcasses. Perhaps animals had learned to avoid the water, though it didn't explain the well-worn path.

The pool was too wide to jump across. It didn't seem to have an outlet, nor was it passable at either end. They turned back, nauseated from the stench. The sight of all that undrinkable water made them nearly wild with thirst.

It was impossible to cut their way across to the path they should have taken. Thorns bushes and tall, matted grass blocked the way. There was nothing for it but to retrace their steps.

Nobody said anything until they were back where they started. They'd lost most of the day with no water to show for it. "Gracie," said J.D., his mouth was so dry he could hardly talk. "You're a brick not to say 'Told you so.' Don't know if we can get to river before dark. Should have listened." The others said more or less the same thing as they started down the narrower, overgrown path that they should have taken in the first place.

It was slow going. They were weary and discouraged. Just before their path turned back toward the river, they came to a boggy area that reached as far as they could see in the direction of the river. "Careful," said J.D. "Might be quicksand." As they walked alongside it, they noticed more animal bones bleached white by time. They were big bones, not so large as the Coelophysis bones, nor so complete a skeleton. But they were bigger than any animals they knew anything about. Nobody said anything. They were too desperately tired and worn to think about it.

After about an hour, the new path left the bog behind, turning steadily toward the river. It was clear of brush and grass now, but they were so weak they could hardly go on. Without warning, Grace sat down. "Can't," she said. Her voice was raspy and hoarse.

Mary Carol knelt beside her, putting her arms around her.

"Come on, Gracie, have to go on. Carry you," said J.D. thickly. "Too close to give up." He was so weak he wondered if he could stay upright, much less carry Gracie. But they had to. He and Mary Carol each took an arm and lifted her up. Slowly they struggled along the path. Robert went ahead, carrying the blanket for J.D. and doing his best to lead, despite the fact that he was feeling a bit light-headed and nauseous, too.

Chapter 22

There were dark green patches in the prairie grass ahead on one side of the path. As they got closer, Mary Carol said, "Grain. Maybe eat." Her voice sounded raspy, too. They all did. Their mouths and tongues were dry and hurting.

Robert stopped in his tracks. Between them and the grain, a large coyote stood looking at them.

"Hold Gracie." J.D. nodded to Robert as he pulled the slingshot from his pocket. He stooped down on the path, picking up a couple of rocks.

"Not afraid of us," said Mary Carol as they struggled to hold Gracie upright.

"No sudden moves," said Robert thickly. "He's just curious."

Slowly and with certainty, Grace said, "He doesn't want to hurt us." The coyote abruptly turned its back on them, plunging into the grain. Suddenly, two large birds flew up.

"Hunting," Robert said.

"Wait," advised J.D.

Something curious happened then. As soon as the birds flew up, the coyote turned almost indifferently, walking away toward the river. "Not hungry," said Robert.

Grace was too weak to walk unaided. She leaned

on Mary Carol and J.D., while Robert forged ahead.

"Look," he called. They hurried as fast as Grace could go. It was a nest with seven eggs.

"One each," Grace said firmly. "Leave others."

"We're starving," protested J.D.

"Birds won't come back," said Robert. They talked in short bursts with no unnecessary words.

"Will too." said Grace. "One each."

"That on the map?" Robert spoke sharply.

"Take mine then," Gracie pleaded. "Have to leave three."

"Please, Gracie knows things," Mary Carol said, "Take mine, too, but leave three."

"One each, then," J.D. said reluctantly. He didn't have any energy for arguing. Besides, Mary Carol was right. Ever since she started reading the map, Grace seemed to know things she wouldn't ordinarily know. He couldn't explain it, but he knew it was happening.

Robert carefully collected four eggs, trying not to disturb the others. They were so desperately hungry and thirsty that they ate them on the spot, licking the shells clean. "You can eat ground-up eggshells," said Robert. "Read somewhere." They saved them in his knapsack.

Even that little bit of liquid nourishment helped. Their spirits rose. Their tongues didn't feel so thick. "Should have listened," said Mary Carol. "Gracie isn't being difficult. It's, it's the magic."

Grace leaned on Mary Carol. Robert and J.D. tried to collect grain as they made their way back to the path, but they were too weak.

"Green. Don't eat," said Mary Carol. "Have to cook it. Come back later."

Grace wasn't the only one ready to collapse. Their desperate need for water sent them on. When they finally caught sight of the river, in the distance, it was nearly dark. J.D. said it was too risky to approach it at night since they weren't sure of the path. Robert agreed. "Should have brought flashlight."

They had to be content to camp in the shelter of a clump of gnarled cedar trees, desperately thirsty and hungry. Robert laid their handkerchiefs on the grass nearby. They couldn't afford to ignore any source of water, even this close to the river.

Mary Carol tried telling a story, but her throat was too parched. Even so, they went to sleep with more hope than they'd been able to muster since they jumped off the train.

Weak and exhausted, they overslept. The sun was

already well up when they stirred. Everyone woke up thinking of water: water to drink, water for a bath. After four days living in the same clothes, they looked tatty. They felt even worse than they looked. They sucked the little water that had gathered on the handkerchiefs. Most of it had already evaporated.

Mary Carol noticed patches of lambs quarter growing here and there. She began gathering it to cook at the river. She was slow, but determined.

Robert and Grace were seated with their backs to a large rock. He held the map on one side and she held it on they other as they studied it. The sun warmed their backs.

Opposite them, J.D. was about to cover the campfire. Suddenly, he commanded, "Everybody freeze. Don't move."

Chapter 23

A Close Call

"Stay calm." J.D. spoke slowly and deliberately. Suddenly clear-headed and decisive, he could feel his strength returning. "Gracie, Rob, stay frozen. There is a large snake on the rock behind you. Looks like a rattler. We've alarmed it. It will strike at the first moving thing. I'm getting the slingshot—slowly."

Frozen in place, Grace wondered if the snake sensed her heart beating faster and the sudden energy that seemed to surge throughout her body. Robert knew J.D. was really good with a slingshot. He also knew J.D. would probably only get one chance. If he missed, the snake could strike one of them before he had time for a second shot. They had no way of treating snakebite.

J.D. was confident he could hit the snake in the head if nobody moved. But once he hit it, there was no predicting what would happen. "Mary Carol," though raspy, his spoke calmly and with authority. "Slowly get three or four smooth, good-sized pebbles. You are far enough away it will be okay. No sudden moves. Stay frozen, Gracie, you are doing great. You, too, Rob."

Mary Carol slowly scooped up the pebbles, handing them to J.D. It felt like watching a movie in slow motion.

J.D. put one rock in the slingshot. Slowly pulling back the sling, he took aim. The snake was making a sound like popcorn kernels in a tin pan. "On the count of three, drop the map and roll to the side, away from each other. Then run for it. If he strikes, it should be at the map moving in front of him." Every movement J.D. made was steady and deliberate, though his heart was pounding.

The rattling continued. "Okay, ready? One, two, three!" He released the rock. Instantly, Grace and Robert hurled themselves to either side, scrambling to their feet and running. There was a thud. Gracie threw herself into Mary Carol's arms. J.D.'s shot hit the snake right on the head. Wounded, the snake struck at the map as it rolled back into a scroll.

Without pausing an instant, J.D. took another shot. "Got him again!" The snake jerked and twitched, trying to recoil. J.D. issued orders like a coxswain urging his crew through the last 500 yards of a boat race. "Good, Gracie, stay put with Mary Carol. Rob, well done. Don't get your knapsack until we have him pinned down."

Mary Carol had her arms around Grace, who was shaking all over.

"Mary Carol, Gracie, find two big sticks with a branch I can break to make a Y. We've got to hold his head down so he can't strike again. About as long as you are tall, Gracie."

Rob picked up a large rock. "I can smash him."

"No, don't try until he's pinned down." J.D. ordered. "He's still dangerous. He's a big one. He can strike as far as two-thirds of his body length, maybe even now." J.D. took a branch from Mary Carol. "Sturdy enough." He stripped away unnecessary twigs and leaves. Stepping on the end, he broke the ends off to make a shallow Y. "Rob, get another branch from Grace. Break it down like this." J.D. took the stick, slowly approaching the snake. It was writhing on the ground, where Robert and Grace had been sitting, still trying to recoil. Staying clear of the head, he plunged the stick down, trapping the snake at the base of its head. The snake lashed violently, almost knocking him off balance.

Mary Carol gripped the branch, giving J.D. support. "Let's just get away from here!" She was nearly frantic, but she kept her head. It was all she and J.D. could do to hold the snake down.

"Rob, pin him with the other stick," J.D. yelled, breathless. "Near the middle. We can't let him get away. When you've got him, Mary Carol and Gracie can take your place. Then you can use your rock."

"Just cut his head off," said Robert.

"No, it will put you too close if he breaks free." J.D. could tell the snake was weakening, but it was still strong enough to be a threat.

Altogether, it was a messy, terrifying, and dangerous business. Everybody was more afraid than they'd admit. When they were sure the snake was dead, J.D. said, "I know you should never, ever try to kill a rattler, but he was too dangerous to let go. Besides, we need the food. We'll take him to cook at the river."

A few days ago, they'd have gagged. "People say it takes like chicken," said Robert weakly.

"Poor, poor snake," said Grace. "He just wanted to live, too."

"I know, Gracie," said Mary Carol, holding her close. "Sometimes Mother Nature seems cruel. But he might have killed you or Robbie. We couldn't take the chance."

"I don't know how long it would have taken him to move away," said J.D. "He was in striking position. The least movement from either of you would have been deadly."

Hope and the rush of adrenalin that got them through the crisis were all that kept them going. The boys draped the snake over the sticks they'd used to trap it. They carried it between them. It was longer than J.D. was tall and surprisingly heavy.

They were about an hour away from the river, moving as slowly as they did. As they got near, they saw J.D.'s wisdom in insisting they wait until daylight even though they were desperate for water. A canyon rim stood high above the river, making a sharp unexpected drop to the river below. It looked as though there had been a path, but it stopped abruptly, covered by rock most of the way down. "Landslide," said J.D., trying to hide the discouragement in his voice. He felt weak again. Now that the crisis with the snake had passed, they all felt weak and spent.

"Footing looks treacherous," said J.D., struggling to get the words out. "Leave snake. Come back. Never get down with extra weight."

Before they started down, Robert said, "One small drink. Just one. Get sick if we go too fast."

"Get wet first," said J.D., vaguely remembering something Mr. Nichols had said.

"Wash first," said Mary Carol, who hadn't been particular when there wasn't any water.

Below, they could see a wide grassy bank that gave way to rocks and gravel below, then the river. It was enough to keep them moving. As they carefully made their way down, all they could think about was getting to the water. But it was impossible to hurry. The way down was too perilous. Loose gravel gave way under their feet, sending rocks scattering before them. When they finally reached the bottom of the canyon, everybody helped everybody else, holding each other up, dragging each other toward the water.

The river ran swift, pooling along the bank where it swirled momentarily before going on its way. They didn't need anybody to tell them it was safe to drink. Still holding each other up, they splashed into the nearest pool and threw themselves down into the shallow water. They scooped it up in their hands, splashing it on their faces, then lapping it. Nothing before or after ever felt or tasted better than that cold, refreshing water. It was hard not to drink and drink and drink.

Grace began vomiting. They carried her to the shade, themselves nauseated and hardly able to walk. "Small sips of water," said Robert, getting the cup from his knapsack. He fell back in the shade, not sure he could get up again to get water, he was so nauseated. He began vomiting, too. As careful as he'd tried to be, he'd taken in too much water too quickly.

Mary Carol put her wet bandana over Grace's head and loosened the one around her neck. She was so weak and nauseated that she could hardly sit up, but she began wiping Grace's arms and legs, then Robert's with a wet bandana.

"I'll get more water," said J.D. He dragged himself back to the river, holding down Robert's canteen to let fresh water pour in. Then he and Mary Carol wet all the bandanas for Grace and Robert, putting them on face, arms and legs.

Grace smiled weakly at them. Mary Carol lay down beside her, putting a wet bandana over her own aching head. J.D. wet a bandana for Robert's head before he collapsed in the shade, too.

After awhile Mary Carol sat up to pass around the cup of water. Everyone took a small sip, letting waves of nausea pass over them. "Now I know what Mr. Hackworth meant when he said he had a busted head," Mary Carol said.

Robert groaned, "Me, too."

"Me three," said Grace.

"We'd better make this our headquarters for a day or two until we recover," said J.D., too weak and nauseated to do anything more.

"Keep sipping, J.D.," said Mary Carol, passing around the cup.

"We have to figure out how to get across the river, too," said Robert, trying to keep his mind off of feeling sick.

They had found an ideal spot. A small grove of young trees, on the grassy bank they'd seen from above, promised protection from sun and wind. The grassy bank was high enough above the river that they didn't have to worry about a flash flood sweeping them away, but very near the bottom of the canyon. An easy path led to the river. There was plenty of dry driftwood. The water was shallow along the bank, but you could see that it got very deep nearer the middle. From somewhere upstream came the roar of a waterfall. They lay in the shade close to the river for a long time, Mary Carol sitting up now and then to order another sip of water all around.

"We've got a long journey ahead," said Robert grimly, sitting up at last. "We'd better use this chance to prepare for it."

"If we'd all been as prepared as you were, we'd have been a lot better off," said Mary Carol. "I'll never criticize you again for carrying that knapsack everywhere. We couldn't have made it without you."

Chapter 24

Nobody Would Believe It

Grace sat up. "I'm hungry."

"Me, too," said Robert, reaching for his knapsack. Suddenly they all felt ravenously hungry. They ate everything left in their reserves—which wasn't much—scraping every bit of peanut butter from the jar with their fingers. It still wasn't enough and it made them feel nauseous again.

Afterwhile J.D. said, "Lets go get that snake before some animal claims it, Rob. It will be slow going and I want to be back before dark."

Grace didn't want them to leave for fear they might not come back. "You can see us," Robert reassured her.

J.D. was right. It was a slow climb. Both boys were weak and still feeling wobbly on their legs. They took their time, turning to wave every now and then, resting when there was a place they could lean into the steep bank, or actually sit down.

Meanwhile, Mary Carol and Grace set up camp under the trees on the grassy bank. Mary Carol put the small bit of green grain they had gathered in Robert's cooking pot to soak. "We can have it for our supper." It was easy to see that it would take the boys a long time to reach the top of the canyon, not to mention the trip back down. Once Grace was reassured that they would be safe enough without her eyes glued to them, Mary Carol said, "Now would be a good time to have an actual bath and wash our clothes. I'll bet they'll dry quickly in this sun." They found a shallow place downstream where the water was shaded. They washed their clothes first, spreading them on bushes where the hot sun could reach them. Soap would have been nice, but even Robert hadn't thought to put soap in his emergency supplies.

"Where do you think Mamma is?" Grace asked as they let the sun-warmed water lap over them.

"Well, let's see," Mary Carol had to think. "We were on the train two days, counting the day we jumped off. It took us four days to get here."

"It feels like more than four days," said Grace.

"No, unless you count two days on the train. We can ask Robbie. Anyway, we know that by now

Mamma is on a ship somewhere on the Atlantic Ocean getting close to England. She may even be with Daddy now."

"Good," said Grace. "If Daddy died, we'd know, wouldn't we?"

The question threw Mary Carol. "I don't know, Gracie. I've heard grown-ups say they knew when somebody died. Maybe we'd know."

"I think we would," said Grace. "Old Shep would tell me."

"I wish Old Shep were here," said Mary Carol.

Grace sighed. "I haven't seen him since before the stop at LaJunta, except once in a dream. I guess we've lost him forever." She didn't cry. She seemed stoic to Mary Carol, much older than when they left Kansas City, too.

Once they were out of the water, Grace exclaimed, "Clean underwear!" as if it were the best thing that could ever happen to anybody. It was the most animated she had sounded since they set out from the rock pile.

"And it's dry!" said Mary Carol, shaking the water out of her hair. "That's one good thing to say about desert heat and wind! Our slips are dry, too. We can wear them while we look for food. We'll pretend they are sundresses. I didn't think I'd ever feel clean again."

They turned their dresses over to dry on the other side. "Let's look for food," said Mary Carol. "We'd better build a fire, too, and find a long branch we can use to make a spit for roasting that snake. Remember how Grandpa Matthias made a spit when we camped out with him on the farm?"

"We roasted a chicken," said Grace, "It took ever so long."

"He taught us a lot," said Mary Carol, "I wish I'd paid more attention. I used to tease Robbie about taking it so seriously. Now I'm glad he did."

They walked upstream. They waved at the boys, who were slowly making their way down the bank with the snake. Upstream, just a few yards away, the water swirled into a deep, clear pool. "This looks like just the sort of place Grandpa Matthias and Daddy would go fishing," said Mary Carol. Sure enough, as they sat looking down into the pool, they could see movement.

"I see one!" exclaimed Grace. "But we don't have a fishing pole."

"No, but I'll bet Robbie can make a spear," said Mary Carol. They pulled watercress on their way back. "Maybe if we cook this, it won't upset our stomachs so much."

They built a fire in the shade of the grove, using one of Robert's precious matches and piling the fire with dry driftwood. "It will need to burn down a bit before they get here," Mary Carol said.

It was approaching late afternoon by the sun when the boys returned. They were exhausted. The fire had burned down to a heap of bright coals that the girls steadily fed. "Well done!" said J.D. "Look, Rob. They've dug holes for the sticks to hold the spit, too." Once they had the snake over the fire, Mary Carol and Grace kept watch over it while the boys rested and had a chance to bathe.

"Why didn't I think of soap?" asked Robert wearily, as he wrung the water out of his clothes and spread them out on bushes in the sun. They were too worn out to talk, even to think. They stretched out in the pool Grace had already named "The Bathtub," and let the water wash over them, soaking away the dirt of four hard days. Afterward, they wore their shorts and undershirts, leaving shirts and trousers on a shrub to finish drying. "I'll never complain about having to take a bath again," said Robert, as he turned over his trousers to sun.

"Have you noticed any large animal tracks along the river so far?" asked J.D., his mind always on survival. "They might come to water here."

"No, but maybe we'd better have a look before it

gets dark."

They did a thorough search up along the river as far as the fishing hole without finding any signs of animals. Later, Robert notched a long, straight branch and made a spear with his arrowhead. The boys tried a hand at spearing a fish. After several tries, Robert succeeded. They threw the fish directly on the coals and ate it ravenously when it was cooked through.

After that, except for Grace who couldn't bear the thought of killing anything, they took turns fishing and tending the roasting snake. "Maybe we should call it quits," said J.D. when they'd speared another fish. "We don't want to scare them away. We'll be stronger tomorrow. Our aim will be better."

It was almost dark when they decided that the snake was cooked well enough to eat. "Nobody would believe it if we told them we're eating rattlesnake," said Mary Carol. But when the snake was roasted to their satisfaction, everyone ate until they felt full. They were too starved to be squeamish. They finished off with cooked watercress and the boiled grain, eating with their fingers. "This would taste pretty good, fried in butter," Mary Carol said, crunching on the grain.

"At least you haven't lost your sense of humor," said J.D.

"I wasn't being funny," said Mary Carol matter-of-factly. Nobody complained, though. It was food. And the fishing hole promised more food tomorrow.

Robert wrote in his notebook, *At a river. Survived nearly a week. Fifth night out. End of day 5 from the rock pile. Day 7 from the train. Day 8 from home. We made it to water. So far, so good.*

As the stars began to come out, they assessed their situation. "We haven't seen any sign of other people," said J.D. He broached the subject gently. He didn't want the others to be alarmed, but he thought it was better for them to know. "There are lots of places out in the country where they don't have electricity, but we haven't even seen smoke from another fire."

"Where do you think we are?" asked Mary Carol, fearfully.

"It isn't just where we are, but *when* we are," said J.D. carefully. "I wonder if we're, I don't know, maybe in another time? It's like we jumped out of our time and place into another."

They sat taking in what he'd said. Mary Carol broke the silence, "What was it Celeste said about not being able to go backward? Maybe she meant backward in time."

"She said, 'He knows I can't go back,'" said Robert.

"There were those Coelophysis bones," said J.D. "We've seen a lot of bones that probably belonged to prehistoric animals. Think about that bog we passed yesterday. It seems like someone would have found it if we're where we're supposed to be, you know, in 1944."

"She said the coastline on the map was a prehistoric coastline," said Robert. They sat in silence, wondering.

"People don't go back in time, really," Robert said at last. "There has to be a logical explanation for this."

"Maybe there doesn't," said J.D. "Maybe there are some things we can't explain."

"It's the magic," said Grace.

"So what it boils down to is that nobody's going to find us or help us," said Mary Carol, feeling her last hope against hope sinking.

"It doesn't really make any difference," said J.D. "Gracie has the key, so we just have to keep on. That's all I know to do."

"But the map only got us this far," Grace said.

"Most of the stuff on the map is across the river," said Robert. "Celeste talked about the Canadian border. I think we have to try to get across the mountains to the coast and go north. That would be the safest route anyway. We'll be closer to food and water sources once we get there. It's more or less what Mr. Nichols marked on my map when we were talking with him, remember?"

"We have to be prepared for more desert before we get to the mountains," said J.D.

"Wouldn't that depend on when this is?" asked Robert.

"Sure, except we don't know where we landed, not for sure," said J.D. "But you're right. Think how different it looked from the train. We were in desert on the train, but we ended up in grassland."

"Yeah, but hot, dry grassland," said Robert.

It was a staggering thought. Attempting to accept their situation, even if she couldn't understand it, Mary Carol said, "The last four days were just the beginning, weren't they. It isn't going to get any better."

Robert nodded in agreement. "J.D., we can have a look up and down-stream tomorrow morning. Maybe we'll find some natural bridge across the river. We have the map and the compass. At least Gracie's map shows mountains and rivers and the ocean."

"And Gracie's glass," said Mary Carol. "Let's not forget the magnifying glass."

"But it doesn't show me anything on the other side of the river," said Grace.

"But you said it says, 'Child, I will show you the way,' and I have to think it will," said Mary Carol, hope rising again. "The night sky is the same, so we can't be too far off, even if the countryside is different. We know there are mountains to cross before we hit the coast."

"Except the night sky isn't the same," said Robert. "Sure, we can see the Big Dipper and some of the constellations we know. But I was serious about my compass. The compass shows that star as being closest to north." He pointed to a bright star. "Look, if you follow over here to the Little Dipper, there is Polaris, right at the tip of its handle. See, the compass isn't pointing toward there. It's pointing to that star."

"It has to be Thuban," said J.D. "See how the two inner stars of the Big Dipper point to it?"

"Miss Spright was asking about the North Star," said Grace.

A startled look crossed Robert's face. "If Thuban is the North Star, that means we're way back in time. Thuban was the North Star in the time of the ancient Egyptians."

J.D. was less startled than anybody else. He'd

been working it out since the Santa Fe Chief vainished into thin air.

"The thing is, we haven't found one of those tokens Gracie is supposed to be collecting," said Mary Carol.

"Not to mention that we don't know what they are or how to find them," Robert added.

"Maybe Mary Carol's right. The map says it will show me the way," said Grace. "So maybe that means tokens, too."

"We just have to keep up our courage and go on," J.D. said. "Think about what we've already done. We have a long way to go, but we can do it."

"What other choice do we have?" asked Robert.

"I wonder if Uncle James knows we're gone," said Grace.

"That's another thing," said Mary Carol. "In all the old stories, time isn't the same once you step into another time. So we don't know how much time has passed for Uncle James."

"But there is a difference between fairy tales and reality," said Robert. "This is real."

"Maybe fairy tales are real," said Grace.

"There was a time when I would have disagreed with you, Gracie," J.D. sighed. "But now, I don't know what I think. I wouldn't be surprised if I saw Little Red Riding Hood skip past."

"Well, if she does, let's ask her if she can spare some bread," said Mary Carol, cryptically.

And hope the wolf isn't behind her, J.D. thought, but he didn't say anything for fear of alarming Grace. He didn't feel as confident as he sounded. *Rob's right. What other choice do we have? Except to give up, and I'm not going to let anybody do that!*

Robert made another note in his notebook: *Thuban was North Star in about 3,000 BC. Compass has to be off. Maybe magnetic field is different out here. Ate snake. Not so bad. Hope Daddy is okay. Mamma, too.*

The sun dropped behind the red-brown sandstone hills on the other side of the river, leaving them dark purple below a bright pink and gold sky. Along a sandbar on the bank just across from them, a lone coyote stood in the shadows. They couldn't see him, but he could see them.

Chapter 25

Doing the Right Thing

There was no easy way to cross the river either upstream or downstream. After three days of rest and collecting provisions, however, it was time to be off. They were feeling stronger and more hopeful. The children agreed that in the absence of any information on Grace's map, their best bet was to follow the stream up past the waterfall until they found a place to ford. They spent the afternoon before they were off packing and improvising ways to store things.

Mary Carol had insisted that they climb back up to the place near where they killed the snake and gather as much grain as they could. That took most of one afternoon, though they found the going much easier now that their strength was back. They tried rolling the heads between rocks to separate the grains from the straw. Since the grain was green, it was slow work. They took turns.

Then there was the problem of storage for their supplies. They tried their hand at weaving baskets with reeds growing along the river, but they weren't skilled enough to make anything usable except loosely woven mats. Mary Carol thought they could use them to store the dried fish. "We can heap up the fish between them, Rob. It will keep your knapsack from smelling fishy."

"That isn't exactly our main worry, is it," said Robert cryptically. "Just stack'em up and I'll figure out how to fit them in."

They put green grain in the jar that the peanut butter came in, but all their other packaging had been used as kindling. "I don't need my undershirt in this hot country. How about we tie grain up in it? I'll carry it," J.D. suggested.

"I can sew the bottom closed so we can fill it like a sack," Mary Carol said. "I have my sewing kit."

"We don't exactly have enough grain to fill a sack," J.D. said. "But I'll tell you what. Robbie, how about we make both undershirts into bags and we can take the extra grain heads."

"That doesn't solve the problem of carrying them," said Robert. "You can't use your belt, J.D.

You've lost so much weight, your pants will fall down without a belt."

"And I'm not sure that shoulder is well enough for you to add any weight to your load, J.D.," said Mary Carol. She was worried about the place where Celeste had dug into J.D. with her fingernails. When they arrived at the river, it was angry-looking and painful to the touch. Soaking in the river had done wonders, but Mary Carol didn't want to take any chances.

Such discussions dominated their waking hours. At night they talked about Mamma and Daddy, the war, Old Shep, Dolly, Uncle James, and all they had left behind. Robert wrote in his notebook every night, keeping track of the days and trying to come to terms with their situation.

"Why did Daddy have to go to war anyway?" asked Grace, inturrepting his thoughts. "Couldn't he be a conscientious objector like Mamma and Uncle James?"

"I think he might have been, if it weren't for what the Nazis are doing to the Jews," said J.D. Seeing her puzzled expression, he explained. "The Nazis are the people who are in charge of Germany now. The first I remember about it is when you were about two-years-old. We heard on the radio that the U.S. and Canada—Cuba, too, I think—turned away a shipload of Jewish refugees. They left Germany because Jewish people were being persecuted. Mamma and Daddy said it is our duty to take care of people—they thought it was wrong to turn away all those people."

"Why wouldn't the United States and Canada want to take care of people?" asked Grace.

"Gosh, Gracie. That's a bigger question than I can answer," said J.D.

"What happened to them?" she demanded.

"I don't know," said J.D. "That was just the beginning. We kept hearing about the war, I wasn't paying that much attention then. Mamma says we didn't hear much about what was happening inside Germany until later."

"Gracie, it's a really terrible thing, but the Nazis are killing millions of Jewish people," explained Mary Carol. "Daddy said that war is wrong, but sometimes it is the only way to stop something even worse than war. He enlisted in the Army Air Force the minute President Roosevelt declared war. He said it was the right thing to do."

"But why would the Nazis want to kill Jewish people?" asked Grace, still puzzled.

"Oh, Gracie," said Mary Carol, "I can't understand it either. I think you'd have to have a really bad heart to want to kill people because of their religion or because of the country they came from."

"So how come Uncle James and Mamma are still conscientious objectors?" asked Robert.

"My brain can't handle all this!" exclaimed J.D. "I'm just a kid."

Everyone was up with first light the next morning. Grace had another look at the map while the others broke camp, covering the remains of their stay. To her surprise, the map had changed. The route they followed to the river was no longer visible. Now a trail went from their camp to the waterfall and along the other side of the river for some time, breaking off west before it ended. "Look at this!" she exclaimed, realizing as she said it that the others couldn't see.

"Must be a natural tunnel underneath the falls," said Robert, when she explained the route.

"Should we catch some more fish before we go?" asked Mary Carol. Once you've been as hungry as they'd been, it's hard to leave a food supply behind.

"We'll be fine as long as we follow the river," said Robert. "We have the dried fish. And there's a lot of grain and dried greens. And we have the eggshells I ground into powder for when we get desperate." His knapsack was full. Their water bags were full.

J.D. tied the grain up in his undershirt and

fastened it around his waist. Mary Carol thought it was a bad idea to use the undershirts for the grain heads that were still full of grain. There was quite a large pile they hadn't gotten to despite their steady effort. "Unless we can wash your undershirt, you'll get the itch when you put it on again."

In the end they tied it up in Mary Carol's skirt, some on each side. "Saddle bags and no horse," she laughed. Looking at her dress, she gave a sigh. "Anyway, it's not exactly my second-best dress anymore."

They felt hopeful as they set out. It was the second week since they jumped from the train. They were far more prepared for extreme conditions than they had been and much more confident in their ability to cope.

"There's that coyote." Robert pointed to a large coyote looking at them from across the river. "Wonder how he got across?"

"Assuming it's the same coyote," said J.D.

"Maybe it is," said Mary Carol.

"It is," said Grace, matter-of-factly.

They could feel mist from the falls before they could see a long curtain of white, tumbling from high above. They had to be extra careful. The wet rocks were slippery. There was no natural path.

Robert had them hold on to his rope. He went first, with Grace following, then Mary Carol, and J.D. bringing up the rear as they made their way parallel to the river. "This must be how that coyote got through," said Grace.

"There are coyotes everywhere in this country," said J.D. "Besides, how would he get over these rocks?"

"Look!" Robert spotted a ledge well behind the falls. "It may be slick. Stay in single file and stick close to the wall. Don't let go of the rope."

As it turned out, the ledge opened to a large cavern with plenty of space to walk. The spectacular sight of the waterfall from behind with the sun shining through mist and rainbows was something the children never forgot, long after their adventure was over.

They came out onto a path following the river. The going was much easier. There were more trees now, too, pine and aspen. Soon they came to high outcroppings of chocolate-colored sandstone, where the river had carved its way through, changing courses, leaving wind and rain to do the rest. They climbed steadily above the riverbed, winding around more chocolate-colored rock formations.

It was at one of these rock formations that Grace gave the others a terrible fright.

A massive bird circled above. "Must be a vulture," said J.D., shielding his eyes from the sun to look up.

"No, a condor. Look, a white patch under its wings," Robert said. "That's one huge bird!"

"There are two of them," Grace said. "They're worried about something."

It did look as if the condors were upset. They repeatedly flew at the rock cliff. "Maybe it's a snake after their egg," said Robert. "Condors only lay one egg every two years."

"We have to help them," said Grace.

"How? They'd attack." J.D. said.

"No, we have to help," insisted Grace. "There's something terribly wrong."

"How do you know, Gracie?" Mary Carol asked.

Grace was already climbing up the rocks. "I just know," she called.

"Come back here, Gracie." J.D. yelled. "You'll get hurt." It wasn't at all like cautious little Grace to go off scaling a cliff.

"No," yelled Grace, already out of reach.

"What if it's another rattlesnake?" called Mary Carol.

"I'm coming with you," called Robert. Handing

his knapsack to Mary Carol, he started up the rock behind Grace, rope in hand, spear slung across his back. "Keep that slingshot ready, J.D."

The climb wasn't difficult. As Grace got closer to the top, she could hear the birds making a grunting, raspy sound. A raspy sound also came from somewhere just above. Near the top, she saw why the birds were so upset. It was their chick. Old enough to start wandering about, it had fallen between the rocks. The parent birds could see it, but they couldn't get to it. Left alone, they would have had to watch their chick die. It was an unbearable thought.

She motioned for Robert to stay back. When she was even with them, she spoke very quietly to the condors, "I think I can get your chick for you, if you will let me." It was as if they understood. They stopped their frantic flapping and grunting to watch. Grace crawled onto the ledge. The condors didn't have anything you'd call a nest. It was just a sandy place sheltered by overhanging rock. On one side it opened to the steep climb from the path. On the other, it faced a sheer drop all the way down to the river gorge below. She hadn't realized how high above the canyon they had climbed since they left the river. Suddenly she felt afraid, looking down at the drop to the river canyon. "Robbie, I need to hold something so I won't fall," she called. She knew her voice was shaky. She felt shaky.

Robert threw her an end of his rope. Bracing himself against the rocks he held on as she inched her way to the crevice, rope tied around her middle. Reaching down, she lifted up the ugly little bird and got a sharp peck on her hand for her trouble. But she managed to pull the squirming chick out. "Don't ever go in there again, you little scamp," she said, setting it back on the sandy ledge. It ran to its parents. They were enormous, ugly birds, frightening to look at. Yet Grace could see that they were as glad as any parents would be to have their child back. They looked at her. She couldn't help smiling at them. "Now, don't go walking off that side until you're ready to fly, little one," she said to the chick. The little condor waggled his grayish-pink, baldhead at her. She turned and started back down the rock face, shaky but satisfied.

When she and Robert were back again, one of the condors glided down, alighting just in front of Grace. It stood there, looking at her, holding its head this way and that, as if it wanted to say something. Then it reached back with its long feathered neck and plucked a feather from one wing, dropping it on the path. Grace respectfully picked up the feather. "Thank you," she said. The condor blinked at them and flew away. Its mate swooped down, alighting on the path. She, too, paused for a moment to look at them from one side of her head, then the other. As certainly as if it had spoken aloud, Grace knew the bird said that if she ever needed help she now had two condor friends who would come to her aid and the aid of her family. "Thank you," Grace said, very solemnly. The bird flew back to her chick.

"The condor feather, Gracie! A condor's on the map. You didn't ask for one or take it. How did you know?" asked J.D.

Grace held the feather almost reverently. "I didn't, J.D. I just knew those condors needed us. We had to help them. It was the right thing to do."

"And a wing feather!" said Robert. They decided that his knapsack was the best place to keep the feather, feeling sure they had the first of the tokens. For the first time it felt as if they just might be able to do it. They were on the right track.

Chapter 26

Trusting the Trickster

"It is the same coyote," said Mary Carol. A lone coyote stood on a rock formation in the distance, looking their way. "It's like he's following us."

"I wouldn't exactly call that following," said Robert. "He's always out there ahead of us in the distance."

"I suppose it could be the same one," said J.D. skeptically. "What are the chances? This is coyote country. There are plenty of coyotes to stand and look at us."

"Not to mention other animals we haven't seen," said Robert. The thought gave them all a chill. They couldn't help thinking of all the bones they'd seen on the other side of the river. They occasionally saw bones now, some of them large, but no complete skeletons. They saw hawks, and now and then a lone raven, but very few animals. There weren't as many insects as in the tall grass, but they did come across clouds of little midges—sometimes the midges bit, leaving them with welts that itched like fire. Occasionally, a startled rabbit leapt away. They saw herds of pronghorn at a distance, but nothing bigger. Robert knew it was just the country for mountain lions. Their only hope was that with the four of them, they would frighten away predators in the daytime. At night they kept a fire burning.

Following Grace's directions, they set a course west, leaving the river. Their days settled into a pattern, always dominated by the need for food and water. They ate what they could gather when they found it, rationing the provisions they'd collected at the river. Every night, Grace and Robert planned their route. Grace always found just enough information on the map to guide them on the way. Robert wrote in his notebook, but sometimes there wasn't much to write except, *More of the same*. He kept count of the days, though. The days and weeks were piling up.

Sometimes they felt so tired and weak from hunger and thirst that it seemed impossible to go on. J.D. drove them relentlessly. He knew that if they were to survive, they had to find a place where it was easier to live than in this wilderness. Spring wouldn't last forever. Streambeds would dry up. He hoped they'd find other people, though they still saw no sign of human life. At every vista he searched the horizon, eyes hungry for the sight of smoke from fires in some friendly village. He figured if they were somewhere following the Ice Age in time, they ought to find other people, or at least a sign of nomadic tribes passing through.

One afternoon, when they were having a rest break, Robert saw J.D. standing on a high rock, looking. "I haven't seen a single footprint or arrowhead or any other thing, J.D.," he said as he joined him. They said no more, not wanting to worry the girls. They didn't know that Mary Carol did her own silent observation, searching the horizon for what could not be found.

A mountain range now loomed in the distance. Like the Rockies they first saw from the train, these mountains looked close. Yet day after day, they seemed to get no closer.

A month passed, then two, without a sign of anything they could call a token. Their route alternated between forested land covered with pine, spruce, and live oak trees, and bare plateaus with little more than a brush and short grass covering. Fortunately, they never went more than two or three days without finding water. They continued to gather dew at night.

The mountains stood in the distance, aloof shadows on the horizon. Then, unexpectedly, foothills appeared before them. The mountains that stood between them and the coastline grew larger and more formidable.

They were well into the foothills, when a thunderstorm hit. They'd had more than one good wetting in the rain, but nothing to match this. Wind whipped the trees. Black clouds boiled overhead. They found cover under an overhanging rock surrounded by pine trees, piling branches around to make a shelter before the storm hit. Wrapped up in Mary Carol's blanket, they watched as lightening tore jagged gaps across the sky. It struck frightfully close, splitting one of the trees nearby. Horrific claps of thunder followed almost instantly. Torrential rain fell sending a river sweeping past, almost at their feet. There was little to eat. The storm left them wet through, cold, and miserable. Worst of all, Robert's notebook was missing. He remembered having it out before the thunderstorm hit. They searched the area, but there was no trace of it. They did find pine nuts in some of the cones that had fallen to the ground in the storm, however, and they were able to refill their water containers.

Mary Carol, Robert, and Grace wanted to hunker down in their misery. J.D. insisted that they keep moving. He was becoming like a tyrant, relentlessly pushing them to keep going.

They were always hungry. They had to content themselves with what they could forage. They were usually lucky enough to have fish when they were in forested areas. They caught grasshoppers, crickets, lizards, and snakes when they could find and catch them, cooking them in the evening when they made camp. Mary Carol was getting good at spotting edible plants, remembering things Grandpa Matthias had taught them.

One morning after they'd slept huddled under trees in a misty rain, they found a ring of coyote tracks around them. Robert said it was only one coyote, not a pack. "Maybe our coyote was watching over us," said Grace. Later, they found bear tracks not far from where they'd camped, just outside the ring of coyote tracks. They wondered if Grace was right. They came to expect to see the coyote somewhere in the distance.

"Maybe he's our guardian angel disguised as a coyote," said Mary Carol one night.

"It doesn't make sense," Robert said. "In all the old stories, the coyote is the trickster. If we believe them, we shouldn't trust him at all." They were sitting around the fire after their meager supper.

"I trust him. He's our only friend in all this wide country," said Grace.

They had a regular nighttime ritual: supper, such as it was; looking into the fire; thinking about the day; wondering where Mamma and Daddy were, talking about the war; and what happened when they didn't show up in L.A. Robert scribbled something in the little notebook Mary Carol gave him after his notebook was lost—his pencil grew steadily smaller. Grace played the music box, they said their prayers, and Mary Carol told a story. One night Grace's music box gave out. It had been slowing down for days. Maybe it got too wet in the rainstorm or maybe it just wore out.

The next morning, Grace declared that she would leave the music box behind. Every ounce of extra weight and space had to be given to food, when they found it. They buried it between the roots of a pine tree and marked the grave with a cross. Grace's lower lip trembled, but she didn't cry.

As they approached the summit of the mountain range, they came upon a field of tumbled boulders. Trees had been thinning out as they climbed. Now they gave way altogether. A path cut through the field, leading into a high mountain meadow. Wild flowers were everywhere. Mary Carol and Grace couldn't resist picking along the path as they went. By the time J.D. called a rest halt, they both had cheerful bouquets.

They sat on one of the boulders, taking in the view. It was a clear day. The sunshine felt much warmer than they expected so high up. "It is the first time I've felt hot since we've been in the mountains," said Robert.

Grace rested her bouquet on a neighboring boulder. All of a sudden they noticed that it was moving. A rabbit-like animal stuck its little head and ears up, pulling on the long stem of one of the flowers.

"Sh-h-h," said Robert. "It's a pika, you can tell by the short ears." They quietly watched as the pika took the flower, carrying it to a tiny stack of flowers and grass several yards away.

"What a little darling," said Grace. They watched as it returned for another and another.

"They don't hibernate. So they make little hay stacks for winter food," said Robert.

A shrill cry came from the meadow. The pika disappeared into its hole. "I think that's their danger cry," said Robert. "One of them must have spotted a hawk. Or maybe we spooked it."

Mary Carol left her bouquet for the pika, too, and they started out again, hoping to reach the summit and start down the Western side of the mountain range before nightfall. They hadn't gone more than a few steps when Grace paused. "Listen. There's that cry again." Their eyes followed the sound. A pika was caught in a tangle of blackberry vines, struggling to free itself.

"Hold it," said Robert. "Something has frightened this fellow so badly he's caught and can't get free. From what I've read about these little critters, it's hard to trap one."

"She," said Mary Carol. "And she's nursing young, too, by the look of it."

"Probably that raven," said J.D., pointing to a large black bird hovering at the top of a gnarled pine tree. "He'd make short work of one of these little guys. Looks like he's just waiting for us to get out of the way."

"It's getting warm. They can't stand heat," said Robert. "This mamma will die and her babies will die if we leave her here."

"We can't let that happen," said Grace.

"We have to be careful about interfering in nature," said J.D. "If she's injured, we could do more harm than good."

"What can we do, Robbie?" asked Grace. "You know about animals."

Taking out his jackknife, Robert took command. "Gracie, I'll cut away the thicket. You be ready to catch her in your hat. We don't want to stress her any more than she is, and we don't want a pika bite."

Grace began talking to the pika in soft tones. "We'd

like to help you, Mrs. Pika. Don't worry. We'll find your babies." The pika froze, eyes bulging in terror. Grace kept talking to it while Robert carefully cut away the vine, staying clear of the pika's teeth.

"Okay, Gracie," he said softly. "I'll cut this last bit. She may be too hot and tired to get back to her nest, but we can release her in the shade. Careful now."

Grace scooped her into the hat where the pika sat without moving.

"I don't think there is much we can do for her. Her leg looks like it was hooked in the brambles. We need to get her back to her nest, though," J.D. said.

"She may have a limp and some bruises," said Robert.

Grace talked softly to the pika as she cradled the hat.

"Over here," called J.D. "It must be a pika community. Look at all these piles of hay. Maybe we can release her nearby and she'll find her way to the right nest."

One leg dragged a bit as the pika crawled from Grace's hat, but soon she disappeared into an opening.

"It must be a happy reunion," said Grace. "She wouldn't go in if they weren't her babies, would she?"

They took a few minutes to pile a few plants like those the girls had picked, leaving them by the pika's doorstep. It would provide food if she needed some time to recover. As they started to leave, Grace leaned down, "Goodbye, Mrs. Pika. We hope you feel better soon."

The pika stuck her head out of the nest, looked at them, then pulled a stem of purple fireweed from her hay pile. She dropped the flower at the door to her nest, went inside, and looked out at them, waiting.

"Gracie, I think she's giving it to you," said J.D.

Grace leaned down. The pika didn't move. "Thank you, Mrs. Pika. We are glad we could help." Grace took the flower and the pika disappeared.

"Do you think the flower is one of the tokens?" Robert asked.

"Well, the pika seemed to be giving it to her," said Mary Carol. "She didn't ask for it or take it for herself. It is one of the flowers on the map. We haven't had anything else that qualified as a token since the condor feathers. At this rate. . . ."

"Don't say it," said J.D. "We're going to find all of them. Once we get over this pass we'll be headed down toward the ocean. With any luck, we'll see the Pacific in a matter of days. Then the going won't be so hard."

They put the dried flower in Robert's bag with the condor feather, just in case. With that they turned to face the mountain again. Ahead, the raven took wing. "Guess we cost him a meal," said Robert.

"Is that a raven or a crow?" asked Mary Carol.

"It's a raven," said Robert. "Crows usually travel in larger groups. Their tails make a fan shape. That bird has longer middle feathers in its tail. See, it looks wedge-shaped."

"I know, you read about that somewhere," teased Mary Carol.

"Haven't we seen quite a few lone ravens?" asked J.D.

"Big ones, too," said Mary Carol.

"That's all we need," said Robert. "Another trickster."

"Don't talk about our coyote that way!" scolded Grace.

They were still in high mountain country, densely covered with trees, when Grace tripped over a fallen branch, cutting a deep gash in her leg. Mary Carol did her best to clean it, but next morning it looked angry and red. They'd just about used up Robert's first aid supplies. Mary Carol put the last drops of Mercurochrome on the wound. But it didn't seem to heal.

As they neared the coastal region, the map led them up through a natural pass in the mountains. But it was away from sources of water.

They hadn't seen a stream for a couple of days. The forest floor around them was dry and in need of a good rain. "We're bound to find water as we start down the westward side of the pass," J.D. encouraged. Meanwhile, they were back to rationing food and relying on dew to replinish their water bags. Fortunately, dew was more plentiful in the mountains. But it wasn't enough to help Grace.

Her wound looked angry and swollen. It hurt, too. The pain slowed her down. One morning, not long after, she simply couldn't bear to put any weight on the leg. Mary Carol elevated the wounded leg on a pile of pine boughs, cushioning it with the blanket. "If we could just find water," she said. "I don't like the way this gash looks. A good soak in fresh water would help."

"We'll stay here and let Gracie rest," said J.D. "This forest is as dry as kindling. But we'd better keep our fire going. Rob, you and I will find a stream. If it isn't too far, we'll carry Gracie."

The boys must have been out for a couple of hours. They returned discouraged. All they found was a dry streambed.

"We need to draw the infection out," said Mary Carol. "Mamma would make a bread and milk poultice to put on it. What can we do?"

"Grandpa Matthias made a poultice of wild strawberries once when I stepped on a nail," said J.D. Wild strawberries were growing everywhere a few days before. Now, all they could find were dry shriveled vines.

Until then, the coyote had kept his distance. Now, he came so close it was alarming. He stopped just out of reach, looked at them, then walked away and sat down, facing them.

"That's odd," said Mary Carol.

The coyote came back and did the same thing over again.

"He wants you to go with him," said Grace.

Robert was worried. "I wouldn't be so sure, Gracie. It's nice to think that we have 'our coyote,' but when a wild animal comes too close, it can be dangerous. J.D., get your sling shot. I'm going to make a fire branch. If the coyote attacks, we'll defend Gracie."

"No, Robbie. You have to go with him," insisted Grace.

The coyote sat down, watching them, undisturbed by the threat of fire.

"Don't shoot, J.D. Can't you see he's waiting? Please?" Grace begged.

"Look, we can't explain it," said Mary Carol. "But Gracie knows things we don't know. She hasn't been wrong yet. That coyote is trying to tell us something. If he wanted to harm us, he'd have done it before now."

"But can we trust him?" Robert was skeptical. "The trickster?"

"I think we have to," said J.D. "Maybe he'll take us to water. Splitting up is a bad idea, but we don't have a choice. We can't take you, Gracie. We're too weak to carry you any more than a short distance and you can't walk. We'll bring water back when we find it. So who's going?"

"I'll go," said Robert. "You all stay with Gracie."

"Not by yourself," said Mary Carol.

"J.D. can stay with me," said Grace. "Our coyote is going to help us. You two go."

J.D. agreed. "Gracie can keep her foot up and rest until you come back. I'll keep the fire going so you can find us again. Rob, leave trail markers. Meanwhile, I'll see if I can make a poultice of dry strawberry vines. Maybe it will help. It won't take that much water."

It was decided. Mary Carol and Robert left all the supplies, including Robert's knapsack and took the empty waterbags.

The coyote trotted ahead and waited. When they came near, he trotted further. He was leading them well off the path Grace had plotted on the map, much farther to the south. Robert broke twigs and dropped stones in a pattern along their path. If the coyote turned out to be a trickster, they could find their way back.

Chapter 27

The Shaman

They walked for nearly two hours without any sign of water. Robert was beginning to wonder if they should go back, when the trees ended abruptly on the edge of a high cliff. Below was a long valley. Out of their reach, a fast-flowing river poured down the mountain to join a small river in the valley. Far beyond that were rolling hills, then, sparkling in the sunlight, was the ocean. Nestled in the valley near the river was a village. Smoke rose from in front of cone-shaped structures that looked like large beehives. Clusters of these structures were arranged in neat rows. The walls of the valley were so steep they couldn't see any possible way down. Yet the coyote went ahead, pausing to wait for them.

Mary Carol took a deep breath. "Oh, Robbie, it looks like we have to follow him."

"That's what it looks like," said Robert. They started a descent more treacherous than any they had yet made. "I actually think it's easier if you look at the coyote instead of your feet," Robert advised.

He was right. Looking down was terrifying. Mary Carol followed, trying to keep her eyes on the coyote. He led them safely down the side of the mountain. Looking back, Mary Carol wondered how they'd done it.

Once they were well into the valley, the coyote stopped in a clearing within a few yards of the village, waiting for them. Just as they approached, he gave a long cry followed by a series of sharp barks. Then he left, trotting back in the direction they'd come from without waiting for them to follow.

Human company! Food and shelter, help for Grace—the thought erased all fear and caution from their minds. Robert and Mary Carol walked as quickly as they could toward the village.

Startled by the coyote's bark, a group of women gathering reeds along the bank of the river stood up. Seeing the two children, they ran toward the huts, yelling. Almost immediately, half a dozen men came running. Naked from the waist up, they wore a kind of apron skirt that hung from a belt at the waist. Long hair was pulled back in a low ponytail.

"They look like cave men!" Robert exclaimed. "I guess we have gone back in time!"

Chapter 27

"What if they're hostile?" Mary Carol asked, suddenly frightened.

"We're children. What threat could we be?" Robert took a deep breath. "Whatever you do, don't act afraid."

"Easy to say," said Mary Carol, bracing herself.

After more than two months of living outdoors, their clothes were in tatters. Their stockings were long gone. Their shoes were full of holes and about to fall apart. They couldn't have looked other than what they were, destitute.

When the men got near, they stopped. The eldest of the party came forward to meet them, a very old man with long gray hair who leaned on a long staff. He called to them in a kindly voice. Robert held up his hand in a sign of peace, "We have come for help," he said. All that did was establish that they couldn't understand each other.

The old man motioned for them to follow. Soon a crowd surrounded them, keeping a respectful distance. Had Mary Carol and Robert understood the language, they'd have known that the villagers were in awe. The women heard the coyote and looked up to see Robert and Mary Carol standing there, as if by magic. To them, it seemed as if a mystical herald had announced the coming of mystical children.

The Shaman

The crowd made way for a man wearing a feathered cap and a kindly looking woman. The man greeted them. A girl brought the woman two tightly woven baskets, each about the size of a large cup. These she gave to Robert and Mary Carol. They were full of delicious, hot soup that tasted like pumpkin.

Through gestures and picture drawings on the ground, Robert explained their dilemma. The woman seemed to understand immediately. Talking rapidly to the man in the cap, she gestured for three of the men to go with Robert.

Mary Carol wanted to go, too. But the woman motioned for her to stay behind, leading her to one of the beehive-shaped structures that turned out to be a house. Mary Carol was too exhausted to argue. If she went, she would slow the party down. Besides, she felt safe. It was as if she'd known the woman all her life.

The woman's name was Chawnaway. It meant discoverer of profound mysteries in the Chumash language spoken in the village. She was a shaman, or medicine doctor. A loving, gentle person, she used her powers for good. Chawnaway was not of the Chumash people who lived there, but long ago they became her people. The shaman before her, a kind and wise woman, reared her from childhood. She taught her plant lore and many powerful spells for healing. Now, as shaman, Chawnaway had brought most of the children in the village into the world, held them under the stars, and given them the secret names by which they were never called. She took care of her people, treating their injuries and nursing them to health when they were sick, just as the shaman before her had done.

When she heard that two strange children appeared from out of the grass, Chawnaway was surprised. She had been expecting four children. She knew they weren't gods. She understood that they came from far away and they had far to go.

One of her responsibilities was to read the stars for signs. No important decision was made in the village until she consulted the stars. She didn't have to consult the stars to see that Mary Carol and Robert were half starved and in need of human kindness. Nor was it necessary to consult the stars to know that she must help these children before sending them on their way. As difficult as the first part of their journey from far over the mountains had been, the last part would be hardest of all. They must be prepared.

She might have let Mary Carol go with Robert, but Chawnaway knew something Mary Carol thought nobody knew. Mary Carol had been giving most of her food and share of the water to Grace ever since she'd wounded her leg. Chawnaway recognized the sunken eyes of one suffering from going without enough water and food. She feared that Mary Carol was close to death, perhaps even closer than the sister she was so worried about.

Along the circular wall of Chawnaway's house were covered baskets of all sizes. In the center was a pile of stones where a low fire glowed. A hole in the roof allowed smoke to escape. Chawnaway didn't give Mary Carol more food or water right away. She knew that Mary Carol needed slow, steady care. After Mary Carol had rested for what seemed a long time, some of the women helped her get undressed. They were interested in her clothing, especially the few remaining buttons, the buttonholes, and what was left of her tattered cardigan.

When they saw the turquoise around her neck, there was excited chatter. Chawnaway was more concerned with Mary Carol than what she was wearing. She noticed the turquoise, smiling. The children had needed all of the protection from harm that the turquoise could bring—and more. She rubbed Mary Carol down with some kind of ointment, taken from one of the pots. It felt like it had sand in it. Then the women handed her a blanket to wrap around herself. Chanaway motioned for her to follow.

They led her to a low dome-shaped structure covered with packed sun-baked earth. A notched pole ladder led to a large hole in the top. Chanaway climbed the ladder, beckoning for Mary Carol to follow. The other women stayed outside. As she began to climb down another pole ladder inside, Mary Carol saw it was bigger than it looked from the outside. Most of it was below ground. Four large poles around the center gave support to the domed roof. Inside it was hot and steamy. A bank of coals glowed on a hearth at one end. Mary Carol was never sure what happened after that, if she fainted, or fell into an exhausted asleep. All she could remember was the sense of steam rising, a pleasant smell of sage and something else she couldn't identify, the sound of Chanaway's voice, and a feeling of deep peace. The next thing she knew, they were climbing out of the hut where the women who waited outside led her to the river. She and Chanaway splashed in its sharply cold water.

It was the only time Mary Carol ever visited the steamlodge. She learned later that it was primarily used by the men.

When they returned to Chawnaway's house, a clean apron-like skirt awaited her. It was made from some kind of plant fiber. Mary Carol felt cleaner than she had since they'd left their campsite on the river. She had another bowl of soup. Then Chawnaway spread out a mat for her, putting a fur-covered pillow under her head. The women covered her with a blanket. But she was too worried about Grace to do more than doze.

Meanwhile, Robert went with the men. They knew another trail up the treacherous canyon walls. It took longer, but it was well-used and less dangerous. J.D. was flooded with relief when he saw them. One of the men gently lifted Grace from the ground, carrying her in his arms like a baby. The other men helped J.D. and Robert cover the fire. There was no sign of the coyote.

It was almost dark when they reached the village. Chawnaway and Mary Carol waited with the rest of the villagers. Chawnaway directed the men to put Grace on a mat she'd placed by the fire in her house. A woman was sent to get soup. She brought a large basket of hot soup and a basket bowl for each of them. The boys drank heartily, but Grace was too weak to try. Chawnaway looked at her wound and sent the boys away. As the women removed her ragged dress, the crystal around her neck caught the light of the fire and sent out a shower of color. The women stood back in awe. Chawnaway examined it, and smiled, leaving it around Grace's neck while she bathed her with a sea sponge. She nodded approval as she removed the strawberry poultice J.D. had put on the wound. Grace was all skin and bones. They all were. It was a wonder they'd made it so far and were still alive.

A pillow covered in animal fur was propped under Grace's head. Others were placed under the wounded leg. Chawnaway took some ointment from a basket and rubbed it directly on the wound. Grace flinched, but didn't cry. Chawnaway wiped this off and packed the wound with some kind of leaf. All the while, she sang a haunting tune. As she finished, she moved her hands over Grace from head to feet without actually touching her. When this was complete, she placed a blanket of woven fiber over her. Grace smiled at Chawnaway, but she didn't speak. For the first time since she and Robert left to follow the coyote, Mary Carol knew that Grace would be all right. "Thank you," she said, blinking back tears.

The men who had gone with Robert took the boys to the sweatlodge and stream. When J.D. took off his shirt, the men saw the silver owl around his neck. They seemed to take it as something of great importance. Afterward the boys were given woven aprons to wear and taken to the chief's hut. They were directed to sit outside. The chief came out, ceremoniously greeting them. "Do you think we should give him a gift?" J.D. asked.

By now, just about everything but the blanket was in Robert's knapsack, including the girls' purses. Both boys had holes in their pockets. "Yes, but what?" Robert asked, digging into the knapsack. The first thing his hand grasped was the kaleidoscope. He gave it to J.D., who presented it to the chief. It was a big success. The chief passed it around for the men to see. "Good work, Rob!" exclaimed J.D.

It was dark outside when Chawnaway sent for J.D. and Robert. She signaled that they were to sleep in her house. Setting out sleeping mats, she left the children to themselves.

"They think our coyote's call was a sign that we're sent from the spirit world, because we're so pale," Grace said weakly.

"Pale!" exclaimed Mary Carol. "Look at my suntan."

"Chawnaway doesn't think we're gods. She was expecting us."

"What makes you think so?" Mary Carol wondered.

"It's what they were saying," said Grace.

"Don't tell me that crystal glass helps you understand other languages!" exclaimed Robert.

"I don't exactly understand the words. It's just what she was saying."

"It makes sense," J.D. affirmed. "They've treated us like royalty."

"Maybe that's how they treat any visitor. Besides,

we're just kids. We looked in pretty sad shape, too," said Robert.

"You two look odd enough in those aprons," said Mary Carol, surpressing a giggle.

"Speak for yourself." J.D. cringed. "I feel silly enough. I'd hate for anybody at school to see me in this."

"You can say that again!" said Robert. "We'd never hear the end of it."

"They probably think our clothes looked pretty silly," said J.D. "I guess it's what you're used to."

"We looked a sight," said Mary Carol. "They've been so nice. I haven't felt this full since we ate that snake! And we didn't even have to eat anything disgusting."

"Anyway, we'd have been up a creek if we hadn't run into them," said J.D. "Gracie, you really needed some medical attention. You look worlds better now."

"We didn't exactly run into them," Robert said. "The coyote brought us here. Does anybody still doubt that it's the same coyote who's been with us all this way?"

"Not anymore," said J.D.

"Our guardian angel coyote," said Grace.

They were about to sing their evening song together when Grace realized that Kitty was missing. The last anyone remembered Kitty was before Grace hurt her leg. Grace's eyes welled up with tears. "Sometimes it feels like we've lost everything we ever loved!" she said.

Chapter 28

The Coyote's Call

Grace's leg mended rapidly. Mary Carol's color returned, and she began to lose the dehydrated look. They were all thriving in no time.

They spent over two months with the kind people of that village, learning their language and their ways. When Grace began to recover, they no longer slept in Chawnaway's house. They shared a beehive shaped thatch house with about twenty other people, including children, though none of their own ages. They were of the family of Konoyo, whose father was the old man who had welcomed Mary Carol and Robert. Later, Grace explained that Konoyo's wife, Leqte, was good with languages. She was eager to host them. Soon Leqte had all the uncles, aunts, and cousins who shared the house, helping them with the language.

There was a fireplace in the middle, with a

smokehole above, though cooking was usually done outside. Their beds were made on platforms built above the sand-plastered floor, with space underneath to store their things. Beds were around the edges of the house and enclosed by mat partitions. "It's like having our own room," Mary Carol observed. They slept on mattresses made of woven plants and fur pillows stuffed with feathers.

The boys fished with the men and other boys, learning to throw nets out to catch river fish. Sometimes they went by tule boats for a day's journey to the ocean where they spent the night, bringing back baskets of clams. They seemed to thrive on these excursions.

They helped gather tule reeds from along the river marshes and lay them out to dry or soak to make them pliable enough to weave into rope. Drying reeds had to be turned every day until they were completely dry. They were put together into bundles with grape vine. These bundles were used to build the tule boats. The reeds had to be handled carefuly. A punctured reed wouldn't float.

Once a boat was tied together, it was coated with black tar-like substance found nearby. Most of the boats had room for one to three passengers at the most. But there were larger boats that held up to five passengers. These were used for longer journeys up and down the coast. Boat building was an on-going activity, as reed boats did not last as long as the small wooden canoes used for river travel.

Their only complaint was a boy about J.D.'s age whose name was Muhu. He was arrogant, lazy, and cheated at games. There was a large sports area where the boys met to play games when work was done. The other boys didn't like Muhu, but they never left him out. They seemed to take his behavior in stride. They'd say that he was the chief's nephew and gestured in a way that said, "What can you expect?"

"As if that makes it right," J.D. fumed on one of the rare evenings when the children had an opportunity for some time alone. "He's always picking at you, Rob. But he's so sneaky, it's hard to catch him in the act. I'd like to give him a pounding to remember."

Robert, usually the more reactionary of the two, said, "He hasn't ever hurt me. I don't think he will. The last thing we need is to start a fight and get kicked out of the village."

"He's probably jealous of the attention you all are getting," said Mary Carol. "He's taller than you, Robbie, so he thinks he can get away with it. But I think you're right."

"Anyway, Mamma would say you should try to ignore him, if he doesn't actually hurt you," said Grace.

Mary Carol spent her days helping the women and girls gather acorns to pound into flour, as well as roots and green plants. The other girls taught her how to make flat bread cakes on a hot rock and to string shell beads. Sometimes, when there was time for play, they took her exploring around the village, teaching her the names for things.

Chawnaway took a special interest in Grace. She taught her how to find healing plants. Grace mixed special recipes for upset stomach, colds, and fever. Chawnaway taught her how to understand animals and birds, something she already seemed to be good at—at least since they'd jumped off the train. Grace helped set broken legs and wings. She learned quickly.

Every time he had a chance, J.D. reminded them that they needed to be off. He was nearly frantic with worry that they'd never leave. He seemed to be the only one who felt the urgency of their mission. Weeks passed. The others wouldn't budge. He knew they were afraid of setting out on their own again. *But if we're ever to get home, we have to find that crystal.* Sometimes he saw the coyote standing on the bluff above the village. *Maybe he was a trickster after all, he thought. He saved Grace, but we'll never be able to leave here. That was the deception.*

One morning everything changed. Just as they were rousing from sleep, they heard the sharp, unmistakable bark of the coyote, close to the village. "I dreamed about Old Shep last night" said Grace. "I haven't dreamed about him since our first night off the train. It was like he was saying, 'It's time.' Now, the coyote's calling us. You're right, J.D. We have to go."

"We'll ask the chief for permission," J.D. said. "After all they've done for us, we can't just walk away." *Besides*, he thought, *if we make our intention to leave official, the others can't keep putting it off.*

The chief had heard the coyote's call, too. "It is an omen," he said. He took them to Chawnaway to see if the stars were right for their departure. Chawnaway already knew it was time for them to go. Once they were alone, she astonished them by speaking in English.

"How did you learn English so fast?" J.D. was stunned.

"You've known all along, haven't you," said Mary Carol, "before we ever got here." She felt as if she was grasping at an idea that she couldn't quite reach.

Chawanaway's eyes sparkled. "You see, Grace is my name, too. It was given to me long before I came to live in the village. It was my mother's name. But that's another story for another time. Perhaps you will know one day, but we will not speak of it now."

Changing the subject, she said, "There is much work for you to do. Now you must show me the map, Grace." The children looked at each other. Nothing had ever been said about the map.

Like Grace, Chawnaway was able to read the map through the crystal magnifying glass. Somehow it didn't surprise them.

Grace traced with her finger, showing them how it was now marked all the way up the coast. It turned along a great river that opened to the sea, going upriver and ending at a mountain in the far north. Chawnaway pointed to Bear in the border, "Beware. Do not trust the Bear-People. They will stand in your way. The people who live along the coast and in the north are few and peaceful. Not the Bear-People," she said.

"Long ago, many people came across the frozen land bridge from beyond. Tradition says they came in animal form, becoming people when they got here. It is told that the Bear-People refused to give up life as bears. Some believe that, to this day, they change into bears and raid other villages to get slaves. They make war, not peace. Your way will take you there. You must have presents for them. Accept their gifts, but be wary. Tell them only what you must."

They selected Mary Carol's mirror and Grace's

glass beads as gifts. Chawnaway gave them small bags of yarrow and white sage, too. "The Bear-People prize these. They are symbols of healing and peace, even to them. I wish that you did not have to do this great thing. But it began long ago and must be taken to completion. I have tried to prepare you for what is to come. All I can do now is to bless your journey."

"Will we ever get back home and see our father and mother again?" Mary Carol asked.

"That I do not know," said Chawnaway. "Some things that seem impossible turn out to be possible. But if for some reason you cannot go home, there's a home for you here with me among my people."

"I wish you could come with us," said Mary Carol. "I wouldn't be afraid."

"I cannot," said Chawnaway. "That was decided long ago, too. I could not be trusted with that which you seek. I have been damaged by its magic." Then, as if understanding the surge of fear that swept through all of them, she added. "You need not fear the magic. Nor do you need to fear her who wields it. Do what you know is right and good. Only fear the one who led her to this great mischief. For he may yet present himself."

"Who is he?" asked J.D., alarmed. "How will we know him?"

"What form he will take, I cannot say. Listen with your hearts as well as your minds, for he will not ring true. Most of all, remember, he cannot enter where he is not wanted."

That night there was a special ceremony held in the sacred space. It was enclosed by mats held by tall flag-bearing poles. Only Konoyo's father, Chawnaway, and a few other men went inside. Everyone else sat around the outside. Afterward there was a feast with dancing in the packed-earth dancing circle. There was singing, and presentation of gifts, too.

After studying their ragged clothing, the women had made trousers and shirts for the boys from animal hide. The girls were given simple and comfortable hide dresses and leggings they could wear when they left the coastal lands. There were boot-like shoes to replace the woven grass slippers they'd been wearing. Their own shoes were beyond repair. There was a hooded cloak for each of them, too—something Chawnaway designed and had the women make for them.

"These are too plain," apologized the woman who presented their clothing. She looked at Chawnaway as she said it.

"The women wanted to decorate with shell beads and fringe. It is a way of showing honor," said

Chawnaway. "But, you may need to hide and slip away unseen. Beads and fringe fall off and mark a trail." Last of all, there were large woven baskets for J.D., Mary Carol, and Grace to carry on their backs. The baskets were packed with all manner of provisions: dried fish mixed with berries, dried squash powder, mats for sleeping, and their well-worn water bags.

Last of all, they gave Robert provisions for his knapsack. It had been carefully mended.

J.D. spoke for them, thanking the chief, Chawnaway, and everyone for their kindness. "You saved our lives. We will never forget you." Leqte had helped him prepare.

Chawnaway gave them a special blessing. Then the chief spoke. It was a long, hard-to-follow speech about the history of the Chumash—how they had come across the sea on a rainbow bridge—and the blessing brought by the four children. *How can we have been a blessing?* wondered Mary Carol, who struggled hard to follow. *We're the ones who have been blessed.*

The last part was the best. "You will not go all of the way alone. We are taking you to the Great River in the north that opens to the sea. We have never traded so far north before, but we have long desired to do so. Konoyo and Leqte, will accompany you to where the country of the Bear-People begins, for she is of a northern tribe and knows their language and ways. She will teach you."

That was the best news possible. Leaving the safety of the village was a terrifying prospect. Except for J.D.'s constant prodding and the bark of the coyote, the others might have given up the quest. Too much time had passed since they jumped off the train. Their journey was too hard. And, most terrifying of all, they feared the quest was doomed from the beginning.

By Sea

Chawnaway asked them to meet her early the next morning before they set off. She had a covered basket about the size of a large apple for Grace. She spoke in English again, "You will need this. It is yarrow. I have taught you how to use it, Grace. Use it only in great need. When you reach your destination, it will be required of you along with the condor feather, the flower, and two other tokens you have yet to discover."

"The third token?" asked J.D. "You know about the tokens?"

"Chawnaway knew," said Grace, smiling up at her. "You already knew about us and our journey before we ever came."

"But not how it will end," said Mary Carol, "or what the tokens are?"

"No," said Chawnaway, "I do not know how it will end, nor what you must find on your way. Yet, I have hope. You must do this for yourselves, but never imagine that you are alone."

She cautioned them, "Do not show the tokens to anyone until you are at your journey's end. Keep them close and beware of anyone who asks for them, no matter who. Only the Keeper has that right, and he must be true to the magic that holds the Last Crystal, whether or not he wishes to do so." Then she gave them all hugs, as Mamma would have done, before they went outside to the boats.

When they arrived at the river, large tule boats were waiting along with almost everyone in the village. Pshokn, who had carried Grace to the village, had been chosen as leader. He and another man were assigned to their boat.

One other crewmember was Muhu. Their hearts sank when they saw him. He was the only other boy allowed to go. His job was to scoop out water when it splashed into the boat. The other boys would have given nearly anything to go along and be a bailer. It was important work, but Muhu sneered as he stepped into the bailer's position. Everybody knew he would never have been chosen, if he weren't related to the chief.

Two other boats accompanied them. Konoyo led

one of these. The plan was to go up the coast to where the Great River meets the sea. It would be a long trip for the men, but it would put the children well on their way to the North Country. The men would trade with costal tribes on their return trip, bringing important goods back to the village.

As the reed boats began their journey down-river to the ocean, Grace pointed to a high, wind-swept bluff. Their coyote stood watching. "He's seeing us off," she said. They waved. The coyote stood looking for a moment, gave a series of long barks, and trotted away. It was the last time they saw him.

The reed boats skimmed along the coastline just past where the tide spills into breakers, the shore always in sight. Every evening, the boats were pulled out of the water into a protected place and examined for deflated reeds. The boys helped build a fire, except for Muhu, who made a point of doing nothing. The girls helped Leqte cook squash soup and fish. There was plenty of fresh fish. At night, they curled up in fur blankets. They were up by dawn's light to set out each morning.

The children had never been on the ocean. It was enchanting. Gulls called from overhead. The tide passed under their boats, before breaking against the shoreline. The water was never quite the same shade of blue. Sometimes dolphins raced them, leaping and diving near the boats. Pshokn pointed to them, "Our brothers. When our people crossed the rainbow bridge, those who fell into the sea became dolphins. To this day, they are our brothers." One day he pointed to whales far out to sea, coming to the surface and spouting.

The trip would have been a wonderful adventure except for three things. One was knowing it wouldn't last and they would eventually have to go on alone. That thought never quite left them. Another was something they hadn't talked about. Weighing on them was Chawnaway's mention of one they should fear more than Celeste. Then there was the immediate problem of Muhu.

J.D. and Robert took their turn rowing with wide-paddled wooden oars. Muhu complained that he should have been assigned to row. Grace and Mary Carol helped him with the bailing so he could have a turn, but he didn't really want to row. He didn't want to do anything but complain. Sometimes he let the water rise to an alarming level before he started bailing. He laughed when the girls became worried or he'd shrug his shoulders, throwing them the bailing basket. He was careful to look busy if Pshokn happened to be watching, though, making them even less trusting of him.

Muhu said rude and disgusting things to them, too, but never where anyone else could hear. The girls decided against telling J.D. and Robert. "If we ignore him, maybe he'll get tired of it," said Mary Carol. "It's just another way of being a bully."

Grace agreed. "He probably wants us to tell so he can pick a fight."

"But if it gets any worse, I'm telling Pshokn," said Mary Carol. "We shouldn't have to put up with it. If he so much as touches you or me, for that matter, I'll slap his face. Then we'll let him explain it to Pshokn."

One morning when it was time to leave, Muhu disappeared. A search party combed the woods. They found him at the bottom of a mudslide. He was scraped and had a sprained ankle. He couldn't walk on his right foot. When the men brought him back to camp, Leqte helped Grace clean his wounds and wrap his ankle. One of the wounds was a nasty gouge. Grace used some of the precious yarrow to prevent infection and gave him white sage tea to drink.

When Pshokn questioned him, Muhu was sullen, saying little, except that his uncle was the chief and people ought to remember that. Pshokn couldn't be bullied. "Your uncle has done you great honor in allowing you to come. You should remember that."

Muhu didn't make any effort to help after his injury. Once they were on the water, he rested while the girls bailed. He said he was too injured to do anything. But he wasn't too injured to be first to eat when they made camp. Nor was he too injured to wander about.

One day Robert discovered his rope was missing. It was a real blow. Losing it was like losing a piece of their daddy. Everyone helped him search, but it wasn't to be found. Muhu said it probably fell overboard. He seemed to take pleasure in knowing Robert had lost something he treasured.

Soon mountains appeared in the distance beyond the shoreline, their peaks topped with snow. Trees were taller than any they had ever seen. Huge boulders stood in the sea and along the shore. The men said they were getting closer to the Great River. Only Leqte and Konoyo had been so far north before.

That afternoon, they put into a protected cove earlier than usual. Leqte explained that they were going to build a lightweight canoe like those used by people in the north. "We'll need the canoe to go upriver. The reed boats will not be so reliable in the swift waters of the north. We can carry the canoe around rapids and waterfalls, too."

Some of the men helped Konoyo look for the right sort of branches for the canoe: strong, but flexible. Others took skins from one of the reed boats where they'd been stored. Everybody but Muhu pitched in. He said he was too weak from his wounds to do anything, even though Grace had long since pronounced him well.

Mary Carol became more and more suspicions. Grace's gold beads were missing. One of the men complained of losing his best spearhead. J.D.'s slingshot disappeared. Mary Carol talked with Leqte about it. "We must look in his basket," Leqte suggested. Muhu was stretched out on the sand. "He'll be asleep soon. Then we'll have a look."

As soon as Muhu was fast asleep, Leqte took his basket. Everything was there: the rope, the beads, J.D.'s slingshot, the spearhead, and many other things, including something that looked to Mary Carol and Grace as if it were a solid gold necktie clip. It was strangely out of place among the other things—something out of time.

Leqte, looked at the tie clip in puzzlement. "This is a most curious device."

Mary Carol tried to explain that men wore a necktie and used the clip to secure it to their shirt or for decoration. But Leqte didn't seem to be able to visualize it. It was too complicated to try to explain being in another time.

"If we confront him about these things," said Leqte, "he'll say someone put them in his basket. We must be wise and choose the right time."

Chapter 30

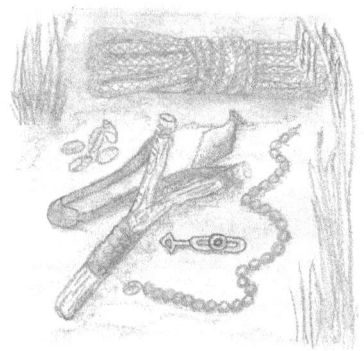

Muhu's Doing

The girls were exploring tide pools around one of the large boulders when they came upon a dolphin stranded on its side. A fragment of fishing net around its pectoral fins was caught in the rocks in one of the tide pools. A spear protruded from its dorsal fin. Grace approached it as Chawnaway had taught her. "Brother Dolphin, I can help you if you will let me." The dolphin didn't resist. They splashed water over its drying body, avoiding the blowhole, then carefully untangled the net so they could turn the dolphin on its belly in the shallow tide pool. Grace sent Mary Carol for Leqte. "Bring the yarrow. We'll need a knife and bailing baskets. The water is too shallow for him to return to sea until the tide comes in."

Grace spoke gently to the dolphin, splashing water over it until Mary Carol returned with Leqte and a bailing basket. They kept the dolphin's skin wet while Grace went to work on the wound. She gently pulled the spear shaft from its fin. She gasped as she held it up. It was Robert's.

Mary Carol recognized it, too. There was no mistaking the arrowhead Mr. Nichols had given him. "He wouldn't do such a thing," she said.

"No, he would not," said Leqte.

Muhu, who hadn't been anywhere to be seen all afternoon, suddenly appeared. "You do not wish to hear what I have to say," he began in an uncharacteristically polite manner. "The tide was going out. I went for a walk in the surf. I know you think I am being false. But my ankle pains me. The sea water helps. I came around these rocks in time to see him standing over the dolphin. It was caught in the fish netting. Dolphins are sacred to my people. I think it was cowardly, even if he is your brother."

Grace and Mary Carol didn't want to believe him. But it was Robert's spear. They'd seen him carrying it that morning as the work started on the canoe.

"We shall see," said Leqte, inspecting the net. "Now we have work. These nets are used by people in the north to catch the salmon at sea." After they'd cut away the netting, Grace directed Mary Carol and Leqte to keep pouring water over the dolphin. She made a paste with some of the precious yarrow, putting it over the wound. A smirking Muhu watched.

Konoyo and two of the men came running up to help. They'd been on a hill above, looking for flexible branches for the canoe, when they saw Muhu wading around the boulders. They returned with the branches just in time to see the girls trying to help the dolphin.

With the men's help they soon dug out the tide pool so it was large enough for the dolphin to submerge its pectoral fins and tail. Grace had them make a shade for it with Mary Carol's blanket. She refused to leave, pouring water over the dolphin's exposed back until the tide began splashing in. Mary Carol stayed with her, taking turns. The tide was well past their knees when the dolphin flipped around and swam out to sea.

Back at the campsite, Muhu repeated his story, saying he'd seen the whole thing. Robert had come upon the trapped dolphin and speared it. Leqte, who carried the spear, said nothing. She began preparation for the evening meal, her mouth set in grim silence.

Having finished their work on the canoe for the day, the men were relaxing in anticipation of a delicious meal. Pshokn looked at Muhu intently. "What you say is not possible. The boy has been with me working on the canoe all afternoon. Until now he has not been out of my sight." He demanded to know how Muhu had come by Robert's spear.

Muhu shrugged his shoulders. "I told you what happened."

"I think you have a number of things that others are missing," said Pshokn. He ordered one of the men to empty Muhu's basket on the sand. All the things that had been reported missing were there. "What is this?" he asked, holding up the tie clip.

"Nothing," said Muhu. "I found it."

The children looked at each other. Nobody claimed the tie clip and nobody could explain it. Pshokn tossed it back to Muhu. "Your conduct will be brought to the elders when we return. They will decide what's to be done. Perhaps, as you say, spearing our brother dolphin was the most cowardly of all." After that, Muhu was very subdued, even pitching in to share in the chores.

"We never believed it was you, Robbie," said Mary Carol when the children had a few minutes to themselves. "It was your spear, but you wouldn't do anything so cruel and cowardly."

"I'd hate to lose the arrowhead," said Robert, "but it was the rope that upset me most. I'm glad to have it back."

The other three knew he was thinking about Daddy and Mamma. "The rope is a reminder of why we're here," said J.D. "We have to get back home. If Daddy doesn't get well, Mamma will need us more than ever."

"I just hope she doesn't know we're missing," said Robert.

"Sometimes I go the whole day without thinking of them," said Mary Carol. "That scares me. What if we forgot about them? What if we forgot to pray for Daddy to be well?"

"We won't forget," said J.D. "We won't let ourselves forget, no matter how long this takes."

"You were right, J.D.," said Robert. "We needed to get back to business. We were getting too comfortable."

"I don't think Chawnaway would have let us forget," said Grace. "She knew a lot about what we have to do. She didn't rush us because she wanted us to be ready."

"What do you think about her name being Grace?" asked Mary Carol.

"I don't know," said Grace. "It is something important, something to do with us and maybe with Uncle James."

Chapter 30

"That doesn't make any sense," said Robert.

"A lot of stuff isn't making sense," said J.D. "What about that gold clip? Wonder how Muhu got that? I haven't seen anything like gold. The Chumash didn't use gold."

"It is a tie clip. I can't think of anything else it could be," said Mary Carol. "I don't think Mr. Lawton wore a gold tie clip, did he?"

There was no way to know how it got there. The thought of somebody from their own time wandering around, maybe even knowing about them, was unsettling.

"Don't forget Chanaway's promise," said Mary Carol. "We aren't alone."

"Not now," said Robert grimly, "not until Konoyo and Leqte leave us."

Three days later the canoe was finished and secured to the side of one of the boats. Muhu was about to get in their boat when Pshokn said, "You will ride in Konoyo's boat. Their bailer will come to this boat in your place. You will bail for Konoyo. See that you do it properly. You are well able to work. Don't presume upon our mercy."

Despite beautiful weather and a sparkling, calm sea, the children's morale was low. The worry about their father, always somewhere at the back of their consciousness, had come to the surface again. The older three, who had secretly read the second telegram, were desperately afraid that their father had died without them knowing. In her heart, Grace still hoped that the water from the Last Crystal would make him well.

As they were pushing out to sea, a dolphin played just past the tide line. When they passed over the breakers, it approached the boat, bobbing up next to Mary Carol and Grace. "He has something on his nose!" Mary Carol exclaimed.

Balanced on the dolphin's bottlenose was a red abalone shell, shining with iridescent beauty. It was the most splendid shell they'd ever seen. Grace reached down and took it. "Thank you," she said. "Your fin looks ever so much better now." The dolphin swam away from the boat, gave a leap above the water and disappeared.

"Uncle James has a red abalone shell," said J.D. The thought of Uncle James sent another wave of homesickness through all of them.

"It's a token," said Mary Carol. "I think the tokens come after a special act of kindness, even the basket from Chawnaway. She helped us, but you really helped her, too, Gracie."

"She was kind to us," said Robert. "Maybe that's what makes something a token."

"Uncle James' red abalone shell was for remembering," said Mary Carol. "Mamma said it was for remembering his sister—the one from his family before he was adopted. I hope that if—when—we get home, we will always remember this."

"Her name was Grace," said J.D. "The sister from before he was adopted was Grace."

"And Grandpa and Grandma gave Mamma her middle name to remember Uncle James' other sister," Mary Carol added breathlessly. The children looked at each other in wonder.

"It really couldn't be Chawnaway, though," said Robert. "Not really." It seemed too implausible, even to Grace.

It took most of the day to reach the Great River. The mouth of that river spread across a vast area bordered by tall fir trees. The current was strong here where the river met the ocean. They camped on the near bank, well into a protected area backed on one side by rocky cliffs. They lit no fire. Leqte said many people depend on the river. Most of them were peaceful, but others might be too interested in their business. "It is better to be unseen."

The sun was not yet up the next morning when Pshokn and the men said farewell. As the reed boats set out for the south and home, the children felt their hearts sink. The only good thing was being rid of Muhu. He sat in Pshokn's boat, looking strangely pleased and self-satisfied. "How can anyone who has so thoroughly disgraced himself hold his head up?" J.D. wondered aloud.

Had it not been for Leqte and Konoyo, it would have been very hard to go on, despite the sense of urgency. Leqte tried to cheer them up. Pointing, she said, "Look, a great white owl is chasing a raven from that tree."

They looked up in time to see an enormous raven taking flight as a white owl settled in the top of the tallest fir tree. "A very good omen," said Konoyo.

"Raven is a trickster," said Leqte. "But the owl is more powerful than Raven."

Chapter 31

Disaster Strikes

Konoyo was in no rush to leave. J.D. asked why they didn't start right away, especially since the tule boats were off at first light. "Tide's out," Konoyo explained. He was a man of few words. It wasn't until they started, sometime before noon, that J.D. understood. Konoyo was waiting for the incoming tide to carry them up through the mouth of the river rather than fighting against both current and tide.

As evening approached, Leqte said they should start looking for a place to stop for the night. They were near the middle of the river, close to its widest point. Konoyo and J.D. were paddling when disaster struck.

"The canoe's leaking!" said Robert. Water was coming in from one side in a steady trickle. The canoe had been tested before Konoyo pronounced it finished. It was a light, swift craft. The men were pleased with their work. Something was terribly wrong. "We'll go to shore," said Konoyo.

The leak was getting bigger, but they were making good progress. With Robert bailing they weren't in great danger until suddenly, unexpectedly, the current caught and spun the canoe around, capsizing it. Everyone was dumped in the swift-moving water.

Gasping for breath, they all scrambled to stay afloat. Thinking quickly, Robert grabbed the oars before they were swept away. He and J.D. were expert swimmers. Mary Carol knew how to keep herself afloat. But Grace was no swimmer.

"Help!" she gasped, struggling for air as she went under. Konoyo acted instantly, grabbing and pulling her up. Choking and sputtering, Grace caught ahold of the canoe.

"Hold on to the canoe! Save your strength," Konoyo gasped.

It was a few minutes before Konoyo caught his breath. "Let it drift," he said. "Leqte, hold Grace. We'll right the canoe." Leqte took Grace and floated out of the way. Following Konoyo's directions, J.D. helped him right the canoe. But it was taking on water too fast. There was no use trying to climb back in.

Konoyo took the oars from Robert, securing them

under the seats and thwart. They drifted rapidly with the current. Gradually, Konoyo and Leqte swam toward shore, not fighting with the current, but steadily guiding the canoe closer to shore. J.D. and Robert were able to help. It was all Mary Carol and Grace could do to hang on. When they reached shore, thoroughly exhausted, they were not far from where they'd started.

Once the canoe was beached, Konoyo had a careful look. "Cut," he declared.

"Muhu's work," said Robert. "My jackknife's missing. I thought he was being awfully helpful when we were tying down supplies."

The good news was that their supplies had been well secured. They lost very little. However, Robert's knapsack was wet through so the contents had to be emptied and spread out to dry. The condor feathers, dried flower, shell, and Grace's precious basket of yarrow were safe thanks to Chawnaway, who had wrapped them in an oiled fiber bag. But to their horror, the map was thoroughly soaked. It was impossible to make any sense of it, even for Grace, with her crystal magnifying glass. "This is terrible!" exclaimed Mary Carol.

"It's my fault," said Grace in despair. "I took it out of the bag to look at it before we left this morning, and I didn't bother to return it. Now I don't know what we'll do!"

Robert was practical, "Look, Gracie, you and I have studied that map nearly every day since we jumped off the train. You spent a lot of time looking at it with Chawnaway before we left. So did I. I'll bet you remember more than you think you do. Between the two of us, we can do it. I have my compass. We follow the river. We have to find a smaller river and go toward where the Bear-People live. We're headed for a particular mountain. After that it wasn't ever clear, but that was the end point."

"What happens when we get to the mountain and there's no map?" J.D. asked.

"The drawings circle back to where we started at the rock pile, right, Gracie?" asked Mary Carol. "Didn't Celeste say that's one of the confusing things about the map?"

"She did," admitted Robert. "Quit blaming yourself for getting the map wet, Gracie. We've all made our share of mistakes."

"Maybe it will be more clear when the map dries out," said Mary Carol.

"Even if it isn't, we have to go on," said J.D., trying to sound hopeful. He he didn't feel hopeful, but he didn't know what else to do. "Then at some point we have to start asking for the Keeper of the Crystal. I think you'll know when, Gracie. Chawnaway said the journey ended at the mountain. I have to think that you'll just know, like you've known so many things all along the way." With or without hope, they had to go on.

They were a gloomy party, though. Konoyo said they'd have to replace the broken section of the canoe. It would take at least a day to stretch the skin, stitch it in place and seal it with spruce gum. Then it had to dry. This meant building a fire, something Konoyo wasn't happy about. They pulled the canoe well off shore, out of sight.

The canoe was repaired without incident, though it cost them the next full day. Leqte made good use of the time by drilling the children on the language of the Bear-People. She'd had them working on it since they left the Chumash village. Now she redoubled her efforts.

Once the canoe was ready, they set out again with the incoming tide to carry them along. They traveled up the Great River for three days. Where there were rapids or the current was too strong, they carried the baskets on their backs and everyone helped with portage of the canoe, getting it to the next safe place on the water. At night, Konoyo insisted they shelter on sand banks, under the graceful branches of fir trees. They made no fire. Konoyo insisted that they carry the canoe well out of view of the river at night, too.

Mary Carol and Leqte searched for edible roots to supplement the dried squash powder they had with them. Blackberries were ripe. There was plenty to eat, though they all longed for a hot meal.

"Why can't we have a fire?" Robert asked. "Anybody can see us on the river. How is that different?"

"True." Konoyo said no more.

"Seeing us pass along the river and tracking us down by following the smoke from our fire are two different things," Leqte explained. "On the river we can go fast at need. We're too few to risk being surprised on the land. Such a mistake led to my capture by the Bear-People."

Leqte belonged to one of the many tribes who lived in the vast woodlands north of the river. As a girl, she and her four brothers were returning from a trade mission with people near the ocean. One night they were surprised by a raiding party, looking for slaves. It was only after several years with the Bear-People that they escaped to the south where they met a Chumash trading party.

"We must keep practicing the language of the Bear-People," Leqte said. She began speaking to them only in that language. It was a struggle, but they understood more and more.

"The thing about learning a language," Robert said one afternoon, "is that once you learn one new language, it's easier to learn another. At least I hope that's true."

Leqte reprimanded him for speaking in English.

On the morning of the third day, as the canoe was re-launched she said, "We're drawing close to the river that we follow north." They passed several rivers, always going on.

"How will you know your river?" Robert wondered.

"When the mountains are in the right place," she said. Far ahead they could see the cone shapes of tall, steel blue mountains, their tops covered with snow. "Soon we will enter the ring of fire that circles the northland. When the gods are angry, they send out flame and ash to punish the people."

"Volcanoes!" exclaimed Robert. "I hope we get to see one in action."

"Not me," said Mary Carol. "I don't want to be trapped by a lava flow. I've already had enough adventure to last me the rest of my life."

"An erupting volcano would be pretty amazing," said J.D. "But I'd rather see it from a safe distance."

Leqte interrupted to remind them that they should be speaking in the language of the Bear-People. Sometimes, in their excitement, they lapsed into English, even when they weren't talking among themselves.

Konoya looked at them all in disapproval. They'd been far too loud. He insisted that they keep their voices low at all times.

"Look, the snowy owl," said Grace, remembering to use her quiet voice. "He's been with us ever since we started out on the river."

"The snowy owl is a good omen." Konoyo gave Grace a rare smile.

Chapter 32

A Different Kind of Ladder

It was early afternoon when Leqte pointed ahead to a small river that opened into the Great River. "Ours," she said softly. They made for the northern bank near the mouth of the small river. Konoyo directed them to pull the canoe ashore. They could hear the roar of a waterfall upstream. It couldn't be too far away; the water was still white and foamy as it spilled into the Great River.

"The river is too rough for the canoe. We must carry the canoe past the falls," Leqte said. They left the task until morning. It was immediately apparent that there was to be no exploring along the bank or relaxation in the warm evening sun despite their early halt. Leqte drilled them on the language of the Bear-People. The closer they came to their destination, the more frantic she seemed, pushing them every spare minute.

The next morning Konoyo announced that the falls began high above, plunging from a steep bank. He had already been to see. Getting to and climbing above them was going to be tricky.

They carried the canoe along a natural spillway that ran parallel to the river. It had developed over the years, creating a smaller creek bed that carried a trickle of water winding its way from the river above the falls. After awhile they had to climb out of the spillway. Several deep pools made it impassable. The steadily rising hill along the spillway leading up to the falls was covered with loose rocks. Climbing up and following the spillway close to the edge was dangerous, especially with a canoe on their shoulders. A step in the wrong place sent an avalanche down the hill into the spillway creek bed.

Once they were even with the falls, however, the water was smooth enough for travel up river. Konoyo pointed, "Salmon."

"They will be battered and bruised by the falls, but they must return upriver to lay their eggs in the place where they were born," Leqte explained. This time she spoke in the Chumash language. "The new fish make their way down the river and out to the sea, only to return to lay their eggs. Soon people will come for the salmon run. They will catch fish and trade all along the Great River. It is a joyful time. But it is good that we are here before they come. They would distract us." Then she repeated the whole thing in the language of the Bear-People.

"It must be hard being a salmon!" Grace watched as a salmon plunged into the frothy standing wave at the base of the falls, flipped up in an arc toward the falls, body thrashing, tail moving wildly. "What can we do to help them?"

The salmon hit about halfway up the falls. A moment later is rose again, flailing to the top where the water was calm.

Konoyo gave Grace a puzzled look.

Mary Carol said, "We could build a fish ladder." She tried to explain about fish ladders.

J.D. helped, using his hands to explain. "In our land, people build pools by the river. Each pool is higher than the one before. The fish can jump to a pool, rest, and go on to the next."

Robert studied the spillway as they stood near the falls looking down, "What if we rolled a few boulders down the side of that spillway? We could take advantage of the gradual incline and the pools that are already there. I think we could get a couple of small avalanches going. We could turn this trickle into a stream and create three or four pools that take the salmon up past the falls."

Grace clapped her hands, in her enthusiasm,

"Then they wouldn't have such a hard swim!"

"But we'd have to figure how to divert water from the river," J.D. said. "It wouldn't be so easy."

"I'm serious. Look at those large rocks. They're big, but we could use a tree branch as a wedge. I think we could do it." Robert was determined.

"Besides, beavers build perfectly lovely dams with little more than sticks and mud," added Mary Carol.

"Then more of the salmon can return to their home," said Grace.

Leqte chided them for speaking in English. But it was hard to provide detailed explanations in the language of the Chumash village and impossible in the language of the Bear-People. Once they'd explained as best they could, Konoyo was skeptical. Leqte reminded him, "We must do as the young child says. She is like Chawnaway. She knows things."

Konoyo reluctantly had them make camp near the top of the falls. They spent the rest of the day working on the fish ladder. He entered into the work wholeheartedly, even though he'd expressed his opinion against it. He was good at calculating where to start rockslides, too.

Massive clouds of dust rose as rocks tumbled down, collecting others before settling into the creek bed. Konoyo was untroubled by the sound. Rock avalanches were not unusual along the river.

It took the better part of the morning and a good bit of sneezing from the dust before they got the trajectory right. Without Konoyo's help, they couldn't have done it. They piled brush around the existing pools and shaped their rock piles with more brush. Konoyo said it would wash against the rocks and hold them in place. Three days later they were finished. By this time, more salmon were gathering in the river below.

In the end, they were able to divert a small stream from the river above the falls with much less difficulty than they'd imagined. It gathered momentum, sending a wide swath of water down the spillway. The pools began to fill, each creating a little waterfall to the next pool as it overflowed. One of their dams didn't hold, washing brush to the next, it created a large pool, and left a greater leap up to the next pool. "But it isn't so bad as leaping up the big falls," said Mary Carol.

"Now, the question is, will the fish try it?" J.D. wondered, as they made their way down to stand at the first pool.

"I think they will." Grace pointed to a large salmon exploring the mouth of their stream. All of a sudden it rose into the air, flipping into the first pool.

Another followed. They couldn't take any more time, but they felt confident that the fish would find the new way easier.

"Here," said Konoyo. Reaching down, he fished an unusual silvery green stone from the edge of the first pool, handing it to Grace. "The fish thank you."

"They thank you, too," laughed Grace. She took the stone, looking at the others. They were all thinking the same thing. *Is it the fifth token?*

Konoyo was anxious to be off, fearing to be in one place too long. Even though it was late afternoon, they made ready to leave. A great snowy owl hooted and rose from one of the trees near their encampment, flying up-river. Konoyo nodded at it, smiling at Grace.

They stayed near the shore, out of the current until they were far above the falls. The canoe had to be hauled out of the water and carried around cataracts and rapids along the way, slowing progress. Konoyo didn't permit conversation when they were out on the river. Leqte said, "Sound carries on the water. It's better not to be heard."

When they were off the river, they pumped her for information about the Bear-People. She told them how the men dress in elaborate animal costumes to go hunting. "It is told that when they hunt, they change into bears."

Later, the children talked this over. J.D. said, "Think about it. If your enemies think you can change into a bear and you dress up like a bear, you've already won."

"Chawnaway didn't think they really turn into bears," said Grace.

"We ought to have some kind of noise maker to scare off the real bears," said Robert, "But I don't think Konoyo would be keen on that."

One afternoon, the trees along the river gave way to a large meadow on one side. Konoyo let Leqte take them into the meadow. There was a good view of the surrounding countryside. They were now well within the ring of fire-mountains. One stood apart, larger, more foreboding.

"That's Talol, the largest of the fire-mountains," said Leqte.

"Our mountain," said Grace.

Leqte exclaimed, "There are bad spirits at the top of Talol and a lake of fire!"

"But that's where we have to go," said Grace. She was certain of it.

Leqte looked alarmed. "I wish it were not so," she said. "I fear it more than the Bear-People."

"It's the mountain on the map," said Robert,

struggling to speak in the language of the Bear-People. "Gracie and Chawnaway say our path ends there."

Chapter 33

The Skirts of Talol

The river ran faster with more rapids. They were spending less time on it, carrying the canoe as often as not. Bright red vine maple signaled arrival of autumn. Mornings were crisp, afternoons pleasant.

Soon they would be at the skirts of Talol, the point at which Konoyo and Leqte were to turn back. The day came all too soon.

Leqte fussed over them, making sure their baskets and bags were full of provisions, worrying about autumn rains, reminding them to wear their cloaks. "We must go. I might be remembered. It would bring harm to you. Don't try to find the Bear-People. They will find you. When they do, treat them as if they were bears—with caution, but don't act afraid. Tell them you're on a quest, but under no circumstance tell them what you seek." Her advice was much like what Chawnaway told them. "The Bear-People may not help, but you must ask. They will be offended if you do not. Listen, but do not follow their advice. They may try to keep you from your quest, but you must go even if they refuse to help—though I wish it were not to Talol."

Konoyo and Leqte took the canoe. It was no longer useful in the high country and it would help on their return trip. The morning they left was cold and gray. Everyone felt gray inside, too.

"We've been pretty lucky to have help this far," said Mary Carol, lapsing into English. It was small comfort.

"The snowy owl is still with us," said Grace. "We aren't entirely alone."

High above, a great snowy owl rested on a branch. "Do you think it really is the same owl, Gracie?" Mary Carol asked.

"Yes," she said. "Now, we have a guardian owl. He's watching over us."

"I miss the coyote," said Robert. "I mean, in a pinch, wouldn't you rather have a coyote on your side? How much good could an owl be?"

"We need to be talking in the language of the Bear-People," Mary Carol reminded them.

The map was long-since dry, but no more easily

read than when they'd fished it out of the water. Grace gave up trying. They wandered in the thick forest for days, following Robert's compass as a guide, going north when the land permitted, sometimes doubling back and trying another route, but always climbing and always moving closer to Talol. Occasionally, they saw an animal that looked like a deer, though smaller. Squirrels and birds chattered above them. Sometimes, they saw the owl. There were times they felt certain they were being followed by some large animal, but they never saw so much as a track. Nor could they shake a nagging feeling that they were being watched, yet there was never any evidence of a watcher.

It started drizzling steadily. Every step was soggy. They followed a trail near the river, going north and up. At night they camped well off the trail, longing for a fire. But, following Konoyo's advice, they took no risks. Even if they'd been tempted, they'd have had a hard time finding anything dry enough to burn. "I always heard that if you get lost in the forest, you should look for the side of the tree the moss grows on because that will be north," said Mary Carol, lapsing into English. "But here the moss grows all around the trees."

"I think moss is growing between my toes," said Grace. At night they curled up in their cloaks, finding them surprisingly rain-resistant. They slept huddled together to conserve warmth. They felt damp all of the time.

A terrible rumbling awakened them one morning before dawn. The ground shook. Trees waved in all directions. It stopped as suddenly as it started. "What was that?" Mary Carol asked, sitting up in alarm.

"I think we can safely say that was an earthquake," said J.D.

"Thank God, nothing crashed on us," said Mary Carol. "I wasn't sure we'd live to tell the story." They'd experienced smaller tremors, the first well before Leqte and Konoyo left. Leqte said they were to be expected in the Bear Country.

"We got a good shaking," said Robert. "Expect an aftershock." He tried repeating himself in the language of the Bear-People, but he didn't have a word for "aftershock."

Despite the quake and fear of an aftershock, it was a glorious day. Soggy gray sky gave way to sunshine. A high meadow opened before them. Late summer flowers sparkled with dew. Talol's summit towered above. There was no question now. They were on the mountain. Snow-capped mountains ringed the crisp, blue horizon, their symmetry interrupted by the snowy expanse of Talol's summit rising before them.

The ground under them became unsteady just as they started across the sun-warmed meadow. Though short-lived, the aftershock was unnerving. "That's over," said Robert. "I hope."

They set off again, spirits lifted as they felt the sun warming them through. Suddenly, with no warning and from out of nowhere, frightful creatures—birds, goats, and bears with over-sized heads—surrounded them. "The Bear-People," said J.D. "Whatever you do, don't act afraid."

"I think I'd rather face the quake," Robert said.

"Or a volcano," said Mary Carol.

Grace was silent.

J.D. stood tall, taller than when they'd left home on the Santa Fe Chief. He looked fearless, though he felt all jelly inside. They were all frightened. Had they been able to see themselves, they'd have been surprised. J.D. wasn't the only one who'd grown taller and stronger. Dressed in the clothing of Chumash people, cloaks thrown back, heads held high, they looked courageous and confident.

"We come in peace." J.D. spoke the words Leqte had taught him in the language of the Bear-People.

A man dressed in bearskins removed his mask. "Come," he said. That was all. He set out and they followed, a frightful procession behind them.

"Try to think of it as a Halloween parade," J.D. muttered to the others.

"If this ends with cider and doughnuts, I'm for it," breathed Mary Carol.

Robert rolled his eyes. Grace said nothing. Her jaw was set, a determined look on her face.

The leader took them on a path across the meadow and further down the mountain toward the west where smoke rose from a village. Long bark huts, each with its own totem pole, dotted a clearing. They were led to a bark-covered longhouse standing at the center. Soon it filled with men, seating themselves in a circle. Women and children peered in.

They weren't experienced enough with the language to follow the rapid talk. But they caught the drift. Grace, who understood, said the village associated their coming with the earthquake. "They think we're sent by the spirit world."

"Don't let them blame that quake on us!" exclaimed Robert. "Think what they'll do if the volcano on their front doorstep erupts."

"Sounds like time for the presents," said J.D. They spoke in English for fear someone might understand the Chumash language.

"Tell them we've come to see the one who keeps the Sacred Fire," said Grace.

"Sacred fire?" asked Mary Carol. "What sacred fire?"

"It just came to me," said Grace. "It's what we have to say."

"If you say so, Gracie," said J.D. Nobody argued with her about such things, not anymore. Grace was no longer the darling, but spoiled, little girl who left Kansas City on the Santa Fe Chief. She spoke with maturity, kindness, and authority.

They were given presents of clothing and blankets. J.D. presented their gifts to the Chief, whose face lit up at the yarrow and sage. He put on the beads, but didn't know what to do with the mirror. When J.D. showed him how to look into it, he dropped it like a hot coal, calling for the shaman. The shaman thought it possessed powerful magic. It was left in his care, along with the yarrow and sage.

When J.D. said they'd come to see the Keeper of the Sacred Fire, there was complete silence.

"Are you certain?" asked the Chief at last.

"We must," said J.D. This was met with some animated talk around the room. Then the Chief motioned for silence, nodding to the shaman.

The shaman spoke so rapidly they couldn't follow. "He's reminding them of a lake of fire at the top of the mountain," explained Grace. "Nobody who goes there returns. The Keeper of the Sacred Fire seems to be a powerful shaman who protects them from the mountain. Otherwise, it will hurl rocks of fire down on them. They're afraid we'll anger the gods of the mountain."

"Oh, great, just what I thought," said Robert. "They're going to blame us for the earthquake."

"We need to be respectful," said Mary Carol, gently.

"You're right," said Robert, subdued. "We have to try and see things from their point of view."

Grace was firm. "J.D., you tell them we've been sent. Tell them that if we don't go, the gods will be angry. It's better if you speak."

J.D. spoke simply, and clearly.

When the Chief answered, they couldn't mistake his meaning. He was avoiding the subject. "We will talk more of this tomorrow. Tonight we feast and tell stories of our people."

So they feasted. Story followed story about mountains controlled by very disagreeable gods, who hurled rocks, trees, and fire at each other. The children were nodding long before the storyteller finished a wonderful story about a man who turned into a bear at night and tricked his brothers. They slept where they fell on the floor of the longhouse, the first time they'd felt warm and dry in days.

After more talk the next day, the Chief said, "We will not go with you, nor will we show you the way. We will speak more of this tomorrow." So another night was spent in the longhouse with feasting and stories. The long strips of roasted salmon were delicious. The stories were spellbinding, but the children couldn't enjoy themselves with the pressure of their mission bearing down on them.

Quietly, they agreed. There could be no more delay. The next morning, J.D. thanked the chief. "We go today."

This seemed to distress the Chief, who spoke against it. They were about to leave over his protest when a young man approached the Chief. He had returned that very morning from two weeks higher up on the mountain. He had been on a vision quest, part of his initiation into manhood. When he saw the children, he stopped, wide-eyed. "These children appeared to me in a vision," he said to the Chief. "I must help them."

The Chief was still against it, but promised he wouldn't interfere. The boy's vision was not to be taken lightly.

They left before the Chief could change his mind. The young man took them on a circuitous path, leading to a wild part of the mountain much higher up than they had been before. They camped there for the night.

Setting out at sunrise, they passed the tree line. Their climb was difficult. The young man spoke little, becoming more and more anxious as they went. He would not give them his name, even the name by which he was called, obviously fearful of speaking it in their presence.

About mid-morning, they reached the snow line. He pointed to a cave above. "In my vision, you were at this place. I will go now." He gave them a small totem of Bear, Raven, and Thunderbird. "The Chief sent this to guide you in the mountain."

They thanked him, sorry to see him go. He'd done what nobody else in the village had been willing to do. Suddenly he stopped. Looking back, he pointed, smiling. "A good omen." A snowy owl flew overhead, settling on a large rock above the entrance to the cave.

"A token?" asked J.D., fingering the totem.

"No." Grace said. "We will leave it at the mouth of the cave. The Chief meant well. The totem is for the Bear-People, not for us."

Going into a dark hole in the side of a volcanic mountain was a terrifying prospect. But they'd come too far to turn back.

Chapter 34

Deep Into the Mountain

They followed a narrow tunnel for some time, coming to a place where it branched into three separate passageways. "Looks like there's a fire in that one," said Robert.

"Somebody's roasting salmon," said J.D. It was unmistakable, the delicious aroma of salmon roasting over hot coals.

"Then, obviously, that is the direction we have to go in," said Robert. "That smell is making me ravenously hungry."

Grace wasn't so sure it was the right way, but as the fire looked to be only a short distance away, she agreed to see. It would be easy enough to return to the branching-off place and choose another path if they needed to.

"We're bound to find the Keeper soon," said Mary Carol. "Maybe it's him."

Soon they could see the silhouette of someone sitting at a small, open fire. When the path opened into a small cavern, they were almost overcome with joy and relief. By the fire was none other than Mr. Nichols, turning strips of salmon. He was dressed in buckskin trousers and shirt. He wore a headband beaded with porcupine needles. They would have thrown themselves on him had he not held up his hand. "Wait. I'm glad to see you, too, but we have important business. Hugging comes later."

"It can't really be you!" exclaimed Mary Carol.

"You are surprised, but as you see, I've been expecting you." He pointed to the salmon. "You've done well against all odds."

While they ate roasted salmon from long sticks, he asked about their trip, eager for details. "So there was a coyote that saved you, then? But you haven't seen him since you left the village. That's good. I agree with your first impression—the coyote is a trickster. You were lucky. Left to him, you would still be in the Chumash village. I wouldn't trust to luck again." Then as they told him about their trip up the coast, he puzzled over Muhu, "It looked like a gold tie clip, did it? You wouldn't find that kind of workmanship among these primitive people."

"The Chumash have silver, but not gold," said J.D. He fingered the silver owl Mr. Nichols had given him. It caught the light of the fire.

"There must be mischief at work," said Mr. Nichols. "Have you seen any other evidence of time travelers? There are few who can do so, and usually to no good purpose. It is just as well that we are all back together again. You may be in greater danger than I feared."

Looking at him, Mary Carol wondered why she had never noticed how handsome Mr. Nichols was. She had always thought of his face as kind and merry, for he was quick to laugh. Now, there was no laughter in his eyes, but he was more handsome than any movie star she'd ever seen on the cover of movie magazines. The others noticed the same thing in their own way. On the train they'd felt his goodness and warmth. Here, they felt his greatness and authority.

As they finished the salmon, they put the sticks into the fire to burn. "I brought something you probably didn't think you'd ever see again," he said. He gave each of them a very large chocolate bar with caramel. "A taste of home."

They would have eaten them at once, but for Grace. "We will save these for later," she said, setting hers aside. The others reluctantly set theirs aside, too. Even though she was the youngest, in some ways, she had become the leader.

"As you wish," Mr. Nichols shrugged, smiling at her. "So now that you are here at last, it is time to finish this quest. Gracie, I must have the tokens before we can go on."

Grace didn't move.

Robert started to take off his knapsack, but Mary Carol stopped him. "We mean no disrespect, Mr. Nichols, but Gracie is not allowed to show them to anyone but The Keeper."

Smiling, Mr. Nichols said, "I'm not just anyone, Mary Carol. And what makes you think I am not the Keeper?"

"You are not the Keeper," said Grace, matter-of-factly.

"Excellent!" exclaimed Mr. Nichols, rubbing his hands together in pleasure. "You have passed that test. Are you ready to come with me, then, Gracie?"

"I am," she said.

Mr. Nichols stood, offering her a hand. She took it, standing with his help. There was a strange expression on her face, but she said nothing.

Getting to his feet, J.D. said, "I'm glad you're here to go with us. This is the part I've been dreading most of all."

"No," said Mr. Nichols, motioning for him to

stay seated. "Only Gracie is permitted to enter the domain of the Keeper. You don't need to be afraid. I will be with her all the way. We will need that knapsack with the tokens, Rob. Relax, enjoy the fire and your chocolate. We'll be back before you know it."

"They have to come with me," said Grace, firmly.

"My child, you must do as I say," Mr. Nichols said tenderly. "Everything depends on it now."

"If they don't go, I don't go," repeated Grace stubbornly. The others stood in stunned silence. Grace was sounding like the old bratty Grace, making no pretense of being polite to Mr. Nichols.

"Look at me, my dear," said Mr. Nichols. "I don't think you understand how serious this is."

Grace looked at her feet. "I understand," she said firmly. "You are not Mr. Nichols."

The others were dumbfounded. J.D. looked at him intently, suddenly understanding Grace. "You may look like Mr. Nichols, but you are not him. In fact, I don't even think you look like him," he said.

Suddenly, the man's appearance changed completely. They all wondered how they could have mistaken him for Mr. Nichols. "Such clever children. Mr. Nichols will be proud of you," he said. "I couldn't meet you here as a complete stranger, so you must forgive me for impersonating your friend. It was absolutely necessary to determine if you are the children sent for the crystal, especially with the threat of other time travelers as a possibility. You have passed every test that I have set for you.

"It is only fair to tell you who I am. My name is Sandastros. I am the Keeper of the Crystal. I have come to help you find your way through the mountain, for it is a long and perilous way. Let us go now, and we will complete this difficult quest. You can claim the crystal and return to your home. That's what you want most, is it not, to go home and for your father to be well again? We must not delay any longer."

J.D., Mary Carol, and Robert could feel the rightness of what he was saying. They picked up their things to follow.

"NO. You may not go with us," said Grace, fumbling for something in her bag. She still looked down at her feet.

Smiling at her patiently, he asked, "And what gives you the authority to tell the Keeper of the Crystal how to do his work?"

"You are not the Keeper," said Grace resolutely.

"Oh, but my stubborn little friend, it is I who must take you to the Keeper." There was an ever-so-slight threat in his soft voice.

"You cannot harm anyone who will not let you." This time Grace looked at him, a stern expression on her face. Stamping her foot, she said, "Now go! Be gone!" With that she threw a handful of something on the fire. The smell of sage, juniper, and cedar filled the cavern as the fire crackled and smoke rose.

Suddenly, Sandastros' beautiful face contorted into cold fury. "You have had your chance. Fools! And you, most of all, you proud *little* girl. Never think for a minute that you can do this without me." With that, he vanished.

Grace sat back down hard, shaking all over. Mary Carol wrapped her own cloak around her and held her.

"The one Chawnaway said we should fear," said J.D.

"What was that you threw on the fire?" asked Mary Carol in awe.

Regaining her composure, Grace said, "It's for driving away evil spirits. Chawnaway gave it to me."

"He had me fooled," said J.D. "But then, when he didn't recognize the owl he gave me, I had a strange feeling. And he called the Chumash people primitive—Mr. Nichols would never have been so disrespectful."

"Maybe this would be a good time to eat that chocolate," said Robert, hopefully.

"Throw it away," said Grace. "Throw it on the fire where it can't harm anyone."

Reluctantly, they threw the chocolate bars onto the fire. There were four sharp cracks and a foul smoke rose into the air.

"Let's get out of here," said J.D. "Cover your faces with your cloaks."

"That smoke is toxic. Back to the entrance," said Robert.

They reached the entrance to the mountain gasping for breath. "So how did you know it wasn't him, Gracie?" asked Robert, when he'd caught his breath.

"It felt wrong. Mr. Nichols called me Grace. He said, 'Gracie.' He'd been by the fire, but he was cold as ice. He didn't want us to hug him because he has no warmth in him. He is ice all through."

"More beautiful than anybody I've ever seen, but cold as ice," said Mary Carol. "You could see it in his eyes. He is even more beautiful than Celeste."

"Chawnaway says that evil has no power over us if we don't let it into our hearts," said Grace.

"I never thought about evil looking so kind and,

well, so beautiful," said Mary Carol, at a loss for words.

"Think about it," said J.D. "Who'd want to follow somebody who looked all snarly and wicked?"

"I hate to think what would have happened if we'd given him the tokens," said Robert.

"Or eaten that chocolate," said J.D.

"But we didn't!" said Mary Carol. "We stuck together."

They allowed themselves a short rest, giving the tunnel time to clear of smoke. When they entered again, it was as if they were entering an altogether different place.

Chapter 35

The Keeper's Due

Dark tunnels and passages led every which way. Several times they stopped, so Grace could decide which path to choose—it seemed to go around and around, but always downward, deeper into the mountain.

After what seemed like hours, they began to climb up again. Nobody was sure how long the path wound upward. Mary Carol was wondering if they'd go around and around forever when the narrow tunnel curved sharply and opened into a cavernous room. High above, fissures in the rock let in fresh air. A shaft of light streamed down, giving the cavern the feeling of a domed cathedral.

A pool of red-hot lava bubbled up from a wide fissure along one side of the room. "The Lake of Fire," whispered J.D. Without cool drafts from above, the heat would have been unbearable. Near the center of the wall to the right of the pool was a large raised platform. This dais was built from stones so skillfully placed that its floor was nearly smooth. At the back of the dais a carved wooden screen extended across its entire length. A handful of men and women sat on fur pelts on the floor below the dais, silently watching.

Robert whispered, "It's like being in a palace."

"Or a church or temple or something," Mary Carol said in awe.

"What do you think, Gracie?" J.D. looked at her intently. Ever since they'd left Sandastros and entered the long winding tunnels of the mountain, he'd been worried. He had the strong impression that this would be the hardest part of their journey, harder than going without food or water, harder than being without their parents. He felt something sinister that he couldn't name. He was pretty sure Grace felt it, too. But her jaw was set.

She sighed. "We're at the end."

An old man stood. His long, white hair and flowing, white leather garments gave him a magical look. He spoke kindly, "Welcome, children. All is ready." With that he clapped his hands sharply, three times.

The people who'd been sitting around the room

snapped into action. The children were offered cushions and motioned to sit on the dais. Pottery bowls full of steaming soup, flat bread, and a mixture of dried salmon, roots, and berries were brought. When they'd had their fill, they were taken to bathe in the waterfall of an underground stream. Long white tunics of the softest leather were laid out for them to wear. The old man beckoned for them to sit with him, this time on fur pelts below the dais and facing it.

He sighed a great sigh, looking at Grace. "I will speak with you in the Chumash language, for you know it better. I have lately dreamed of your coming. I am the Keeper. The crystal is bound by its own rules. We must observe them. Are you absolutely certain, child? This must be of your free choice."

"I am certain," said Grace.

"Then so it shall be." The Keeper had a look of great sadness. Mary Carol thought that parting with the crystal must be very hard for him.

The sinister feeling weighed more heavily on J.D. He wondered if Sandastros was nearby. He had a feeling it was something else, though, something no less sinister.

The man clapped his hands sharply again. With that, a series of costumed dancers appeared on the dais, each performing a dance accompanied by drum, shakers, and wooden flutes. A bird dancer swooped and whirled. The bird was followed by another, more fierce looking, two-headed bird. A wolf dancer and a black bear leapt and snapped huge jaws. Other dancers were not in full costume, but wore frightening masks with leering faces. As they danced, the music became more frenzied, going faster and faster. Suddenly there was silence. The dancing stopped as abruptly as it had begun.

The Keeper stood. Taking Grace's hand, he led her to the dais. There he spread out a white fur pelt and bade her to sit, facing J.D., Mary Carol, and Robert. The musicians began a mournful chant, accompanied by a stringed instrument this time. The music rose and fell like the wind. Mary Carol thought it was the saddest melody she had ever heard. Tears welled up in her eyes.

The Keeper drew a circle around Grace with colored sand, placing a garland of leaves on her head. "What gifts have you brought?" he asked.

Grace nodded to Robert, He handed her the condor feather, the dried flower, the basket of yarrow, the abalone shell, and the rock from the river. The Keeper took each of these, placing them on the dais inside the circle with Grace.

Disappearing behind the wooden screen, he returned. A boy accompanied him carrying a beautifully carved wooden box. Kneeling, the boy placed it on the floor in front of Grace. She opened it, lifting out a golden box covered with precious stones. "Open it, child," said the Keeper. "It is your right and your burden."

Grace lifted the latch that held the golden box closed. A soft light shone from the box as she raised the jeweled lid. Inside was a rock about the size of the Keeper's hand and a silver goblet. Grace removed the goblet first. It magically filled with wine. She set it upright in the golden box so the wine wouldn't spill, then lifted out the rock. It was much lighter to hold than she expected and cool to the touch. Light clung to its surface like an aura. Catching the light from the fire, the rock sent an explosion of colors dancing around the cavern. The Last Crystal! In its center was a bubble, water from the beginning of time to heal their father and take them home.

The foreboding J.D. felt was nearly unbearable. Now Robert sensed it, too. They exchanged fearful glances.

Mary Carol felt it in her own way. Certain that they were missing something important, she tried to remember everything Celeste had said. Tears ran involuntarily down her cheeks.

Grace gravely set the Last Crystal on the fur rug. Watching her closely, Mary Carol felt that something terrible was about to happen.

The Keeper asked Grace to hold the goblet high. As she did so, he waved the condor feather over it, laying it on the wooden box. The flower, yarrow, the shell, and the stone were waved over the wine in turn. Rising, he took the gifts to the pool of lava and threw them in, one by one. Flames leapt up, burning brightly for a moment as the fire received each gift.

Mary Carol heaved a great sigh as the abalone shell met the flame. There was something about losing it that felt unbearably sad.

"Drink, my child." Grace could hear a soft, sweet, familiar voice coming from the goblet of wine.

It was like a dream. Light now shone from the goblet. Looking into it, Grace saw Daddy and Mamma the way they looked before Daddy left for the war such a long time ago. Their image faded. Celeste's eyes were looking at her. "Drink this lovely wine, my dear. It will refresh you. Your work is almost done. Soon your daddy will be well. Drink, and everyone will be home again."

Grace felt as if she were being pulled into the wine. There was something she must remember, but suddenly she was too exhausted. She sighed, still looking into the goblet. She felt sluggish. Everything was in slow motion.

Suddenly, Robert understood. "It's her! It's Celeste! She can see Celeste," he cried. "Don't look, Gracie. She's trying to pull you into her power."

"Drink all of it, dear." Celeste urged softly. "Don't expect the others to understand what you must do. You are the only one brave enough to do this. That is why I chose you. You have come so very far. Now, you must have the courage to go on in spite of them."

As Grace slowly lifted the goblet to her lips, several things happened at the same time. "Don't drink it!" J.D. screamed. Robert took a dive, knocking the goblet from her hand as J.D. leapt into the circle and threw his arms around Grace, pinning her down.

The wine spilled, bursting into sparks that sputtered and shot into the air like aerial fireworks. Reaching the top of the cavern, they exploded into showers of color.

Wrenching free, Grace grabbed the crystal, clinging to it. J.D. pulled her to her feet and threw his arms around her again, holding tightly. "I see what you're doing," he said to the Keeper. "There were five tokens. Gracie is supposed to be the sixth, isn't she? She makes it a perfect number. But you're wrong if you think we brought Gracie in *exchange* for the crystal. You are not going to put her in the fire! We won't let you."

Now on the dais, Mary Carol threw her arms around Grace, too.

Grace struggled to break free, crying hysterically. "Let me go! I saw Daddy and Mamma. Don't you see? It will make Daddy well. We can go home. Let me go! I have to do this. Please. Can't you understand? I'll go in the pool of fire, then we'll be home. I just want to go home."

"No, Gracie," Mary Carol said. Joining them, Robert wrapped his arms around J.D. and Mary Carol.

"Celeste never meant you to go home or for Daddy to be well," said Mary Carol, gently. "What she wants is a terrible thing. Celeste wants to *exchange* you for the crystal. It's a horrible, wicked plan. It's part of her evil magic."

"Gracie," J.D. said sternly. "Daddy would never accept this. If you exchange yourself for the crystal, it won't help him and we'll be in the hands of that evil woman."

The Keeper stood back, making no attempt to intervene. J.D. turned to him, "You said we have to follow the rules of the magic. When you have your perfect number, the magic will work. That means Gracie has to be put in that lava pool like the other tokens. Celeste will have the crystal, and Gracie will be lost to us forever."

"That I do not know." The Keeper spoke calmly. "I know nothing of a perfect number. My part is to keep the Last Crystal until it is claimed. This I have done as did my father before me and his father before him. I do not govern the crystal. It is not my wish to take your sister to the fire. But if she is to claim the crystal, it will be in exchange for her life. It cost a human life to bind the crystal with dark magic. It will cost a life to free the crystal. That is not mine to change, though I would, were it in my power. What happens after is not mine to know."

Letting go of his hold on Grace, J.D. turned to the Keeper, "If a life has to be taken, then take mine. You can't have Gracie. I'm the eldest. It's my responsibility to take care of my brother and sisters. It's a promise I made to my mother." His voice was firm, though he was shaking and pale as a ghost. "I will go to the fire in her place."

Chapter 36

The Pool of Fire

"No, J.D.! Don't do it. It's evil magic!" said Robert. Letting go of Grace, he put his hands on J.D.'s shoulders, looking him directly in the eyes. "This isn't about getting to go home. Don't you see? Gracie has to die so Celeste can have her crystal. That's all. That's the end of it. We could all jump in the fire and it wouldn't change things. It's Gracie she wants. She's planned this all along. She expects Gracie to throw herself in the fire."

Gracie wasn't fighting now. Still holding the crystal, she leaned into Mary Carol, sobbing.

"If you do not wish the crystal, it is not my part to make you take it," said the Keeper. "But if you want the crystal, it must be bought with the life of this child. None other will do."

"NO!" declared Mary Carol, emphatically. "No. Nobody's going to die. Not Gracie. Not J.D. We'll go back to Chawnaway. We've come this far. We can go back. We'll live together. Then maybe we can figure out a way to get home, but not like this. Does anybody really think Mamma and Daddy could bear it if they knew we let this happen? It would be easier for them to think we all died than for them to learn we'd done such an awful thing. It would be better to live without ever seeing Mamma and Daddy again than to let Celeste have Gracie or you, J.D." She smoothed the hair back from Gracie's face. "Oh, Gracie, don't you see? This isn't a fairy tale. Nobody gets to live happily ever after."

"We were lost the minute we jumped off that train," J.D. was grim. Looking at the others, he said, "All we have is each other."

"Gracie, we're a family. If we lose each other, there isn't anything left," Mary Carol said. "We can't let you do this. I think you have to tell the Keeper that you don't want the crystal. You have to refuse, no matter how much you want to make Daddy well. No matter how much you want to go home."

"You have to tell him. He can't listen to us," said Robert. "That's how this nasty business works. He can't change the magic. Remember, Chawnaway said he has to follow the rules of the magic?"

"I cannot change the magic." The Keeper waited

patiently, unmoving.

It was completely silent in the cavern except for occasional shifting in the pool of fire. Not a sound came from the musicians on the floor behind them.

Mary Carol stroked Grace's hair. "Gracie, you have to have the strength to say, 'No,' to the crystal. Then we're free of it. We can't fix this. But we can walk away from it. Whatever happens after, we face it together."

They waited.

"I don't want the crystal," said Grace at last, looking up at the Keeper. "It would be wrong. It was the worst bad luck that anybody ever had when we met that awful woman," she sobbed, offering the crystal to the Keeper. He nodded to his son, who took it.

"I don't want Daddy to die. But I don't want to die either and I don't want J.D. to die. I don't want anybody to die! I want Mamma and Daddy." Gracie burst into violent sobbing again, clinging to Mary Carol with one arm, reaching out to J.D. and Robert with the other.

At just that moment the floor of the cavern began to shake. The children held on to each other. The musicians threw themselves on the floor.

"It's the mountain! They've angered the

mountain," came a booming voice from the shadows behind the musicians.

In the confusion, the boy dropped the crystal on the fur pelt in the circle, where it lay by the golden box. He ran to the Keeper who put his arms around him, shielding him from the quake. It was worse than the one before they met the Bear-People. Rocks fell from above. Lava spewed up from the pool, splashing out onto the floor. The children were terrified that the volcano would erupt or the mountain would collapse. But the quake subsided. All was still.

The voice from the shadows spoke firmly, "The mountain must have its due. Give the children to the mountain, or we are doomed. They must all die!" Leaving their instruments, the musicians rushed up onto the dais. One grabbed J.D. Another jumped on him from behind.

J.D. put up a good fight, but he was no match for two grown men. Others grabbed Robert, Mary Carol, and Grace, quickly binding the hands and feet of all four children.

"NO! It can't end this way," sobbed Mary Carol, "not after all we've been through!"

The Keeper placed himself between the children and the lava pool. He motioned for the musicians to stop. They refused, demanding to sacrifice the children to the mountain. "There will be no sacrifice," the Keeper said. They overpowered him and the boy, binding them, too.

"The girl belongs to me!" called the voice from the shadows. A man wrapped in a dark cloak stepped out of the shadows, coming to the dais. He gestured to the musicians.

Drums began beating wildly. Two musicians carried Grace to the lava pool to throw her into the fire. J.D., Robert, and Mary Carol watched, helplessly waiting their turn. "I love you, Gracie!" screamed Mary Carol.

"I love you!" They all shouted it together.

The man from the shadows stepped up on to the dais, holding his hand up to stay the musicians carrying Grace. "Put her down. She is mine."

"It's him, it's that imposter!" yelled J.D.

"How nice to be recognized," said Sandastros, smiling a self-satisfied smile. Calmly, slowly, as though he had all the time in the world, he stood looking down at them where they lay helplessly tied. His voice was smooth and sweet. "It is so very sad that you chose not to work with me. Now you won't get to go home. Your father will probably die. You will die. The magic holding the crystal will be broken and I shall have it all to myself. Good for me."

The musicians were still holding Grace. He reached to take her from them when an ear-splitting roar came from behind the carved screen. It was so loud and terrible they thought it would shake the mountain. Sandastros stepped back into the shadows.

Out from behind the carved screen lunged an enormous brown bear on its hind legs, the largest they'd ever seen. It turned on the men who were carrying Grace.

"Put her down gently, or you will answer to the Great Bear," said the Keeper from the spot on the floor where he'd been left.

Everything was chaos. An enormous white owl swooped down from the top of the cavern. "The Owl and the Bear!" screamed one of the musicians.

"It's a sign!" screamed another. "The end of all things!" The men set Grace down and ran, holding their hands over their faces to protect themselves from the owl's sharp, curved talons.

"Stop!" commanded Sandastros, stepping out of the shadows again. "We must feed the mountain. The mountain will not forget." Heedless of him, people ran in all directions. The owl swooped around, herding them out. The bear followed, his enormous paws cuffing any who got in his way.

Meanwhile, in the midst of the chaos, the Keeper rolled to the edge of the dais. Rubbing the ropes around his wrists on a ceremonial knife, he freed himself. Staying low to the floor, he crept up to the others, using the knife to make quick work of freeing J.D., Mary Carol, and Robert. "Stay down," he whispered. "This is not over."

Ignoring the chaos, Sandastros calmly lifted Grace from where the musicians had dropped her. "I am sorry that it had to come to this, my dear," he said in the most pleasant, matter-of-fact voice. "It would have been so much easier if you had obeyed me when you had the chance. Of course, you would have had to go into the fire anyway to break the spell binding the crystal. But it would have been so much more elegant. I do so hate inelegance."

Grace said nothing. She didn't struggle.

Without letting go of her, Sandastros knelt by the Keeper's son. He spoke in a gentle, but persuasive, voice, "Now, I must have the crystal. Give the crystal to me and all will come to the end. There is no reason you and your father should have to go into the fire, too."

But the Keeper's son did not have the crystal.

"Where is the crystal? I must have the crystal," Sandastros demanded.

The boy nodded to the circle where the crystal glowed softly, resting between the golden box and the empty goblet where he had dropped it. They all saw it at once. Robert was the closest.

"Get it, Robbie," cried Mary Carol. "We can't let him have it!"

Robert jumped up, racing across the dais.

In his eagerness, Sandastros dropped Grace, who landed on a fur pelt. Leaping over her, he threw himself at the crystal like a short-stop diving for first base. Knocking Robert off his feet, he grabbed it with both hands before anyone could intercept him. In the same instant, Sandastros realized his fatal mistake. Magic still clung to the crystal.

The Keeper now stood, "Neither Angel, nor Immortal, nor Mortal Man, nor Beast," he intoned.

Sandastros tried to drop the crystal, but he couldn't. It was like an electric field with a current running through him, shaking him. For an instant he shone through like a light. Then he dropped the crystal and vanished.

The Keeper hastily untied Grace and his son. The last of the musicians had already disappeared into the tunnels. The owl flew to a perch high above in the cavern.

The children were never quite sure what happened

next. The owl gave three short, raspy hoots and swooped down. There was a burst of blinding light and where the owl should have been stood Mr. Nichols—the real Mr. Nichols with his kind eyes and warm arms outstretched.

Grace and Mary Carol threw themselves at him. Robert and J.D. were right behind. "It really is you!" said Grace. There was no mistaking.

"You were the owl?" gasped J.D.

Mr. Nichols laughed his jolly, comfortable laugh, hugging all four at once. "I've been with you every step of the way. But I couldn't interfere without destroying your chances of survival until Grace gave up the crystal. It was part of the magic binding it."

"Then you were the owl and the coyote," said Robert. "I knew there was something. . . ."

"Oh, no. I am always myself," interrupted Mr. Nichols. "Perhaps you've seen an owl and a coyote when you've looked at me?"

The bear now returned, ending further conversation. Still standing on his hind legs, he waited expectantly, like the tamest of beasts.

"Just a minute," said Mr. Nichols. "If you can leave off hugging, there's one more thing to do." He nodded to the Keeper.

The children watched in complete and utter amazement as Mr. Nichols took the bear by the head and began to spin it around and around. Then he and the Keeper lifted it off, handing it to the boy.

There, free of an enormous head mask, stood just about the last person they would have ever expected to see. Uncle James held out furry, bearskin arms. "Did you think I'd let somebody throw you off my train and not do anything about it?" he asked, hugging them close.

"We weren't thrown, we jumped," said J.D., weakly.

"Here, let me get out of this hot bear suit," said Uncle James.

Meanwhile, Mr. Nichols picked up the wine goblet. "I believe Celeste has heard enough," he said, throwing it into the lava pool. The last drops of wine shot into the air like so many Roman candles that fell into the pool in a blaze of crackling lights. He motioned for the boy to pick up the crystal. "You've done well. I'll be back for this. Put it where you think best, but not in these terrible boxes." Picking up the ornate golden box in which the crystal had been kept and the wooden box that held them both, he heaved them into the lava pool. There was one last shower of fireworks as the boxes were consumed by fire.

The crystal no longer glowed. The magic binding it to Celeste was now spent. It was beautiful in its natural light, clear and translucent. The Keeper took it from the boy, wrapping it in a blanket. Mr. Nichols followed him behind the screen. Presently, they returned carrying a roughly hewn plank table with two benches piled on top. The children helped set the benches down. The Keeper spread a white linen cloth over it. The cloth seemed out of place in their rough surroundings.

Then he disappeared again behind the carved screen. "Shall we have some dinner?" Mr. Nichols asked.

"I'm not sure I remember how to sit at a table," said Mary Carol, able to laugh at last.

Chapter 37

Questions and More Questions

"Now about those questions," Uncle James began. The girls sat on either side of him across from the boys and Mr. Nichols. "I think our friend has more answers than I do."

"Okay, okay," Mr. Nichols laughed, holding up his hands as if to defend himself. He told them how his twin sister gave up her sacred charge as Keeper of the Seven Crystals, using them one by one to add beauty and years to her life. "Celeste didn't have magical powers as a mortal except for those she put in place to hold the crystals. But she once did. She knew that her powers would be limited when she became a mortal, so she bound the crystals to herself while she could. Each of the crystals was hidden in a golden box someplace on the Earth where only she could claim it. Neither Angel, nor Immortal, nor Mortal Man, nor Beast could open one of the boxes holding a crystal without forfeiting his or her life and unleashing all manner of curses on the world. It was Grace Willis—she was about your age, Grace, a bit older—who figured out how to get around the magic and take the Last Crystal from where Celeste had hidden it in a black alabaster box. But she did it at great cost to herself. She couldn't finish the work, but in some strange way that I can't explain, the crystal was bound to her and through her to her children."

"That's why Celeste wasn't in want of a boy," asked Robert, "because of the girl who figured out how to take the crystal from the alabaster box?"

"I expect so," said Uncle James. "There were some things about the magic that I don't think even Celeste understood."

Mr. Nichols explained, "Celeste had a lot of control over the people who became involved with the crystal. I figured that the only way to keep it from her was to take the crystal back into time. When Celeste gave up being an Immortal, she knowingly renounced her ability to travel in time. So I found a Keeper. It's been in the family of the Keepers ever since, passing from father to firstborn. Unfortunately both the Keeper and I were bound by the rules of the magic. It took me a long time to understand it. There was a particularly nasty twist. The golden box holding the crystal was sealed at the cost of a life. It could not be opened—not even by

Celeste—without another life being forfeited."

Uncle James added, "But Mr. Nichols found a way around that, too."

"I knew something Celeste didn't know. There's a deeper magic than the magic that bound that box. The dark magic led Celeste to count on selfishness. If the one who claimed the crystal were to show unselfish acts of kindness, then willingly refuse the crystal, the magic surrounding it would be broken completely," Mr. Nichols said.

"Thank God for that!" exclaimed Mary Carol.

The Keeper and the boy returned with bowls of soup and a plate of flat bread. "My friend and his son had to follow the rules, too," said Mr. Nichols.

"We did," said the Keeper. "Terrible rules." He pulled a stool up to one end of the table. His son seated himself at the other.

"Was the wine so she wouldn't feel the fire?" asked Robert.

"Do you honestly think Celeste would give two cents about that?" asked Mary Carol.

Uncle James said, "Its real purpose was so Celeste could command anyone who opened the golden box. It was part of the old magic. She would command them to drink it, they would come completely under her power, and then willingly go to their death."

"That was the hardest moment," said the Keeper.

J.D. felt anger boiling up. "How could you play with Gracie's life! What if she hadn't refused? What if she'd agreed? And what if we'd let her? You'd have watched her throw herself into the fire?"

"We wouldn't have let that happen," said Uncle James.

"I'd have searched for another way." Mr. Nichols looked at the Keeper. "You were counting on us, right, friend?"

The Keeper's face lit up with a smile. "I was."

The Keeper finished his soup and began collecting the bowls. "Now, we take our leave," he said. "You have freed my son from having the burden I have carried these many years. Thank you, all of you."

After they said their good-byes, Mr. Nichols continued, "You didn't let it happen, either. By crying out when you did, Robert, you broke the connection with Celeste and saved Grace before we had to step in and find another way. Grace had to have an opportunity to refuse the crystal. She couldn't have done that if she were completely in Celeste's power. And J.D., it was beyond Celeste to imagine anyone willingly giving himself up to save someone else."

"That one act of selfless love was more important than you can imagine, J.D.," said Uncle James.

Mr. Nichols nodded in agreement. "It was a shattering blow to the magic."

"J.D., what did you mean about the perfect number?" asked Mary Carol. "There wasn't exactly time to ask."

"It's why I thought Gracie was supposed to be counted as one of the tokens," said J.D. "Six is a perfect number. A perfect number is one that's equal to the sum of all the things it can be divided by without a remainder. So $1 + 2 + 3 = 6$ with six as the perfect number. We had feathers, a flower, yarrow, an abalone shell, and a rock. When the Keeper put them in the circle with Gracie, then into the fire, I realized that Grace would make six and she'd have to go into the fire, too. At least it seemed like that would be how magic works."

"Ancient people often gave perfect numbers magical properties," said Mr. Nichols. "I think that's what Celeste thought. She never understood that the gifts had to do with kindness, not with numbers. And in that sense, J.D., when you offered to take Gracie's place, you made the perfect number."

J.D. didn't know what to say.

"I have a question," said Robert. "Why didn't

you just throw us outside the mountain instead of making us walk all the way from New Mexico nearly to Canada?"

"I didn't have anything to do with where you left the train. I could see what was likely to happen. Once you were off, I couldn't interfere. But every step that you took without knowing your path, every act of sacrifice, every bit of courage and act of kindness unraveled Celeste's powerful magic. She thought the map was about directions," said Mr. Nichols.

He paused momentarily, thinking. "You see, we Immortals had something to learn, too. We wanted the earth to be protected. So the crystals were set aside for healing of the earth. But there's more than one way to heal the earth. When you covered your camp sites, when you took only what you absolutely needed to live, you were healing and repairing the earth."

"But that's just being responsible!" exclaimed Robert.

"Being responsible is how we save the earth," said Mr. Nichols. "I think we Immortals had it wrong about the crystals. We meant them for good. Water from the crystals would have healed the earth at times of great need, but it would have protected people from the consequences of their choices. In the end, it is mortals who must care for the earth—

people like you. The Last Crystal shouldn't remain here. I will take it to the Immortals. They will decide what is to be done with it."

"There's something I don't understand," said Grace. "Why us? Why me?"

"Yeah, we're just ordinary kids," said Robert.

"Not to me," said Uncle James. "What do you say to that, Mr. Nichols?"

"I don't know," said Mr. Nichols. "But it was you, and you met the challenge."

"I keep thinking of that red abalone shell," said Mary Carol. "There was something about it—it was so beautiful. I was sorry to see it destroyed. I wish we'd been able to keep it to remember, like your shell, Uncle James. . . ."

"How did you get here anyway, Uncle James?" Robert interrupted. "You haven't answered that question. Are you magic, too?"

Uncle James laughed. "Not me! That's another sort of magic. Mr. Nichols magic, though I don't think he'd call it magic. But that's another story, too."

"Uncle James, you were in this all along!" exclaimed Mary Carol. For the first time, she noticed that there was a twinkle in his eyes.

He laughed, "I guess you could say I've been in it since before I was born."

"What he means," said Mr. Nichols, "is that when he was born, I promised his mother I'd keep an eye on him. And I have. You see, it was his birth mother who opened the alabaster box—Grace Willis. But as he says, that's another story."

"Will we ever get to see Chawnaway and Konoyo and Leqte again?" said Mary Carol.

"And how come Chawnaway's name is Grace? I'd like to know that story," said Grace.

"Once Mr. Nichols has his eye on you, you never know," said Uncle James, grinning. "Here, let me take the rest of these things." He stood, collecting their remaining dishes and disappeared behind the wooden screen.

"Uncle James didn't answer my question," said Grace.

Robert was the first one to notice that their table was shaking ever so slightly. "Oh, no, not aftershock!" he said. It wasn't an earthquake, though. It was a steady motion moving them forward. And there were large glasses of lemonade sitting on the linen-covered table in front of them.

"So what about some dessert?" asked Mr. Nichols without so much as batting an eye. "Do you think they have any more of that chocolate cake?" He motioned for Mr. Elijah. "Maybe with some ice cream?"

"Chocolate cake!" exclaimed J.D. "Chocolate we can actually eat?"

They were in the dining car. People were eating and talking as if nothing more extraordinary than a train delay had happened.

"Five pieces of chocolate cake coming right up," smiled Mr. Elijah, "with vanilla ice cream."

"Where's Uncle James?" asked Grace.

"I expect he'll be meeting you in L.A. I think there's somebody else who'd like to see you," Mr. Nichols said. "She'd much rather ride in your purse than in my pocket."

"Kitty!" cried Grace. "But my purse is all worn out."

"Is it?" he asked, handing Kitty to her.

Grace looked down to see her purse with the kewpie doll face. And she was wearing the same dress she'd had on so very long ago. The others were wearing their train clothes, too.

"Oh!" said Mary Carol with relief. "My second-best dress—except maybe it's my best dress after what we've been through together."

Robert's knapsack was on the seat beside him, though it looked decidedly less stuffed than when they jumped off the train.

"Where did you find her?" Grace asked, hugging Kitty.

Mr. Nichols ignored the question, eyes sparkling. "It was only a slight delay after all. We should be in L.A. before night."

Grace started to put Kitty in her purse. There was her music box safely tucked inside. "Oh, Mr. Nichols, thank you. Does it work now?"

"Well, I don't know about that, but we couldn't very well leave it there buried in the wrong time. If anyone dug it up, they wouldn't understand it at all, would they? Now Robert, your notebook is another matter. I managed to dry it out, but it looks waterlogged all the same. I'm afraid the only part I could save was your army patch collection." He handed Robert the notebook.

"Gosh! Thank you, Mr. Nichols. I thought it was gone forever."

"What about Sandastros?" asked Mary Carol, changing the subject. "He just appeared at the last minute and almost had us fooled."

"That is a part of the story I did not know at first," said Mr. Nichols, pausing for just a moment as Mr. Elijah brought their cake and ice cream. "I always thought that Celeste chose to give up her immortality, knowing the consequence full well. But along the way I learned that Sandastros wanted the crystals for himself. He tricked her into giving up her immortality in exchange for the dark magic so that he could have them. He didn't count on her skill as a magician or her stubbornness as a mortal so he was never able to get them from her as he hoped."

"So maybe the crystal was freed at the cost of a life after all," said J.D. "His life."

"Not exactly. Beings like Sandastros have a way of reassembling and appearing again to do mischief," said Mr. Nichols. "But you need not fear him. He has no power over you."

They were just about to leave the dining car when Miss Spright came in. "I see that you are back," she said. "Well done."

Mary Carol couldn't help looking at her shoes, but they were laced up and tied smartly. "Mary Carol, dear, I think you must have dropped your blanket. I found it on the floor by your seats. I folded it and put it on your seat—such a fine blanket. I'd hate for you to lose it."

Mr. Nichols was with them later, as they gathered their things. As the train pulled up to the station in

L.A., they could see Uncle James waiting for them on the platform.

"It was awfully nice meeting four such interesting and well-mannered children," said Miss Spright, as they waited to get off of the train. "Perhaps we shall see each other again. I'd like that."

"Are you magic?" Grace asked her point blank.

"Magic? Everybody has a bit of magic in them, don't you think?" Miss Spright looked at Mr. Nichols, smiling. "Besides, it would be such a dull world if everything could be explained."

It wasn't a satisfying answer.

When they got off the train, they thanked Mr. Raymond. He told them good-bye, giving them all a big group-hug. "Maybe I'll catch you on the return trip," he said.

Mr. and Mrs. Hackworth hurried past, pausing long enough for Mr. Hackworth to say, "Did you get that Red Cap for our luggage, George?"

"Excuse me, Mr. Hackworth," said Mary Carol politely, "his name is Mr. Raymond Lincoln Moses."

*****

U.S. Army Air Force pilot John David Harrison was at home when the children returned at the end of the summer. He had lost a leg, but he could walk with crutches. Many men and women were unable to return home to their families after fighting in that war. The children felt lucky that their Daddy was alive and well.

One evening at supper Mamma said, "Oh, my! I almost forgot. When your father and I got home, there was a letter from a woman I met when she was a little girl. She said that she met you four on the Chief. She was very complimentary of your behavior. She is working in L.A. for that big aircraft company, Lockheed-Vega. Her family home is Tahlequah, in Eastern Oklahoma. Her Aunt Myrtle was your Uncle James' teacher when he was a little boy. I remember meeting them once when they visited the farm before I left for college. I declare, it is such a small world!

"I wrote back and invited her to come see us sometime when she is back home on vacation. Or we can drive over to see her. It isn't so very far."

"Dolly!" The children cried, relieved to know that she was safe.

One day after school, several weeks later, Mamma said there was a post card from Uncle James. "Mr. Nichols was here," J.D. read aloud. "We were remembering the adventure we had on the Santa Fe Chief. Hope you can come again. Love, Uncle James. P.S. Chawnaway and Old Shep send love."

"Chawnaway? Old Shep?" the four exclaimed all at once. They looked at each other in dismay.

"Does that mean we'll get to see Old Shep again?" asked Grace. "I hope so." In her heart, she had hoped that Old Shep would be with Uncle James when they got to L.A. He wasn't. Uncle James said Old Shep hadn't been there for several years. "You never know with Old Shep," he explained. "Maybe you don't need him so much as you did."

Incredulous, J.D. had said, "Are you saying that Old Shep is the same dog. . . ."

"And he's 350 dog-years old?" Robert ended his sentence.

"Oh, much older than that, I should think," Uncle James had said, eyes twinkling. "I wonder that it surprises you, after your adventures."

Mamma offered them a plate of her oatmeal cookies. She had a puzzled expression on her face. "It was so sad when Old Shep left. Maybe you will get to see him again, Gracie. That would be nice," she put down the plate, hurrying back into the kitchen.

"But how could Uncle James possibly know Chawnaway?" Robert asked, keeping his voice down.

Suddenly, Mary Carol realized, "That's the answer to your question, Gracie. Chawnaway is his sister, Uncle James' other sister, the one Mamma is named for."

Daddy looked up from the evening paper. "Speaking of the Santa Fe Chief, listen to this, you four mischiefs. 'Axis Spy Ring Broken. Married to an industrialist, whose company holds millions of dollars in contracts to furnish parts for Lockheed Aircraft, Irma Hackworth must have thought she had the ideal cover. FBI agents arrested her Wednesday as she was getting off of the Santa Fe Super Chief, shortly after it arrived in Los Angeles. Mrs. Hackworth was found with the names of key Axis operatives in her possession. Mr. Hackworth, who said he knew nothing of his wife's connection to the Axis powers, was rushed to the hospital with a heart attack, where he remains in critical condition. The key tip off that led to her eventual arrest came several months before when an unidentified Allied agent on the Santa Fe Chief to L.A. first discovered the link leading to Wednesday's arrest of Irma and her lover, the infamous Axis agent Rolf Schultz, . . .'"

"Mrs. Hackworth!" The children were bursting with excitement. "We met her. She was on the Chief."

"And she was kissing that man!" said Robert, rushing to look over Daddy's shoulder. "That's him in the picture, that's the man she was kissing."

"Well, listen to the rest of this," said Daddy. "Mrs. Hackworth transported critical information regarding the war effort, written in invisible ink on her white gloves, along with the names of Axis operatives. FBI agents were able to identify and arrest all members of the network she headed. It seems apparent that the ring's mission was to infiltrate highly classified Allied aircraft development operations."

"Well, she dropped her gloves in the Ladies Room when we were waiting for the Chief and got really mad at me when I tried to help her pick them up!" Mary Carol exclaimed all in one breath.

"And she gave Rolf Schultz one of her gloves," said Robert.

"Well, like I said, you never know whom you'll meet on the Santa Fe Chief," laughed Mamma, joining them, a pitcher of lemonade in her hands. "But I wasn't thinking about enemy spies!"

"So, Mary Carol, were you the unnamed operative who turned in Mrs. Hackworth?" asked Daddy, eyes sparkling in amusement. "Or was it you, Robert?"

"You all have grown so much over the summer. Especially you, Gracie," said Mamma, setting down the lemonade next to the nearly empty plate of cookies. "I'm so proud of the way you work together now. I hope it wasn't too awfully boring for you with Uncle James. You must have really made an impression on him this time, though. I couldn't believe my eyes when I saw that he'd sent his red abalone shell home with you."

"He gave it to us for remembering all that happened. . . ." said Mary Carol, not quite sure how to finish the sentence.

"On your visit?" Mamma sighed. "I know how you hated having to stay with him, but there really wasn't any other way."

"Uncle James, boring?" said Robert.

"Let's put it this way," said Mary Carol. "We found out that there's more to Uncle James than we imagined."

"There is more to us than we imagined, too!" giggled Grace.

"And you never know who you'll meet on the Santa Fe Chief," J.D. added, giving the others a knowing look.

"*Whom* you'll meet," said Mamma, smiling at him.

ACKNOWLEDGEMENTS

Many thanks, Colleen Cummings, for reading all three manuscripts in the trilogy and for your encouragement. Thanks to Nathaniel Stork and Isaiah Leach, for reading drafts of the book. Liesl and Amelia Bolin, your unfailing support has made the trilogy a family adventure. I could not have done it without you. Warren Schoonmaker, you talked me through rough points and shared your vast knowledge of the Western United States and its history. Thanks to Nancy Schoonmaker for editorial assistance—you know an independent clause when you see one. Jon and Leslie Dunlap, your encouragement and support have been a light along the way. Kathleen Conry, thanks for your enthusiastic promotion of the Trilogy. Philip and Julia Nichols (no known relation to Mr. Nichols in the book), Nathaniel Stork, and Amelia Bolin for your help with the cover.

ABOUT THE AUTHOR

Frances Schoonmaker is author of *The Last Crystal Trilogy*. She spent her early school years in Western Oklahoma and graduated from high school in Washington state. After teaching in elementary school for a dozen plus years, she joined the faculty of Teachers College, Columbia University where she was Professor in the College's historic Department of Curriculum and Teaching. She retired in 2009 and was granted the title Professor Emerita. When she isn't writing, she enjoys making school visits to meet with girls and boys, traveling, reading, walking, and her garden. She lives with her family in Baltimore, Maryland.

ABOUT THE BOOK

In writing the Trilogy, I have tried to be true to history, as we understand it today. History is our story. How we tell the story changes as we gain more information about the past. It also changes as our values change. For example, how we tell the story of the U.S. began to change when people who were left out of the telling spoke up. People whose lands were stolen, whose lives were stolen because they were slaves, women who were left out because people thought they were too weak to take part in the great affairs of the world—people with all kinds of differences in identity, life circumstances, abilities, and experience help us to understand our own story if we listen. As Papa says in *The Red Abalone Shell*, "We're all in it together."

Though I have driven along much of the route covered by the Santa Fe Chief, many times over, I took a train trip from Kansas City to Los Angeles twice as I wrote *The Last Crystal*. The Santa Fe Chief has long since been retired from service, replaced by the Southwest Chief. But the natural landscape is remarkably unchanged from 1944, the time in which I set the story.

Union Station in Kansas City, is now a center of community and cultural events. But you can see the Santa Fe Chief today at the Railroad Museum in Sacramento. You will also find Pullman train cars just as they looked in 1944. There are many people who are interested in keeping the traditions of railroad travel alive. There are collectors who have true-to-history train sets, people who restore and travel in old rail cars today, and museums devoted to rail travel.

I wondered who would be on the Santa Chief in April of 1944. An article on *The Chicago Tribune* website introduced me to Benjamin Franklin Gaines, a retired porter. Raymond Lincoln Moses is modeled on him and took a lesson from Mr. Gaines when people called him "George." Mr. Gaines is quoted as saying, "My name is Benjamin Franklin Gaines. There's no George anywhere." You can read his story and see a video at *https://www.chicagotribune.com/news/ct-pullman-porter-national-monument-anniversary-met-20160218-story.html*, one of many interesting resources about porters on luxury trains who were among the forerunners of the civil rights movement in the United States.

I have to thank Jennifer Goodwin for Sargent Nakamura, one of the passengers. Her husband's grandfather was a member of the Japanese-American 442nd.

Out of habit, Mr. Hackworth refers to Lockheed Aircraft as Lockheed-Vega. Lockheed-Vega was one of the primary manufacturers of aircraft during World War II. But by the end of 1943, the name Vega had been dropped. The Vega was Lockheed's first airplane, produced in 1927. In 1932, Amelia Earhart flew her transatlantic flight in a Vega. You can find more about Lockheed and pictures of its operation during World War II at *http://www.militarymuseum.org/LockheedAirTerminal.html*.

Also by Frances Schoonmaker
The Last Crystal Trilogy, Books 1 & 2

The Black Alabaster Box
and
The Red Abalone Shell

follow her:
 fgschoomaker
To get on her mailing list,
contact her at fgschoomaker@gmail.com.
Please put *The Last Crystal Trilogy* in the subject line.
You can find out more about her
and her books at www.fschoonmaker.com.
Resources for teachers can be found there and on her blog:
www.fourleavesandtales.blog

Grace Willis stood at the front door looking out, wondering what it would be like tomorrow when she no longer had a home. *Will the robins nest in the lilac bushes this spring without me to watch over them? Who will collect seed pods when the Catalpa trees drop them along the driveway? Will the garden know I am gone?* She was utterly miserable.

Left up to her, nothing would change. But Grace didn't get to choose. With new land opening in the West, her father and mother were determined to go to California. It was their dream to start a medical school. *So tomorrow is the auction. And there is nothing I can do about it.* Grace heaved a great sigh.

Just then, a big black and white dog came bounding up the front porch steps. Wagging all over, the dog looked at her as if they were best friends and he was asking permission to come over and play.

"It's Old Shep!" Grace called, momentarily distracted from her misery.

"Why, he does look just like Old Shep," said Daddy. "It can't be," said Mamma, joining them at the door. "Old Shep would be at least one hundred three in dog years by now. Dogs don't live that long."

Looking at Daddy, the dog held up his right paw. Daddy stepped out on the porch. Shaking the paw respectfully, he asked, "Do you mind if I have a look, old fellow? You all can come out, he's a gentle dog."

The dog sat quietly. Daddy knelt beside him, carefully feeling the paw and all the way up the leg. "Apparently this dog does live that long," he said. "This is Old Shep. His leg healed nicely, if I do say so."

"Really, you can't be Old Shep," Mamma said kindly as she sat down in a rocking chair. The dog went to her, putting his head in her lap. "Why, you are Old Shep!" Mamma exclaimed. "Remember how he used to do that? I'll swear, you don't look a day older."

"Perhaps we misjudged his age," said Daddy. Sitting down on the porch swing, he motioned for Grace to sit beside him.

"Either that or he's magic!" Mamma scratched Old Shep behind the ears.

"I'm not entirely prepared to rule out magic," said Daddy, giving Mamma a knowing look. "There are plenty of things in this world that can't be explained.

Dogs aren't magic, thought Grace. *But, if he was magic, I'd tell him to stop the auction from happening.*

"Old Shep had a broken leg when a friend left him with us, Grace," Daddy explained. "You probably don't remember Mr. C'lestin. You were a little tot then. Old Shep was limping and in a lot of pain. I set his leg. He stayed with us almost a year. Then he just disappeared. That was nearly ten years ago."

"Mr. C'lestin didn't come for him?" asked Grace.

"I daresay he had his reasons," said Daddy. "C'lestin is an unusual person, a bit mysterious—but very nice."

"Old Shep must not have been his dog," concluded Grace. "But why didn't Old Shep want to be our dog? We loved him."

"I'm not so sure you can say that Old Shep belongs to anyone," said Daddy carefully, searching for the right word.

"It is more like we became part of his circle of friends. Now he's come back to see us."

"I smell dinner," exclaimed Mamma. "It's our last dinner in this house. I'd sure hate for it to burn. Come set the table, Grace."

Last dinner. Reluctantly, Grace washed her hands at the kitchen pump and set the table.

She could have stayed with Grandpa and Grandma Willis the next day while the auction went on, but she refused to go. In one last effort to bring things to a halt, she dug her heels in and had an all out, screaming tantrum. But it didn't do any good.

"I know this is hard, Grace," said Mama, sighing. "You are going to have to decide if you are a part of this and ready to accept an adventure, or if you're going to cling to your misery and lock out the world. Either way, we are going to California and so are you."

Old Shep stayed by her side the whole terrible day. He was the only one who acted like he understood how she felt. When she crawled under the porch, he went with her. When she retreated to the carriage house in the back yard, he came along. When she hid in her secret place in the bushes behind the Catalpa trees, he was there.

They watched from her hiding places as strangers hauled off one precious thing after another. By the end of the day the house was completely empty. It was no longer their house. Somebody bought it, too.

After the auction, they stayed with Grandpa and Grandma Willis. All too soon family and friends came to help them load their wagon.

"That's a real fine thing you and the Mrs. are doing, Doc," said one of their neighbors as they stacked supplies on the wagon. "I wouldn't have the courage to go West."

"You sure do have a lot of books and medical supplies piled up in there," said one of the men as they finished loading. "You might ought to take more food. It's a long ways out there from what I hear. You can't eat books!"

Daddy good-naturedly shook the man's hand. "You're right, Paul. Don't worry. We'll be trading for a bigger wagon once we get to Kansas City. We'll stock up on provisions there."

"I reckon they don't have good doctors way out there in California," said an uncle. "Still, we sure will miss you all."

"Amen to that. We'll miss having the best doctor in St. Louis right next door!" said one of the women, giving Mamma a hug. "Lord knows I'll miss you, Amanda. And little Grace, too," she added, wiping away tears.

Little? Grace was offended, but she didn't say anything. Mamma would say back talk is rude.

Grandpa and Grandma Rhoads lived on a farm way out in the country. They stayed over at the Willis house to see them off the next morning. The sun was barely up when their last good-byes were said. Grandma Willis gave Grace a whole tin of gingerbread men. "These won't last you all the way to California. When you get settled out there, I'll just have to send you some more." There were tears in her eyes. Grace gave her a hug. There were tears in her eyes, too.

Grandma Rhoads held her close. "I know you don't have room for another thing, but I want you to have this, Grace. I made it for you. It won't take up much room. When you hold it, just remember how much you are loved. Two thousand miles can't change that." She gave her a linen handkerchief with a wide crochet lace border. It was beautiful, but when Grace thought of all the things she wished she could take, she hadn't thought of handkerchiefs. She thanked Grandma and hugged her just the same. She didn't want to hurt her feelings.

"Reckon you're takin' that dog," said Grandpa Willis. Old Shep stood waiting by the horses.

"Leastwise he seems to think so," said Grandpa Rhoads, chuckling.

"Old Shep makes his own decisions," said Daddy. He laughed, but there were tears in his eyes as he got in the wagon where Grace and Mamma now waited. Mamma wiped her eyes.

****

the rest of The Black Alabaster Box
and The Red Albalone Shell *are available*
through booksellers internationally